W9-BIX-307

THE ACCIDENTAL BRIDE

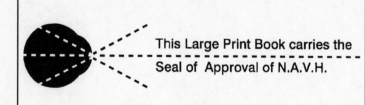

This Large Print Book carries the
Seal of Approval of N.A.V.H.

THE ACCIDENTAL BRIDE

CHRISTINA SKYE

THORNDIKE PRESS
A part of Gale, Cengage Learning

Detroit • New York • San Francisco • New Haven, Conn • Waterville, Maine • London

GALE
CENGAGE Learning·

LIBRARY OF CONGRESS CATALOGING-IN-PUBLICATION DATA

Skye, Christina.
  The accidental bride / by Christina Skye. — Large Print edition.
    pages cm. — (Thorndike Press Large Print Romance)
    ISBN 978-1-4104-5398-3 (hardcover) — ISBN 1-4104-5398-7 (hardcover)
  1. Weddings on television—Fiction. 2. Man-woman relationships—Fiction.
  3. Large type books. I. Title.
PS3569.K94A65 2012
813'.54—dc23   2012037761

Published in 2012 by arrangement with Harlequin Books S.A.

Printed in the United States of America
1 2 3 4 5 6 7 16 15 14 13 12

Dear Reader,
I hope you will join me on a new adventure.

Our travel will take us to fog-swept coves.
To the magic of a special town and special
people. On Summer Island's quiet streets
friendship runs deep, and the love of a good
yarn runs even deeper.

One by one old friends will be pulled back
home to the rugged Oregon coast. One by
one dreams will be lost — and then found.
As the seasons change, each friend will face
secrets and betrayals, along with the healing
gift of love.

Please join me on this journey home.

With warmest wishes,
Christina

A warm thank-you to all my friends
at Tuesday-night knitting for good
patterns, good cheer and great
inspiration.

Thank you to Celia and Caroline —
world-class knitters and friends.
Fiber days rule!

Another big round of thanks for
Peggy and Victoria. You are the best.
I couldn't have typed *The End*
without you!

A deep and hearty thank-you to Phyllis
at Barnes & Noble in Goodyear,
Arizona. You rock! As always, you are
the *queen* of booksellers!

And finally, my heartfelt appreciation
to Debbie Macomber,

wonderful author, wonderful friend.
Thank you for all your kindness and
laughter. And thanks for that amazingly
clever wedding twist!

PROLOGUE

It was a beautiful wedding.

The groom got sick. The bride overslept. The best man was a dog.

And the day had barely begun.

The anxious bride peeked out the door at the back of the crowded chapel, watching more and more people cram the pews. Everything had happened so fast over the past week. It was still hard to imagine how much had changed.

Right now all she wanted was to have the ceremony over. She wasn't used to wearing makeup, and she never fiddled with her hair, but the wedding consultant had taken her job seriously.

Jilly O'Hara was stunned to see her image in the mirror, a tall, serene vision of elegance in a long white silk gown. A cream satin sash framed her slim waist, accentuating her height, and a single satin orchid gleamed in her upswept hair.

She could barely recognize herself. None of her friends would have known her, that was for sure.

A few stragglers were being seated, to the backdrop of restless coughing. Standing at the back of the chapel, Jilly's friend Jonathan made a discreet gesture and smiled as the bridegroom came to stand at the front of the crowd. The groom's big brown dog sat nearby, alert and perfectly behaved, a vision of canine elegance in his red bandanna.

The organ music swelled. Jilly took a deep breath as the instantly familiar strains of the *Wedding March* filled the chapel.

She stared down the long aisle, wondering how everything had happened so fast since she came to Wyoming. Marriage was the last thing she had planned for herself. Down the aisle Jilly saw her groom, lean and a little dangerous in a severely cut black suit that looked very expensive.

"Are you ready?" Jonathan stood smiling at the door.

"As ready as I'll ever be. Explain to me again why I agreed to this," she murmured.

Jonathan took her arm. "You'll be fine. By the way, you look gorgeous. Seriously, I wouldn't have recognized you under all that makeup and puffy hair."

"Gee, thanks. *I think.*"

As they walked outside, Jilly focused on not falling in the strappy evening sandals that the bridal expert had insisted she wear.

Every face turned. The music swelled. The big room seemed to blur as Jilly's cool, thoughtful groom smiled at her from the altar.

CHAPTER ONE

Arizona
One month earlier

The restaurant kitchen was a scene right out of World War III. Pots churned, grills smoked and a dozen harried workers danced to avoid each other. It was cramped, hot and noisy — one step away from chaos.

And Jilly O'Hara couldn't have been happier.

She presided over the hot, noisy room like a choreographer, watching for problems and juggling advice along with her orders. Running a restaurant had always been her dream and her passion, and after years of work, Jilly had her own baby.

Since the first week it had opened, Jilly's Place had been a stellar success. Sometimes Jilly hated how successful her restaurant had become. The social end of the job gave her a headache, and shmoozing with customers was a nightmare. As soon as she could, she

13

ducked back into the crowded kitchen to create magic.

Only here did she feel fully alive. With her wavy black hair tucked behind a bandanna, the rail-slim chef juggled a smoked asparagus risotto and two orders of grilled potatoes with salsa verde. Beside her on the counter, smoky-rich tortilla soup steamed next to a wedge of wood-grilled salmon. The flavors teased and tantalized, every color snapping with southwestern energy.

Another meal done, Jilly flipped a fresh towel over her shoulder and then attacked the next order. One of the kitchen crew caught her eye. Smiling, he poured a thermal cup of coffee and slid it toward her over the counter.

"Caffeine break. After all, you've only had three tonight," he said, well aware of Jilly's particular vice.

"Lifesaver." Jilly took a long drink, savoring the caffeine.

They were crazy crowded tonight, but that was normal. At the kitchen door, her front desk manager signaled his pleasure at the crowd with a big thumbs-up, then vanished back outside to deal with the reservations desk.

The Saturday-night pace was sheer pandemonium, but Jilly was used to that. She thrived on the jagged edge of chaotic energy. Even on her days off, she made it a point to check out new restaurants or help in the kitchen of a friend, working the line with manic energy. And why not? She loved to cook.

She didn't do vacations, and time off was for wimps.

Jilly finished her coffee and scanned the next set of dinner orders. Tugging on Kevlar mitts, she leaned down to grab an eggplant pizza from the wood-burning oven. She had just removed the mitts when the pain hit her.

Jilly looked up blindly at the ceiling, struggling to breathe.

No one in the busy kitchen noticed her shaking or her short, strangled breaths. No one helped her when she leaned forward to grip the counter.

Blindly, she stared at her white hands. No ring. No husband. No kids. Just a pile of debts from her years in cooking school.

A fresh wave of pain struck. Jilly whimpered, clutching at the long granite counter.

A pot was boiling over on the big 8-burner Wolf stove. The foam seemed to rise in slow motion. Bubbling and hissing, it exploded over the copper rim, down into the steel prongs of the burner.

Burn.

Burning.

Her throat and chest on fire, fear striking her like a mallet, Jilly slowly bent double and whimpered.

Her legs gave way. With a ragged cry she fell forward onto the cold tile floor.

CHAPTER TWO

The emergency room doctor was talking to her, but Jilly couldn't make out what he was saying. His lips moved but no sounds seemed to come out.

She squinted at him and tried to focus.

"More tests. But we think it was your heart."

Excuse me? Jilly's mind raced. Her heart? What about her heart?

Lights flashed on the machines that crowded the small white room. She had collapsed in the kitchen. She remembered that part.

Then something about an ambulance . . .

She closed her eyes, feeling dizzy. A little pain in her chest. Okay, nausea. *Lots* of nausea.

What was going on? She was only *twenty-blipping-seven.* She hadn't smoked more than three times in her life. Once when the town bad boy talked her into sharing a

Marlboro behind the old post office. Once after her junior year prom, which she watched dateless and bored from the high school bleachers. And the last time, to celebrate her admission to cooking school in Arizona.

Six bleeping years ago.

So how was anything wrong with her heart?

"Symptoms are consistent . . . still need detailed results of EKG, angiogram. More tests of your heart enzymes . . . Hospitalized until then."

Hospitalized?

Jilly stared at the white walls while the words rained down, sharp and cold.

Rest? More blood tests? No way. She didn't have time to be sick. She had a restaurant to run and debts to repay.

She looked down at her arm stretched out on the white bed. They were good arms. Good muscles. She could whip a chocolate mousse by hand almost as fast as a mixer could. She could swirl perfect frosted flowers over a white chocolate cake and mince a tomato as finely as any machine.

And Jilly loved that work. Every minute she spent cooking was a joy in her life.

But her hands showed another story, too. Jilly saw a sprinkling of fine silver scars from mishaps in crowded kitchens on busy nights. She had always felt proud of those marks as signs of her experience.

Her nails were short. Always clean and unpolished. She was strictly no frills and always had been. Her no-frills life kept her lean and fast, ready to catch that next wave and race on to meet her dream. Right now that dream was to create a natural-food empire by the time she was thirty-five.

Her scarred hands twisted with a tremor of pain and loss. What would happen to her dreams now? She listened to the machines hiss and whisper a warning.

A heart attack at twenty-seven. Why her?

She closed her eyes. More words bounced past.

"Possible malformation . . . MRI. Then exploratory catheterization."

All bad things.

Jilly's mind stuttered and then shut down, paralyzed by the weight of her fear. Only once had she felt this overwhelmed and vulnerable. That had been years ago, on the day she found out her mother had left her in a cardboard box on the steps outside the local fire station at the grand, strapping age of two months.

But she had survived the news. After the crushing pain had passed, Jilly had wiped away her tears and boxed up her mother along with the rest of her sad childhood memories. With fierce determination she had dug a dark hole and shoved them deep inside, where she would never have to think about them.

Because Jilly O'Hara had no time for tears or weakness or *what might have been.* She was too busy racing forward, creating her dreams.

"Ms. O'Hara, can you hear me? We'll need your consent to proceed with the catheterization and other tests. I have the paperwork here."

Jilly blinked and struggled to focus. "I — I'm tired. Maybe we can talk later. Sorry." Her fingers clenched, and she thought of Caro and Grace and Olivia. Growing up together in the small coastal town of Summer Island off the Oregon coast, the four girls had been inseparable. For years her best friends had shared her dreams and she had shared theirs.

They had argued and nudged and supported.

Their circle of strength had kept Jilly going during the worst of times.

She desperately needed them now.

Summer Island
The Oregon Coast

"She still isn't answering her phone. Something's wrong."

Caro McNeal frowned at her silver watch. Her husband, a marine currently deployed in Afghanistan, had given her the slim silver design for her last birthday. Caro wondered where Gage was and what he was doing at that moment.

Was he in danger?

She tried to push her usual worries aside and focus on Jilly. "I've tried calling her half a dozen times, Grace. Why doesn't she answer?"

Grace Lindstrom put down the sweater sleeve she had been knitting. "Jilly gets distracted. Produce. Ovens. Spatulas. Anything can take her into that alternate chef universe."

"Not for this long." Caro frowned at the phone. The women had been closest friends since they had met as girls. When one of them faced problems, all the others seemed to feel it. First Caro had come home to heal from an accident. Then Grace, a respected food writer, had returned to Summer Island after her grandfather had been hurt. "This is different."

"Did you try texting Jilly?"

21

"Four times." Caro looked out at the ocean. Seagulls cried as they circled a trawler anchored in Summer Island's small cove. "Something's wrong, Grace. I've been sending Jilly daily updates on the repairs here at Harbor House. Jilly was excited about coming back next week to work on a design for the new front porch. She sent me a gorgeous picture using local fieldstone and a rustic brushed grout. It was gorgeous, but . . ."

"But what?"

Caro blew out a breath. "I told her to send me more examples so I could work on pricing. Then I didn't hear a thing. That was two days ago." Caro shook her head. "Jilly wouldn't drop out of sight like this. She wants to finish the work here just as much as we do."

In a moment of insanity the women had decided to buy Summer Island's oldest landmark and renovate it to its former glory. They had been nearly finished when an earthquake had damaged the roof, half the rooms and part of the foundation. After serious soul-searching, they had decided to start all over, crazy or not.

Grace rolled her knitting up slowly. "Where was she when you two last spoke?"

"Working at her restaurant. Where else?"

"Silly question. Okay, I'll book a flight. I can be in Arizona before bedtime." Grace stood up and stretched. "The idiot is probably off in a peach orchard taking soil samples, completely oblivious to the time. You'll see."

"But I thought you and Noah were going to spend this weekend together in San Francisco." Caro studied her friend's face. "You've been planning the trip for ages. Is something wrong?"

Caro watched her friend turn, looking south past the old dock, past the restless sea wall. Grace rolled her shoulders but didn't answer.

"Grace? Tell me what happened."

"He was called in to work," Grace said slowly. "Another day, another emergency."

"Can't he get time off?"

"Apparently not. When you're good, everyone wants a piece of you," Grace said flatly. Then she forced a smile. "Don't worry. We'll go on our trip. But it won't be this week."

Something was *very* wrong here, Caro thought. Grace was acting too cool and trying too hard to be convincing. This was more than a simple trip cancellation. "Are you okay about this, Grace? You were so excited when you told me you and Noah

23

were going on this trip."

Grace shrugged and then slid her knitting bag over her shoulder. "I'm almost used to the last-minute cancellations," she muttered. "But I'd better go. I'll call you when I get to Arizona."

Clearly, she didn't want to discuss her problems with Noah.

"You have the address for Jilly's new restaurant, right? She just moved into that new building."

"Got it."

Neither woman questioned that Grace would go to Jilly's restaurant and *not* her apartment. Chances were slim to nil that their driven friend would be anywhere but working. They would have to do something to correct that, Caro decided. "As soon as you hear something, let me know. I'm just sorry I can't help more."

"Let me handle the Barefoot Contessa." Grace cleared her throat. "You've got plenty to do with this renovation. Not to mention the baby to care for."

Caro was certain she heard a wistful note in her friend's voice.

So Grace was thinking about a family. That was interesting, since she and Noah had only recently confided that they were engaged. No wedding date was set as far as

Caro knew.

Caro hadn't seen Noah since the spring and he'd only been in town for two days. He was supposed to be moving to a less demanding job, Grace had explained then. Something without constant emergency calls.

Given the cancelled weekend, *that* didn't seem to be happening.

Caro still had no idea what Noah did, beyond it being difficult and very secret. But she knew that Grace worried terribly about him.

More problems to sort out.

Caro gave her friend a hug. "Say hello to Noah. Tell him I'm still waiting for the Ukrainian Welcome Bread recipe from his mother."

"I'll get it for you." Grace slid her yarn and her knitting needles into her bag and forced a smile. "And stop worrying. I'll call you as soon as I have any news."

CHAPTER THREE

Scottsdale, Arizona

Jilly watched the parking lot fill with silver Hummers and black Range Rovers. Only sports figures, celebrities and the very rich came to this private clinic in the high desert above the sprawl of Phoenix. Jilly had only gotten in thanks to one of her restaurant regulars. When Jilly hadn't been at her usual spot, buzzing between the tables and the kitchen, he had learned about her collapse and arranged to have her transported. But she had received the same cold diagnosis here that she had received in the small emergency room near her restaurant.

Jilly closed her eyes.

Her heart.

Why *now*, when she was on the verge of a huge career leap? Her restaurant was booked out for weeks. She had plans for a cookbook, and she had just received two offers to buy her signature line of organic salsa, Jilly's Naturals. Then, in the space of a heartbeat, everything had fallen apart on her.

No more sixteen-hour workdays, the cardiologist had warned.

Not even three-hour workdays until her tests were done.

She would need at least half a dozen procedures plus a battery of lab tests before the total picture was clear. Something was wrong with her heart, starting with an arrhythmia that triggered a counter beat when she was under stress.

But when *wasn't* she under stress? Maybe during the first few minutes of waking, when her big white Samoyed puppy was curled up at her feet and she had the whole day ahead of her, with all its possibilities. Reality always swept in too soon, carrying in a flood of calls, emails and text messages.

Produce deliveries to inspect.

Employees to placate.

The magic of food had called to Jilly ever since she was twelve. Cooking was the only thing she had ever wanted to do, her first and only dream.

Her fingers opened, massaging her chest above the spot where her problematic heart waited to stammer and skip, sending her back into oblivion.

Did she have a family history of heart disease? Had any relative suffered a heart attack very young? The thoughtful cardiologist had quizzed her for twenty minutes. Were there parents or siblings with heart defects? Any relevant family incidents that she could remember?

Jilly's fingers closed to a fist above her heart. What parents? What siblings? Her genetic profile was a total blank. She had been found red-faced and howling beneath a cheap blue flannel blanket in a packing box on the steps of the local fire station. Less than three months old, the Summer Island doctor had estimated. Healthy. No problems beyond a little dehydration. Just wrapped up and left behind, discarded like an old newspaper.

Jilly closed her eyes. So what if she was alone? In the end you were always alone. You couldn't take anything or anyone with you when you died, and you couldn't trust anyone with your deepest hopes and secrets while you lived.

You did it by yourself or it didn't get done.

Now the future was in her hands. She had to change, and she would work on that. Yet how could she possibly replace the job she loved? Cooking had given her an anchor when nothing else could.

She didn't hear the light tap at her door. She was too busy searching the bright corridor of dreams that had been her compass since she was old enough to understand what *orphan, foundling* and *abandoned on the firehouse steps* meant.

"You *idiot.*"

She jumped when she heard the familiar voice, rough with concern. Then her oldest friend's strong hands slid around her and gripped tight.

"Why do you always have to do everything alone, stubborn as a rabid mule?"

It was a timeworn joke between the four friends. *When I need help I'll ask for it.* It was Jilly's oldest answer to any question. And of course she *never* asked.

She whispered the familiar words now, a tear slipping down her cheek.

"You should have called us! I could *strangle* you." But Grace's hoarse words were full of love and support, despite their anger. "What happened? Were you burned?"

Jilly took a raw breath. No way to lie. Not to your oldest friend. Not to Grace, whose face held worry and irritation and complete, unqualified love.

"It happened at dinner. It was right after the tortilla soup and the wood-grilled salmon. I had a beef tartare entrée coming

29

up. The Wagyu beef was perfect, with little marblings that —"

"Forget the food. What *happened,* Jilly?"

"It was — like a fist at my chest. Nausea. Straining to breathe and dizziness. I lost it. Just plain lost it. The doctors say that . . . it's my heart. There's some kind of atrial valve malformation. And when you factor in the stress of my work, plus the physical demands and the long hours . . ."

"What's the diagnosis?"

"They think — well, that it was a heart attack," Jilly whispered.

"No way." Grace sank down on the bed. "You're too young for that."

"Apparently I'm not." Jilly took a deep breath. "No more busy Saturday nights at my restaurant. No more Jilly's Naturals. No more mango tomatillo tamales with espresso chipotle sauce. What am I going to do now, Grace?"

"We'll be here. All of us. Caro and Olivia and I. It's going to be fine."

"How can it be fine? All I'm good at is cooking."

"Be quiet and listen to me." Grace gripped Jilly's shoulders. "You've got us and you've got the Harbor House. Just remember that. If there's a way to make this work for you, we'll think of it together. And if not . . .

30

then we'll find a new dream for you to catch and hold. It will be even better than the old ones."

"But how will I —"

"Just *trust* someone for once, will you? I learned how to trust again, and so can you. Now tell me everything. Start with what happened in the restaurant and all your symptoms. I'm going to do some research. Then you can get another opinion."

"Don't waste your time," Jilly said softly. Her shoulders slumped as she leaned against Grace. "I saw the X-ray with the shadow. I saw the first lab results. There's no point in hoping —"

"There's *always* a reason to hope. If you say that again, I'm going to deck you, Jilly O'Hara."

Jilly forced a smile. "If you pull out my EKG monitor, I could expire right here. 'Death by best friend!' I can see the head-lines in the *Summer Island Herald* now." Jilly gave a shaky laugh as Grace handed her a tissue and an expensive chocolate bar. "I'm only supposed to eat what they bring me. Nothing else. Tomorrow there are more tests."

"I checked with the nurse. One piece is okay. Now dry your eyes and eat. Then we're going to make a plan of attack."

31

■ ■ ■ ■

"She looked so sad, almost as if she was broken. I've never seen our Jilly look like that." Grace sat stiffly in the hospital's big lounge. Outside, purple clouds swept across the distant foothills. Lightning flashed and shimmered, as restless as Grace's mood.

"I've never seen Jilly give up. She's totally single-minded. *Nothing* stops her," Caro said worriedly. Her voice came closer to the phone.

"This thing has. Her doctor says that she's going to have to change her life 180 degrees or else. No more stress. No more crazy work schedule. Good food, rest and exercise along with medication. Maybe surgery."

"Jilly doesn't know how to relax." Caro sighed, sounding tired. "She never has. This is all so terrible, Grace. I just wish I could be there with you. When can she leave?"

"Probably a week. But I'm staying here, so don't worry. Meanwhile, we're making a plan. Tomorrow I'll talk to her cardiologist and then I'm going to get another opinion. But you need to rest, too, Caro. You sound exhausted." Since Grace's departure, all the Harbor House repair work had fallen on Caro. Grace hated leaving her friend in the lurch this way.

"I'm fine. Things have been intense here, that's all."

"It's that new contractor, isn't it? Fire him, will you? You're too kindhearted by a mile."

"But he has three kids and a new baby on the way. And his mother used to work at the animal shelter. I can't just —"

"You can and you damned well better, Caro. If you don't, then I will. Now go get some sleep. The Harbor House will survive. I'll text you as soon as I know more about Jilly. We'll make this work out right. We always do, remember?"

"I remember." Caro gave a sleepy yawn. "Talk to you tomorrow."

"Count on it." Grace frowned. As soon as she broke the connection, her optimism faded.

She wanted to be positive for Jilly. She wanted to believe in a sunny world full of possibilities. But how did you argue with X-rays and heart enzyme tests?

"Stop fidgeting. Read one of those magazines."

Jilly punched at her pillow. "I tried. They're boring."

"Then read that thriller I left you."

33

"It's stupid. Nobody does ridiculous things like that." Jilly scowled. "I was rooting for the villain by page ten."

"Jilly, I give up. You have to rest. The doctor told you that, remember?"

"I'm *trying.* It's just not easy." Jilly shifted restlessly. "Can't you find me a good magazine? *Cook's Illustrated* would be perfect. Or maybe *Gourmet* —"

"The doctor said no cooking. No more work obsession. You are supposed to relax."

Jilly blew out an irritated breath. "How can I *relax?* My salsa line will be dead if I don't get back to work. And my wholesale produce contact said —"

"Talk to the hand." Glaring, Grace waved her hand in front of Jilly.

"But —"

"*Rest.* Otherwise I'll bang you with that meat mallet I found in your purse."

"Don't knock the mallet, pal. I lock up really late at night and the parking lot is empty. That thing makes a great defensive weapon."

Grace jumped as her cell phone chimed, forgotten in her pocket. It took her a moment to clear her tangled thoughts. "I'll take this outside."

"Sure. Go right ahead. I'll just sit here and let my brain rot slowly."

34

Grace shook her head as she walked outside. But when she glanced at her phone, she felt the instant wave of joy . . . and then the crushing worry.

It was Noah.

She scanned his text quickly.

Called Caro. Got an update. How's the Salsa Diva doing?

Grace cradled the phone. Noah still caused a flutter at her chest, even after all these months. She hoped that would never go away.

Not so good. Waiting for more tests. It looks like her heart. She's upset and so am I. I only wish that . . .

Grace left the sentence hanging and hit the send button. What was there to add? There were still too many questions to predict what would happen next.

Noah would understand. He had read her feelings almost from the first moment they had met. He was smart and decent and also the sexiest man she knew.

But sexy and decent didn't help when his job kept him tied up 24/7. Lately Grace woke up at night in a cold sweat, seeing dark images of explosive death and shattered limbs. Though few people could be told, Noah was a bomb disposal expert and he was the very best. Because of his experience and thoroughness he had cheated death again and again.

Given how important his job was, Noah couldn't turn and walk away. No matter the risk.

And because Grace knew how much the job meant to him, she wouldn't ask him to. While they were perfect together, perfect equals and amazing lovers, a distance had begun to creep between them.

Grace had a suspicion that one day she'd wake up and find the distance too great to cross, and she'd lose the only man she could ever love.

Her phone chimed, and Grace answered breathlessly.

"Hey, gorgeous. How are you holding up?"

"I've been better."

"I'm really sorry. Any updates? Have you seen her medical reports yet?"

"A few. There are more to be done." Grace watched more lightning play over the mountains beyond the hospital window. "It looks like heart problems."

"She's awfully young for that, isn't she?"

"They found a malformed valve. They told

Jilly it was just a matter of time."

"So they caught it early. That's something." Noah took a deep breath. "Tell me how you are doing."

"I'm . . . managing. But Jilly's not exactly in her best mood right now. She lives to work but her doctor says all that has to change. And seriously, Noah, I don't know if she can."

"Everyone can change. All it takes is motivation and commitment."

"You really believe that?" If so, where did that leave *them*? Nothing had changed Noah. His job was still a jealous lover, and any day he could walk out of his apartment and not come back.

"I do believe people can change. Grace, about my transfer . . . I'm working it out. In fact —"

Grace heard muffled voices and then the angry cry of a siren. "Noah, are you okay? Is anything wrong?"

"Everything's fine, honey. I'm just finishing up some loose ends."

"Truly? You . . . wouldn't lie to me? *Never* lie," Grace whispered fiercely. "I can handle anything but that."

"No, all the heavy lifting is done. We're just waiting for the folks from Homeland to arrive so we can sign off." His voice was

37

calm and reassuring. "I wish I had more time to talk." There was no hint of nerves or impatience.

But Grace wasn't reassured. "Be careful. And if you manage to change your schedule, I guarantee you some amazing Chinese dumplings and a cable car with a view of the bay." Grace refused to give way to desperation. They needed to meet halfway as equals — or not at all. If he was locked to his job, what kind of future did they have anyway?

"Working on it, honey. Give me another week. Then let's book that hotel on the hill with a view of the Golden Gate. I want to order room service and wake up every morning with your head on my pillow. I promise I'll make it happen this time."

This was the third time they'd tried, but Grace didn't bring that up. Third time was the charm, right? "Clear the date and I'll arrange everything, just as long as Jilly is doing okay," she finished.

"She's damned tough. Your only problem will be keeping her out of the kitchen long enough to get a diagnosis."

Both of them knew it was no joke. Cooking was the one dream that had kept Jilly afloat during a troubled girlhood and a lonely adulthood.

"We'll think of something. Maybe Caro, Olivia and I should stage a kitchen intervention," Grace mused.

"Hey — that's not a bad idea. Is Olivia finally back from Europe?"

"She got back two days ago."

"Jilly's luckier than she knows. Not many people have friends like you three. And I vote for the intervention," he said gravely. "Life's too short." His voice turned hard. "I know how short, honey. So pin her down and make her do the right thing. Meanwhile, we'll work this out with my job. Just give me a little more time —"

Sirens split the quiet air and Grace heard the swell of urgent voices. "Noah, what did you say?"

"Sorry, honey. Gotta go. The Homeland team just arrived."

"Okay." Grace's heart twisted in her chest, but she kept her voice level. "Be safe."

She heard shouts and more sirens. She bit down all her questions. "I love you, Noah," she said hoarsely. "Remember that. Call me when you can."

But it was too late. He had already gone.

Life was too short, Grace thought. She wasn't going to let Jilly ruin hers. Suddenly an intervention made perfect sense.

CHAPTER FOUR

"You like this idea of Grace's? You don't think it's too drastic?" Caro took a breath and stared up at her friend. "Be honest, Olivia."

"I'm always honest with you." Olivia Sullivan paced the room, frowning. Like her two other friends, she was plotting a way to help Jilly redesign her hectic life.

When Grace had first called with a wild intervention plan, the idea had seemed very extreme. But clearly something had to be done.

Caro studied the border of the baby blanket she was knitting. In the crib nearby, her daughter slept, pink-cheeked and contented.

Could her world have been more blessed and filled with magic?

Sure. You could have your husband safe, home beside you, a voice answered coldly.

"Caro, are you listening to me?" Olivia

Sullivan sat in a bar of morning sunlight, tan and very elegant in a linen dress and Italian silk scarf. Her hand-knit linen shrug matched her dress perfectly.

"Of course I am." Caro managed a smile. Clearly this trip had been a good thing. It had been years since Olivia had looked this relaxed. Her months working and studying architecture in Europe had left her glowing. "You always look so elegant, Livie. I swear if you weren't my oldest friend, I'd have to hate you."

"Hardly." Olivia ran a hand over Caro's unfinished blanket. "You're the radiant one. When you pick up the baby, you actually glow. Someday . . . well, I want to look like that, too."

"You will." Caro squeezed her friend's shoulder. "But you should see me at 3:00 a.m. when I have spit-up on my robe. Not a pretty sight."

"If anyone could carry it off, it's you. And you and Gage are so great together. At the wedding it was almost as if you could read each other's thoughts. I loved watching you two." Olivia frowned. "I know it must be hard without him. I'll babysit or shop or do laundry. You name it."

"I may take you up on that. But now I want to hear about Europe. You went everywhere you planned? Florence. Paris. Tuscany, too?"

"I did. It was amazing." Olivia gave a rueful smile. "Great food, but I gained ten pounds."

"You could stand to gain ten more," Caro said, feeling just a little envious. "So what's in your bag? You keep looking at something."

Olivia dug in her purse and set a plastic container on the table. It was a model Caro had used herself. "Well, well. You've been busy over there in Europe."

Olivia flushed.

"Is there something I'm missing here?"

"Probably."

"So is that a *used* diaphragm?"

Olivia turned the plastic container slowly. "Almost. Very, very close."

"Anyone I know?"

Olivia shook her head. "He was nice and smart and gorgeous. A painter from Paris."

"So what happened?"

"*That* happened." Olivia glared at the plastic. "Everything was gorgeous — a quiet country inn. Linen sheets and moonlight spilling through the windows. He didn't push me, Caro. I wanted to sleep with him. I told him to wait a few minutes and then — then I couldn't get that devil's tool inserted. I finally gave up. We had a fight and ended up driving home in total silence. Not a word the whole trip. It was beyond horrible."

Caro frowned. She could see Olivia was still hurting from the encounter. "I'm sorry to hear it, Livie. They can be tricky."

"I felt like such a fool." Olivia glared down at her teacup. "I refuse to feel so humiliated ever again."

Caro had a sudden memory of Olivia at fifteen, putting on panty hose and trying not to be flustered for her first date. Her father, Summer Island's mayor and most powerful public figure, had been very strict, criticizing every move his daughter made. Over the years Olivia had never been smart enough or thin enough or popular enough for her father. He never hid the fact that he had wanted a son to groom for his real estate investment business.

In his eyes women were meant to stay at home and keep the house clean, anticipating their husband's whims. Women were not meant to be CEOs or senators or physicists.

Caro almost never cursed, but she thought a bad word loud and clear. She had said quite a few of them when Olivia's parents had separated and her father blazed off to become a high-profile mover and shaker in Seattle with a different nubile model on his arm every night.

Good riddance, Caro thought. He wouldn't be around to dig away at his daughter's confidence anymore. Olivia could finally find her feet. The time in Italy and France appeared to have done her a world of good. She looked calm and collected.

Caro wondered if the appearance was only skin-deep.

"Pour us more tea and I'll give you some instructions. When I'm done, you'll be an expert, Livie. But after that, I want to hear all about Europe. Especially your social life," Caro said dryly. "With a husband who has been gone for months, I need to remember what sex is all about," she muttered.

Arizona
Two days later
More lab tests came back.

Negative for cardiac blockage.

Negative for elevated heart enzymes.

"That's good, right?" Jilly dragged a hand through her hair as she studied the print. "This means my heart is okay?"

Jilly's specialist picked his words carefully. "It means the major triggers for a future attack are missing. But we need to dig deeper to find out what did happen. And there's still the question of your valve malformation and your arrhythmia." He studied Jilly's patient records, which were getting thicker by the hour. "Your weight is good. A job that keeps you active, I see." He flipped through more pages and frowned. "A high-stress work environment. We need to remedy that." He stopped as someone knocked at the door.

Grace peered in. "Sorry. I'll come back later."

"No, it's okay." Jilly felt sick at what was about to come next.

No more stress.

No more cooking.

Find a new line of work.

She closed her eyes. "Please come in, Grace."

"You're family?" The doctor closed his file and studied Grace.

"A friend. A very good friend," Grace said fiercely. "I'll help any way I can."

"Good. Your friend has some big decisions in front of her. Having a support network will be crucial. What about family?"

"No," Jilly said coldly. "None."

"I see." The doctor tapped the thick chart. "It could be worse. You're young and otherwise healthy, Ms. O'Hara. No tobacco use. No obesity or diabetes. But your last ECG

45

shows an elevated heart rate. I'm not thrilled about your LDL levels, either."

"What does all that mean?"

"Your heart is working too hard. At this point, surgery is not recommended. Diet, medication and lifestyle changes are the first step."

Jilly ignored the first two items as irrelevant. "Lifestyle? I'm not giving up my work, Doctor. I can't," she said hoarsely. "I could . . . cut back a little. Maybe go in late sometimes."

The doctor looked at her and frowned. "I'm not sure you understand what I'm saying. We only get one heart, by nature's choice. Blowing through it isn't a sane plan." He shook his head slowly. "By all rights you're far too young for us to be having this conversation. But you've had a warning shot over the bow and now you need to pay attention. I'd hate to see you back here in three months. Or in three weeks," he added gravely.

"So you're saying I can't work? I have to lie in bed and vegetate?" Jilly's voice rose with an edge of hysteria. "I'll go insane."

"Then stay busy. Take up a hobby. Find something that relaxes you. For the moment your old life needs to be put on hold while we assess our options and how well you respond to those options." He glanced at the needles sticking out of Grace's bag. "Why not take up knitting? Some convincing tests show that knitting confers a measurable relaxation response."

"Not the way I knit," Jilly rasped. "I'm terrible at it. Can't I just — well, cut back my work hours?"

The doctor crossed his arms. "All I can tell you is what makes the best sense for the long term."

Jilly squeezed her eyes shut. "You don't understand. Cooking is all I have."

"What I understand is your health. For you that means at least six months stress-free. It means medication, exercise and careful medical follow-up. The rest will be up to you and your body." He closed the chart and slid it under his arm. "Get some rest. I'll be back this evening with a detailed health plan. It won't be the end of the world."

He nodded at Grace and then walked outside as his beeper began to vibrate.

Jilly closed her eyes and gripped Grace's hand. In three months her salsa line would be gone, her vendors lost. In four months her investors would bail out. Her business would be destroyed.

"Hey." Grace gave her a mock shoulder

punch, though her eyes shimmered with tears. "It's not a disaster. You've got us. Remember that. We'll work this out together."

Jilly tried to smile.

But Grace didn't understand. It was different for her and the others. They had families and people they could rely on in an emergency. Jilly was alone — and she always would be.

Grace spoke quietly, keeping an eye on the door of Jilly's hospital room. "She's going to have to make huge changes, Caro. That means no stress and no cooking for at least six months."

"She'll hate it," Caro said fiercely. "It will feel like a death sentence for Jilly. Hold on. The baby's crying."

Grace heard rustling and then the sound of sniffling.

"Okay, one hungry baby emergency under control." Caro took a deep breath. "So it was definitely her heart?"

"That's what her doctor said."

"We have to get her through this transition somehow." Caro hesitated. "Can you get email?"

"I'm on my cell right now, but I can get email on that."

"Great. There's something I want you to see. This will make Jilly rest, whether she likes it or not."

"The intervention idea?"

"I think I found the perfect place. There's a lovely resort in Wyoming that specializes in craft retreats. She can enjoy a class in the day and then relax with a spa treatment at night. Lots of nature. Lots of peace. Not a lot of noise or distractions."

"What's this place called?"

"Lost Creek. They hold a highly praised knitting retreat there every year."

"Knitting? You'll *never* convince her." Wearily, Grace rubbed a cramp in her neck. "Jilly hates to knit. And she hates to be manipulated."

"I know." Caro hesitated. "And that, my friend, is where *you* come in. . . ."

CHAPTER FIVE

Oregon
Three weeks later

"Behold the new me. Completely calm. Seriously relaxed."

Jilly scowled at Grace, who was driving. "In fact you see before you the *queen* of relaxed. But there's one problem. You can only take so many walks or read so many fluffy magazines before your brain starts to rot. So listen to me, Grace, because this is serious. I love Summer Island. It was nice for the first few days and totally great to see Olivia again. Your grandfather, too." Jilly tugged back her hair in a vicious twist and dragged a rubber band around the thick strands. "But if I have to endure five more months of this *fun,* I may shoot someone. Most likely myself," she muttered.

"Relax, Jilly."

"Relax how?" Jilly glared up at the gray Oregon sky. "At least in Arizona, it was

50

sunny. These gray skies are depressing." Jilly sat up straighter, watching a road sign flash past. "You just took the wrong turn. We're supposed to be going to that new restaurant in Portland." Jilly's head whipped around as Grace turned onto the freeway and took the exit for the airport. "What are you doing? I thought we were going to Portland."

"Not exactly." Grace pulled into a parking spot and waved at a nearby car. Caro and Olivia jumped out, beaming in excitement.

"What's going on? Why are Caro and Livie here?"

"Because, my dear, sweet, idiotic best friend, they came to see you off. Caro has your suitcase packed and Livie bought you some new clothes."

"Clothes? Why clothes?"

"Because you're going on a trip and you'll need them."

"This is a joke, right? You planned some kind of a girls' night out in Portland. Just don't tell me it's at a Chippendales place because my heart isn't in it. My heart, get it?" Jilly's face was stony. "I'm trying not to spoil the party here, Grace."

"No Chippendales. I promise, you'll like this. It's a cooking retreat that I found on the web. It's only offered every three or four years, so you're in luck."

Jilly began to smile. "Really? I could handle that. I never have time to improve my skills, and I could finally dig in and catch up." She hesitated. "But the doctor told me no work —"

"You won't be working." Grace grinned. "You'll take classes. No worry and no cleanup. Low stress all the way."

"Wow. It sounds great." Jilly waved at Caro and Olivia, who slid into the backseat. "Cool scarf, Livie."

"I got the yarn in Florence. They really know how to live over there." Olivia tapped on the suitcase near her feet. "I've loaded up on your favorite travel food, chocolate included. You'll be in junk-food heaven. Caro packed the rest of your stuff, and I added a few clothes."

Jilly looked shell-shocked. "You mean I'm going *now?* What about Duffy? What about my ticket?"

"All taken care of." Olivia high-fived Jilly. "We'll take care of your dog and everything else. This trip is our gift to you."

"Seriously? You mean —"

"We mean you are going to go and have fun, Jilly. You're going to start over and learn how to relax."

Jilly rubbed her hands in excitement. "You guys are the best. You know that? I've told

52

you that, haven't I?"

Grace coughed and then pulled back onto the road. "Terminal 3, here we come."

"Where is it? San Francisco? New York?"

"Wyoming," the three others said in unison.

Jilly frowned. "I've never heard of any cooking programs there."

"It's all in your travel folder. Olivia will give it to you at the gate." Caro frowned at Jilly. "And remember. No caffeine. No alcohol. No heavy exercise or stress. You're supposed to take it easy."

"Sure, sure. I can go without coffee now. I won't buy a single cup while I'm gone. And no all-night keggers, I promise." Jilly wriggled like a kid, eager for details. "So what is this place called?"

"Stop asking questions and move." Grace eased the car to the check-in curb, motioning to Olivia in the backseat. "Olivia will go inside with you and help with your bag. She can answer any questions, too. We'll circle a couple of times and wait for her. Now get moving." She leaned over to hug Jilly. "Take care of yourself."

Olivia jumped out first, but Jilly grabbed her suitcase away and charged inside.

Caro shook her head. "She'll never change."

"Don't worry, Livie can handle her. By the time she realizes the truth, she'll be on the ground in Wyoming." Grace gave a guilty laugh. "And there are no more flights out tonight. I already checked. Like it or not, Jilly will be stuck there — on the vacation of a lifetime."

Lost Creek, Wyoming
Jilly had only landed ten minutes before, and her head was spinning from the whirlwind trip. So this was Wyoming.

She hadn't expected the mountains to be so big.

And the airport to be so *small.*

She crossed the waiting area and frowned at the row of two dozen seats. "This is a mistake. This *can't* be the airport for Lost Creek. It's tiny."

"No mistake, ma'am." The attendant at the sleepy baggage claim glanced at Jilly and sized her up for a big city tourist. "You going up to the resort?"

"I thought I was going to someplace near Jackson Hole."

The attendant laughed. "Quite a few peaks between you and Jackson. A couple million dollars in real estate values, too." He pointed out to the curb. "You can get a taxi over there. May have to wait a bit. Joe just had a baby so they're short-staffed."

Jilly felt a headache building force. "How long would it take to drive to Jackson Hole?"

The attendant looked as though she'd made a rare joke. "Couldn't do it. Not with all the mountains you'd have to cross. Why'd you want to go there anyway? Overpriced and overpopulated, if you ask me."

"The restaurants for a start. The fresh produce." Jilly closed her eyes. "The coffee," she whispered with a sigh of longing. "Oh, yes, the coffee."

"We got coffee here. Darned good coffee shop over on Main Street. This your bag?" He lifted the bright blue suitcase and sniffed. "Smells like chocolate."

Jilly took the bag and frowned. It *did* smell like chocolate.

"Probably sitting on the heater in the service truck. Must have melted the chocolate."

Another disaster. Jilly closed her eyes and tried to relax. "So how far is it to this resort?" Jilly dug into the pocket of her leather bag and found the big envelope that Olivia had handed her right before she boarded the flight to Denver. Jilly had assumed this place called Lost Creek was near Jackson Hole. Remote but sophisticated.

But there was no point in arguing now.

She was bone-tired and ravenous. Coffee would have been nice, followed by room service and a long soak in a big tub. Maybe even a massage. That's what people did to relax, right?

Jilly didn't know. She'd never had a massage and she hardly ever relaxed.

Something nudged her foot. She looked down and fell into a pair of big brown eyes.

A broad, furry face stared up at her.

The big brown Lab retriever looked calm and expectant, as if Jilly were an old friend who would know what to do next. And just like that Jilly's mood brightened.

She loved dogs. Any color, any size, any breed, they made her day.

Her irritation vanished as she sank down on one knee and rubbed the dog's soft brown fur. "Oh, my. You're a beauty, aren't you? Smart, too." Impulsive as always, Jilly felt no fear. The dog made a rough sound of pleasure as she found the little hollow behind the right ear.

It never failed. What dog didn't like to be scratched slowly, just along that sensitive little ridge?

"Excuse me, ma'am. My dog isn't good with strangers. Touching him is a bad idea."

"He's your dog? Well, we're doing just fine here. In fact —" Jilly glanced up, ready to protest, but her breath tangled up in her throat, lost in a husky gasp as she saw the rugged man looming over her.

CHAPTER SIX

He was tall, at least six-four. His eyes were an uncommon shade Jilly had never seen before. Not quite navy. Not quite gray, either. No, they were an unusual, restless shade warmer than both.

His skin was tan from long hours outdoors. A cowboy, by the look of him. Long legs. *Seriously* long legs. Jilly couldn't help running her eyes up that long, lean length of man with a silent sigh of appreciation.

Okay. This was one ruggedly handsome cowboy.

She coughed and stood up slowly, gathering her wits. The man was almost six inches taller than she was. She wasn't used to that. She also wasn't used to the quiet, focused way he was studying her.

No chatter. No cues of any sort. Totally reserved. But he looked as if he liked being in command of things around him.

Her brain began to race. Maybe he was a

rancher with a few hundred thousand acres, which he personally supervised by Jeep and horseback. On the other hand he carried himself with an almost tangible sense of command. Slow, simmering charisma of a very alpha type.

An actor?

No, not an actor, Jilly decided. His face was too contained. Actors were always on stage, oozing energy and playing to an audience. This man looked as if he could keep his secrets very well. He would give orders, but he'd do it so smoothly you never knew you were being controlled.

Jilly frowned. Where had all *that* come from? She didn't know the slightest thing about the man.

The big dog moved closer, nudging her hand for more petting.

"Okay, honey. You're a big beauty, aren't you? Want another long scratch behind the ears?"

The brown tail rocked hard and banged Jilly in the face as she knelt. "You love that, don't you? Sure you do."

The man's eyes narrowed. "Are you from L.A.?"

"No."

"Las Vegas?"

"No way." He thought she was from *Ve-*

gas? Hello?

"So where?" He slid his hands into his pockets, his eyes slipping to a darker shade of navy.

"I'm from Oregon, as it happens." Jilly stared back at him. "I've been working in Scottsdale for the past few years. That's in Arizona," she said, feeling a little snide. "South of here."

"I know where Scottsdale is." He made it sound like a bad thing.

That cool, assessing way of his irritated her. "What's wrong with Scottsdale?"

"Nothing. Not that I know of. Never been there." He rolled his broad shoulders. "Pretty hot in the summer, I guess."

"So are New York City and Houston and Washington, D.C. And they've also got humidity to crush your soul. Your point is?"

"No need to get riled."

"Who's riled?" Jilly glared at him. "I'm just throwing out some data here. You should visit Scottsdale before you pass offhand comments. It's a great town. They have fabulous spas there."

He tilted back his cowboy hat. "I'm not too big on spas."

"Well, then there's the hiking. You look like the outdoors type."

"Could be."

"Amazing resorts and world-class restaurants, too. I could name a dozen at least."

Irritated, Jilly blew out a huffy breath. Why did this complete stranger make her so defensive and flustered? "And one more thing. You should scratch your dog's head more often. Do it like this. Don't you know about this little ridge?"

The maybe-rancher looked bemused. "Don't think I do."

"Well you should. It's a great way to bond with your pet. It calms a dog and gives them sheer joy. *Any* dog."

"I'll remember that, ma'am," the man said dryly.

Oh, *sure* he would. And the world was flat.

Jilly reached for her suitcase, glancing outside in search of a taxi.

Suddenly a truck backfired. At a terse command from the owner, the dog sat down and went absolutely still in what was clearly part of a familiar routine. All the playful energy vanished. All the good humor disappeared with that low order.

The dog did not move a single muscle, alert for the next command.

Jilly forgot all about her suitcase and stood up slowly. "Wow. How did you do that?"

"Good dog, good training. He rarely takes to strangers though." The man frowned at the dog. "Odd. Probably it's because he's been cooped up for two flights back-to-back."

"Ugh." Jilly ran a hand through her hair. "I know just how he feels. Traveling can be hell."

"I didn't think you were a local."

"Don't get started on that again." Jilly waved her hand toward the front of the airport. "I guess I'll go find the taxis. I'm staying at Lost Creek Resort, wherever that is."

"Not far. You're too early for skiing," the man said slowly. "No real snow will accumulate for a month or so. Not that it's any of my business." The man started to reach for his heavy duffel bag, murmuring to his dog as he leaned over. Then he swung around, frowning.

His dog was looking at Jilly with an expression that could only be called wistful.

"Winslow? We need to go."

Ignoring him, Jilly leaned down to scratch his dog's head and smooth the powerful shoulders. The big dog gave no sign of going anywhere, motionless under Jilly's stroking hand, soaking up the attention.

"That's another first." The man shoved his hat back on his head. "He really does like you."

There was something about the man that interested as well as aggravated Jilly. She sensed a story here, something that would explain his detached manner and why he didn't like sharing anything about himself.

She gave a shrug. "Most dogs do. People not so much. And forget about skiing. I'm here for the cooking retreat."

The cowboy frowned. "Didn't know they had cooking workshops at the resort. But then I'm way out of touch. I don't get into town all that much." He looked away, his eyes on the horizon.

"Why not?" The words just slipped out.

His shoulders seemed to tighten. Then he ran a hand along his arm, almost as if it hurt him. "Lot of reasons."

As she looked at that tanned, lean face, Jilly felt the little hairs stir along her neck. Probably it was from the cool mountain air. Or maybe it was exhaustion from traveling. But there was no mistaking the sharp sense of awareness that hit her when he turned, reaching down next to her to pet Winslow.

Jilly could almost feel the heat of his body. Or was that her imagination?

Did he feel this weird kind of sensation, too? No way to know. His face gave away nothing. He barely smiled.

But his eyes tracked her, and Jilly thought

they had darkened as they watched her.

Again her skin prickled. She was usually excellent at reading people. She had a real radar for lies, secrets or bad juju. Her friends called it her crud-meter, and they relied on it frequently in tackling their ongoing renovation project in Oregon. It had saved Jilly from getting involved with bad business partners and shady construction offers on a number of occasions.

But right now the meter was dead cold. All she picked up was distance and sharp intelligence. Not a single emotion or detail came across from his face or his manner. And that was downright impossible. Jilly could *always* dig up something.

But the cowboy — if he was a cowboy — remained a cipher. By now most men would be impatient to be on their way, unless of course they were trying to make a move on her.

Not this man. He stood as if he controlled the spin of the earth. He seemed to register everything around him but showed no emotion about how it affected him. Just being near him left her feeling oddly . . .

Unbalanced.

But grounded, too. That was the right word. As if he gave her weight and order and security.

And he wasn't coming on to Jilly at all.

There were no covert stares at her legs or clever banter. No sly hints as he tried to mentally undress her. He simply wasn't interested, she decided.

Not that it mattered to *her.*

On impulse she held out her hand. "I'm Jilly O'Hara."

His eyes narrowed. Then slowly he held out a calloused hand. The movement seemed awkward and a little unsure. "Walker Hale. It's . . . nice to meet you, ma'am."

"Oh, call me Jilly. Everybody does, except when they call me worse things."

Their hands opened and met and Jilly felt awareness flare into something sharper. When his rough fingers opened, they seem to fit her hand perfectly, as if they had been made for nothing else. The jolt of contact made her bite back a sharp breath.

Jilly released his hand so fast it edged on rudeness. Even then her skin seemed to burn. "Well, Mr. Hale, I do love your dog."

The dog's eyes followed her, alert and liquid. The first hint of a smile brushed the man's face, and the change stunned Jilly. In that moment his expression softened, open and loving as he stared down. Well, who wouldn't love a big, wonderful dog like his?

He touched the dog's head and said a few low words. Instantly the dog was all energy, dancing at Jilly's side, full of joyous excitement.

"Impressive. He's like a totally different dog now. And you are one lovely ball of fur, aren't you, honey?" Jilly laughed as the dog nudged her hand, demanding more ear-scratching bliss. "What a gorgeous friend you must make."

The man rubbed his jaw. "Not many people call Winslow *honey.*"

"Well, I'm not most people." Jilly raised an eyebrow, irritated that she couldn't read the man. Not even a hint. "And honey is an equal-opportunity endearment. I use it for animals or people I like, male or female."

Something zinged between them. Recognition and possibilities and just a hint of something deeper. Speculation. Man/woman stuff. Jilly's meter spiked hard with that one. Unfortunately the feeling vanished before she could pin it down.

A muscle moved at Walker's jaw. "Give the lady your paw, Winslow. Show your manners." The big dog barked once, rolled over, raced around Jilly and then sat down, one paw raised perfectly.

"Isn't that the smartest thing? You're a real beauty."

Walker scratched his dog's head. Jilly noticed that this time his fingers moved until they found the exact spot she had pointed out at the dog's ear.

Fast learner, she thought. Maybe she had been wrong about him. Again Jilly felt the little stirring along her neck.

"Lost Creek is a small place. Maybe I'll see you around," he said. "Are you staying for the week?"

"Ten days, actually. The classes are supposed to be pretty intensive."

"I see."

The attendant clearing the luggage area glanced over at them, clearly impatient to finish his work. Jilly saw a yellow taxi pull up out front.

"I'd better go before I lose my taxi." Jilly swung her small suitcase off the carousel and wrinkled her nose. The smell of chocolate was unmistakable. Caro and her friends had stocked up on her favorite junk food in vain.

As she lifted the suitcase, two bags of chocolate candy fell out of the unzipped pocket. More candy spilled out, landing on plastic-wrapped bags of snack cakes in various flavors. Before she could turn the suitcase over, two sheer pieces of white lace fluttered to the floor.

Jilly blinked.

A ruffled lace camisole with matching bikini panties? Definitely *not* hers. She didn't do lace, not in any shape or style. Ditto on the ruffles.

"That's some stash of chocolate you have there." Walker looked down at the camisole that had drifted down onto his well-worn brown cowboy boot. A muscle moved at his jaw. "Nice underwear, too." He reached down and lifted the fragile lace carefully. "Sheer."

"Civilized people call it *lingerie*," Jilly snapped. "And hands off, if you please."

But she couldn't take her eyes away from the strong fingers that cradled the frilly lace. The contrast was so sharp it made her feel hot and strangely dizzy.

Okay, time to get moving.

She grabbed at the candy bars and wrapped cakes, shoving them back into the suitcase. Then she reached for the camisole he was holding.

The ground suddenly swayed. Her breath caught.

"Hey."

Jilly didn't answer. Her face felt hot and flushed.

"You don't look so good." The voice came from very close by, but for some reason Jilly

68

couldn't focus. She was fascinated by the little green squares in the carpet, which seemed to jump and dance.

"Sit down." Walker Hale gripped her shoulder and urged her down onto her suitcase. "Steady now."

His voice sounded a million miles away. The floor kept spinning. Maybe it was because of the hours of travel. Or the altitude. Or dehydration.

Winslow pushed up against her chest, licking her face and whining softly. His owner leaned down beside him. "Jilly, look at me." He cupped her chin and raised her face. Concern creased his forehead. "Take long breaths. Go on. Nice and deep. That's right." All his attention was focused on her, as if she were the only thing in the world.

Jilly seemed to slide straight down into his deep gray-blue eyes, as if she were wrapped up in a cool, clean mountain dawn. Now she could sense the warmth behind all his distance. Oh, yes, there were deep emotions here. There was power and need and loss, if you knew where to look and weren't afraid to dig hard.

He was definitely intriguing.

"You're shaking. Jilly, can you hear me?"

She hated that he was right. "I'm just a —

a little dizzy. Maybe it's altitude. Or something."

"Hydration," he said flatly. A water bottle met her fingers. "Drink it all."

Winslow whimpered and sidled up beside her, offering his body for her to lean against. Still shaky, Jilly was glad to accept the support and the water. As she drank, she focused on Walker and realized that he looked concerned.

Really concerned.

Did she look *that* bad?

She tried to be casual. "I forgot to buy water in Denver. I had to run after a gate change." Her throat was dry and the water felt like heaven. She finished drinking and ran a hand over her face, glad when the shaky feeling in her legs began to fade. "That's better. Thanks."

"Elevation can hit you hard. We're not so high as Telluride or Jackson, but it's high enough. Drink more water for the next few days. Don't overexert yourself." His fingers slid over her wrist and he focused on the big wall clock, watching numbers flicker by.

He seemed to know what he was doing, so Jilly closed her eyes and tried to relax, taking another deep breath.

"We're only at 4,500 feet here, but the resort is another thousand feet up. Get acclimated slowly. No alcohol, whatever you do." He continued to watch the clock. "You look okay, BP wise. A little high, but nothing crucial." His voice was cool and soothing.

"Say that again."

"Blood pressure. I've spent a lot of time at altitude and I know standard alpine medicine protocol. Do you have a history of heart problems? Asthma or emphysema?"

She looked away, frowning. "I'm fine." She wasn't going to discuss her health with this aloof stranger whose eyes saw too much. "I feel a lot better now. But I drank all your water."

"Not a problem. I always carry a spare. I can get that one, too, if you think you need it."

She flushed at his simple generosity. "No, but thank you. I really appreciate it."

Winslow bumped at her hand and gave a short bark.

"Hey, Win. Let her catch her breath."

"He's no bother. Are you, sweetie? You're just perfect." Jilly scratched the dog's head, wondering if she'd missed something. But no, she'd passed two exercise tests before leaving the hospital in Arizona. The heart halter she'd worn for a week had come up clean. This had to be a case of simple dehydration and the stress of travel. She did recall her doctor saying she should watch for signs of labored breathing and keep her exercise level low. He had warned her against going above 8,000 feet. But she would be fine here in Lost Creek.

When she got to the resort, she would reread all her medical instructions, which were stored safely in her bag. Since her blood pressure was fine, she wasn't going to worry. Too bad that her plans for a nice latte and a glass of Merlot would have to go on hold.

She stood up slowly, relieved when her dizziness did not return. "I guess the traveling caught up with me. I'd better go grab that taxi. Apparently you don't have a lot of choices for transportation in this town."

Winslow bumped against her leg, whining.

"My dog sure does like you." Walker sounded bemused. "I don't understand it."

"Wait a minute." Jilly gave a sudden laugh and slid a hand into the pocket of her sweater. She pushed past a half-eaten bag of nuts until she felt a sealed plastic bag. "Bingo. All is illuminated." With a flourish she held out a big piece of wrapped beef jerky, which she'd forgotten in the rush to leave. Her own dog, a snowy-white

Samoyed, loved jerky, especially her home-made treats.

Jilly felt a pang of regret, but she knew that Duffy would be happy at Grace's house on Summer Island, where he was boarding until Jilly's return.

What could compare with the love in an animal's eyes or the flow of warm fur beneath your fingers? What was better than the dance of pure excitement a pet gave to welcome you when you walked in the door?

Not even a fine, single variety dark chocolate could match it.

"Jerky. That would explain it." Walker scratched the dog's head. "Don't worry, bud. I've got a week's worth of jerky stowed in my duffel. We'll get right on that."

And then Jilly saw it again, the open, loving warmth that softened the man's eyes. He loved this dog and he didn't care who knew it. They were a real team.

And wasn't it pathetic that Jilly felt jealous of a dog?

She held out the bag of jerky. "This is on me. I don't need them. My Samoyed is back home."

"A Samoyed? Smart breed. Great temperament."

"That's my Duffy for sure."

"Miss him, do you?"

Jilly gave a rueful smile. "Terribly and I've only been gone part of a day. But I don't think he's giving me a second thought. He's probably running on the beach with his pals right now back in Oregon."

"Sounds like dog heaven. Winslow and I don't get to the ocean enough, do we?" Walker scratched his lab under his chin. "Thanks for the jerky." He gave a small piece to the dog, who gobbled it eagerly.

Jilly saw the attendant wave at her and point outside, where the taxi driver was standing up, talking on a cell phone. "I'd better go. Nice to meet you, Mr. Hale."

"Walker." He reached around her. "Let me get this for you." He scooped up her suitcase before she could react. "You've got the tote to carry. Winslow, sit."

Jilly watched the dog move over, sitting while Walker clipped on his leash to lead him outside. She didn't speak as they walked out to the cab. Something about the whole incident made her tongue-tied.

"Have a safe trip, ma'am. Say goodbye, Win."

At the drawled command, the big dog held out one paw. Jilly shook it and then scratched the soft head. "Drop by the resort if you want a food sampling. I make a killer chocolate mousse." She slanted a look at

Walker and frowned. There was something very intriguing about all that distance and cool control. Even now he gave nothing away. And the more he hid . . . the more Jilly wanted to pry out of him.

"Do you live in town?"

"Nope," Walker murmured. With a nod to the taxi driver he stowed her bag in the trunk.

After a moment Jilly slid inside. "Somewhere nearby then?"

"Nope." He closed her door, gave a two-finger wave and tapped on the hood. "Enjoy the resort, ma'am."

As the taxi drove away, he stood motionless, one hand on Winslow's head.

Jilly wondered why he had avoided both of her questions. It didn't feel like rudeness. More like habit. And there was a definite story here. Piecing it together would help her fill the time over the next ten days. Besides, that dog of his was special. Too smart and well trained to be a simple pet.

Nothing wrong with a pet, of course. But Jilly O'Hara recognized a trained service dog when she saw one.

And what did that make Walker Hale?

"Pretty lady, Win. Nice eyes. A little high-strung though."

75

The big brown lab watched the taxi vanish over the hill, then turned to look expectantly at his owner.

"What do you think?"

Winslow raised his head and gave a low howl that rose and fell like wolfsong.

"So you agree about the high-strung part. But you liked her. You made that very clear. And she had a real nice laugh."

Winslow turned and looked after the taxi, tail wagging.

"Great legs, too. Not that I was looking."

But he had looked. And at more than her legs, Walker thought. That lace thing from her suitcase had hit him right in the gut. What man wouldn't fantasize about seeing a woman in something that lacy and sheer?

Walker rubbed his shoulder, which had begun to ache again. Too many long flights. Too little downtime.

He forced away the pain by habit and turned his mind back to the woman. She had long dark hair that curled over her shoulders. Green eyes that glinted when she got angry.

She seemed to get angry fast. He smiled at the way she had ripped into him when he'd said Arizona was too hot. No mincing words, she had stuck up for a place she loved. He liked that kind of loyalty.

Yet when she mentioned Arizona she had looked sad. Almost lost. She had touched her chest as if it hurt.

Broken relationship? Marriage called off?

Hell, it was none of his business. Too long between dates, Walker told himself.

Too long between anything at all. He'd have to do something about that one of these days.

Frowning, he rubbed his neck. He remembered how her face had flushed and how quickly she had sat down. She had recovered fast, at least. But was it because of dehydration or something more serious?

None of your business, Hale.

And right now he had work to do.

A whole mountain of work waited, back at his cabin. He had a new set of mission plans to review. After that he and Winslow had to work out half a dozen new drill scenarios.

The training would help U.S. troops using service dogs in hostile mountain terrain all over Afghanistan. Walker and Winslow were something of a legend in their work. Since his medical discharge from the marines, Walker was in high demand as a combat training consultant. He traveled for work, and coming home to the mountains was always a relief. Everything he needed or wanted was right here in this small town. Nothing would change that.

So he pushed Jilly O'Hara's husky laugh and sexy underwear out of his mind, shouldered his heavy duffel bag and headed off to his Jeep with Winslow trotting alertly at his side.

CHAPTER SEVEN

The fieldstone buildings of Lost Creek Resort hugged a valley between two peaks. Small cottages circled a rugged lodge and two guest wings. Jilly imagined how beautiful the tree-lined slopes would look blanketed in snow.

As the taxi drove up the winding road bordered by pines and aspens, she gave up trying to get Walker Hale out of her mind. "So . . . do you know that man at the airport?" she asked her driver casually. "The one with the dog. He's a local?"

"Walker Hale? Sure. He's been here awhile. He's got a nice place up the mountain. Family's had a place here for generations. His dog is real nice, too. Trained and everything. Heard both of 'em were fighting over in Afghanistan."

"The *dog*, too?"

The taxi driver nodded. "In the marines over there. Dog helped with security. Both

79

got hit. Walker nearly got himself killed saving Winslow. Least that's how I heard it." The driver rounded a curve, and they cruised past low stone fences that framed the last of the year's wildflowers.

Jilly soaked in the beauty while she processed the new information about Walker Hale and his dog. "Wow. I thought his dog looked smart."

"He takes real good care of Winslow. Not too social though. He doesn't come into town much except for food and coffee. We got a new coffee shop this year," the driver said proudly. "You should stop in. They could use the business."

"I may do that." Jilly thought longingly of a frothy mocha latte with a dusting of cinnamon. But she had sworn to cut down on her caffeine, and she didn't want to go back on her promise.

She didn't confess that the real draw was encountering Walker — and his enchanting dog — again very soon.

Her room — a suite actually — was a cabin nestled in a grove of aspen trees. Their white trunks and dancing golden leaves made Jilly sigh in sheer delight. The rustic log design was peaceful and the clear mountain air seemed to calm her soul.

In her old, driven mode she would have rushed off to dig up every detail about her cooking classes the following day. But the new Jilly was determined to slow down and enjoy the scenery. Instead of fuming or worrying, she kicked off her shoes, opened the big French doors and wandered out to the stone patio overlooking the valley.

The view was drop-dead amazing, all green slopes and ridges above the distant valley and town lights. Someone had set out a plaid blanket on the big patio rocker. Jilly wrapped the thick wool around her shoulders, watching the sunset.

Not bad. This was almost peaceful.

Maybe she was getting the hang of this relaxation thing, after all.

A gust of cold air shook Jilly awake two hours later.

The sun had set, and the night sky was a soft purple lit by stars. Yawning, she stood up and stretched, then made her way inside to the living area. Bright rugs covered the walls, across from a fieldstone fireplace with distressed wood mantel.

Whoever designed the place had a real eye for color. With a yawn Jilly glanced at her watch and was stunned to see how late it was. No point in leaving her cabin tonight.

She had her travel food and the little room refrigerator held plenty of drinks.

She drummed her fingers on the table and then dug out her cell phone.

Grace answered on the second ring, sounding breathless.

"Hey, is something wrong?" Jilly asked.

"I'm repainting the upstairs hallway. The electrician finished the rewiring and the new floors are done."

"That's great. What about that kitchen wall?"

"One more week. But forget about the renovation. How do you feel? What do you think of Lost Creek?"

"The town is pretty small. And the resort is definitely rustic." Jilly studied the darkening purple sky. Was that a shooting star she had just seen? "But rustic in a good way. And the air up here is amazing. I feel great. I sat out on my porch and actually fell asleep. In fact I'm going to bed early. No point trying to check on my classes tonight."

"That's right. No need to rush," Grace said quickly. "You can get all the, uh, details in the morning."

"Is something wrong? You sound odd, Grace."

"I'm just a little antsy because I want to finish up and then take a nice, long bath.

I've got paint in my hair and under my fingernails. But Noah finally managed to get away. We're meeting tomorrow in San Francisco."

Jilly smiled at the excitement in her friend's voice. "About time. The hunk will have eyes for only one thing and that's your smiling face." Jilly stretched her arms and yawned again. "As for me, I am totally dead on my feet. But I have to know how Duffy is doing. Is he eating okay? Did he get his exercise? Did he go to see Dr. Peter for his checkup?"

"Let's take them in order. Duffy is doing great. He is eating like a horse. Or he would, if Caro let him. You should see Bogart and Bacall race around with Duffy up in the woods. Olivia is going to take him to her office, too. But you know our Livie. She's a little afraid of dogs she doesn't know well."

"Wait," Jilly cut in. "Olivia's afraid of dogs? I didn't know that. What happened?"

"Don't know. She closes up like a clam when I ask. But Duffy is such a big teddy bear that she seems okay around him. Is that a full enough report?"

Jilly blew out a little breath. "Thanks, Grace. It's just that I miss him. And I worry."

"No need to explain. Duffy's a great dog,

and he'll be here healthy and happy when you get back. But first we want *you* healthy and happy. So just relax and enjoy yourself."

"I'm working on it. I can't wait for my cooking classes tomorrow."

Grace cleared her throat. "Great."

"Well, I just wanted to call and say thanks. You're all the best."

"I'll tell Caro and Livie you called. You have the list of instructions from your doctor, right? No alcohol. No caffeine. No heavy physical exertion."

"I'm up to speed, Grace. Don't worry. Forget about painting the hall. Focus on having a great time with Noah. And tell him I said hi, okay? Remember that I want his mother's meatloaf recipe. She has some secret ingredients I can't figure out. Maybe roasted paprika?"

Grace laughed. "I'll tell him you asked."

Jilly stifled another yawn. "Did I tell you I saw a shooting star tonight? There was a tail of light that burned over the ridge. I'm taking it as a sign that good things are coming." Jilly hesitated. "I . . . met a man at the airport today. He had a wonderful dog. There was something about him." She turned, watching stars twinkle over the dark line of mountains. "Something intriguing. He was so controlled and contained. I

84

couldn't read him at all."

"No way. You can read anyone."

"Not him." Jilly smoothed the wool blanket, wondering why she couldn't get the man out of her mind. "Well, I'd better go. Make sure Caro doesn't work too hard. The contractors will drive her nuts."

"Olivia's taking over now that she's back."

"Good. Caro's too nice."

Grace chuckled. "I'll tell her you said that. You take it easy up there. Have a great time."

"That's the plan."

After she hung up, Jilly leaned against the cool glass doors. Her whole body felt relaxed and somehow lighter. Tonight she might actually be able to sleep. Though she had never told her friends, she had been plagued by crippling insomnia for months. Nothing seemed to help.

But tonight Jilly thought she could sleep for a week.

Yes, she was going to take that shooting star as a very good sign.

Things were finally looking up.

At 6:45 a.m. she was up.

She had slept better than she had for months. Totally energized, she was ready to plan for her classes. She paced back and forth, admiring the huge stone fireplace, waiting for someone to appear at the reception desk.

Her sunny mood began to fade when no one appeared. She tried the offices, but all were empty. Frowning, she followed the noise of rattling dishes back to a serving area. The drifting aroma of coffee and bacon told her the kitchen wasn't far away.

Jilly waved to a harried woman in a resort uniform. "Can someone help me?"

"Dining room is down that hall, ma'am. I'm afraid breakfast doesn't start for another ten minutes though."

"I'm really looking for someone at the reception desk. I want to find out about the cooking retreat."

The woman blinked at Jilly. "Come again?"

"Cooking. The classes?" Jilly said the words very clearly. "I'm signed up but I haven't found any details posted. Who should I talk to about that?"

"Well . . . I guess . . ." The woman put down her tray of clean silverware and gestured to a closed door off the kitchen. "Head chef is back there. Maybe he can help you."

"Thanks. Sorry to bother you." Jilly crossed the hall, noting the outdated cooking ranges and cramped food prep areas. The resort could definitely do with some renovations. Meal service during peak guest seasons would be a nightmare.

Not your problem, O'Hara. You're on vacation, remember? Let somebody else worry about the cleanup and the details of the food prep.

She stopped at an entrance with a carved wooden door, listening to the deep voice inside.

"I know the guest reviews have been good. But how can I upgrade the menus on the current budget, Mamie? And my staff is too small. Two cooks and six kitchen staff for a resort this size? It's impossible."

Jilly hesitated. She didn't want to eavesdrop. And the conversation seemed to be growing volatile.

Suddenly the man's voice boomed out in a laugh. "Sure, sure. I'll just keep asking. So what about the Henderson wedding? Still on for Friday? I know how you love a big resort wedding."

Jilly peeked through the door. A short man was sitting at a postage-stamp-size desk. Cookbooks lined neat shelves all the way to the ceiling. "Check. The cake is baked." He tapped on a computer as he spoke. "We'll start the decorations tomorrow. You still planning for one hundred guests?"

There was more silence, broken by the soft tapping of computer keys. "Will do. Come by at lunch. I made that ginger ice cream you like."

The chair creaked again and Jilly heard the typing resume. She knocked on the door.

"Come on in. It better be important. I've got a wedding menu to finish."

Jilly stepped inside. "Sorry to bother you, but I'm hoping to get some information about your cooking retreat classes. They start today, but I can't find any signs posted. I thought I'd ask back here."

The resort's executive chef swiveled his chair around slowly. "Cooking classes?" His ruddy face slid into a grin. "Very funny. Wait a minute." He tilted back in his chair, studying Jilly. "Do I know you?"

"I don't think so. I arrived last night."

The chef drummed his fingers on the tidy desk. "I recognize you now. You're Jilly O'Hara of Jilly's Naturals. I read an article about you last week. Look at these." He opened a drawer and rummaged excitedly, then pushed a jar across the desk. "Mango Chipotle Salsa. A mix made in heaven. I used it last night as a basting sauce for grilled pork. So why are you here at Lost

Creek Resort?" He made a kissing motion to the air. "Why aren't you in your kitchen producing more great salsas?"

Jilly liked him instantly. She had to smile when he pulled three other flavors of Jilly's Naturals products from the drawer. "It's kind of . . . an enforced vacation. I've been a little under the weather, and my friends set up this trip as a surprise. But they told me I was going to a cooking retreat. There aren't any classes here?"

"Sure, but not for cooking. Somebody must have made a mistake."

No cooking? That couldn't be right, Jilly thought. Could her friends have been confused?

Maybe she should call Caro and —

The chef broke into her tangled thoughts. "Nothing serious, I hope. About you being under the weather."

"No. Just working too hard — you know how hectic it can get in a kitchen."

"Tell me about it." He held out a beefy hand. "Name's Ralph MacDermott. My friends call me Red. Not for the hair, but because I burn. It's the Irish in me. Tell me what you think of the resort so far."

Jilly took the cup of tea he poured from an electric pot behind his desk. "Everything's beautiful. You've got a nice, tidy kitchen. Very clean and well organized." In politeness she didn't add that it was also cramped and forty years out of date. But cooking magic came from people, not appliances.

"We manage pretty well, most of the time. Ski season gets a little crazy. Skimageddon, we call it." He sipped some tea and then studied her some more. "Had a chance to look at the menu yet?"

"No. I fell asleep last night. The air here is amazing."

"It will take off ten years, and that's a fact. Have a croissant." He pushed a plate of golden pastries across to Jilly. "You must be pretty busy with your restaurant and your food line. How did you manage to get away?"

Jilly's smile faded as she remembered her fall in the kitchen and the cascade of bad news that had followed. Right now her business was shaky. A friend from cooking school was filling in temporarily, but she couldn't ask him to help out forever. Soon she'd have to make a decision.

She could let go of her dream and sell everything. Or she could go back to the job that she loved, knowing it could kill her.

What kind of choice was that?

Jilly decided that her call to Caro could

wait. She was having too much fun talking shop with another chef. "I delegated. I'm trying to learn better management skills."

Red refilled Jilly's cup. "And your friends signed you up? Nice idea. They definitely sent you to the right place to relax. Sure, we're not Jackson Hole or Aspen, but for my money, I'll take Lost Creek any day."

He searched through a folder, then glanced up at the wall clock. "How about I walk you over to the building where our workshops are held? It's just down the hill, but the path can be confusing." He flipped off his computer and stood up.

"You've got a kitchen to run," Jilly said. "If you can give me directions, I'm sure —"

"No way. You're a celebrity," Red said firmly. "You get the grand tour."

As they wound past cedar-and-glass buildings, Red filled Jilly in on the town's history, dating back to a rough-and-tumble mining camp in the last century. It was clear that he loved the place. Between questions about produce sources and trends in southwestern cooking, he grilled Jilly about future plans for her salsa line. She managed to be polite despite her fears about the future of her business, but she was relieved when they finally stopped at a big redwood structure with stained glass windows.

Now maybe she would get some answers.

Red glanced at his watch. "Here's where the classes meet. But it's a little early. You have time to get breakfast."

"I never eat much breakfast. The croissant was perfect. Besides, I want to see about the retreat. If it's really not geared to cooking . . ." Her voice trailed off. She looked around curiously as a young woman with a big wool bag strode past, red Keds flashing beneath purple leggings. Two more women rounded the path, both carrying big fabric totes.

Jilly studied their bags. They had big pockets on both sides. Jilly had seen bags like those before.

Caro carried one. It held her current sock project. And extra balls of yarn.

Stitch markers.

Long wooden needles.

Jilly closed her eyes.

They hadn't. They couldn't.

Had her devious friends signed her up for a *knitting* retreat instead of a cooking school?

CHAPTER EIGHT

She was going to skewer them for this!

Jilly shot from surprise straight into fury. They had tricked her with images of cutting-edge cooking techniques and hot new chefs. They'd *lied* to her.

They'd signed her up for *knitting* camp. A bunch of old ladies with blue hair and arch support shoes, Jilly thought furiously.

Oh, she could knit if she had to. She knew the basic moves. But it had never been fun or relaxing for Jilly, and each project attempt left her crazy with impatience.

There was no way she'd be going through that door into those classrooms. Over her dead body!

Red was staring at her in concern. "Are you okay? It's not cooking, but our retreats are very popular. We've sold out three years in a row. You're lucky your friends could find you a spot."

"*Lucky?* Not from where I'm standing. I

knit like a surly second-grader, so my friends tell me. I'm going to kill them for this," she muttered.

"Hey, you might like it. Kinda soothing to see all those needles bobbing around. My wife used to knit. I lost her last year to cancer." The chef cleared his throat. "What I mean is, you should give it a try. I can introduce you, if you want. I know all the teachers by now. We bring pie and chocolate down every afternoon at break time."

Jilly tried to rein in her temper, aware that her friends had set this up with good intentions. They wanted her to rest and they figured this was the best place for it.

But she needed to *cook,* not knit. She needed to stand at a big 34-inch stainless steel stove finessing salsa and coaxing European butter and dark chocolate into sinful new concoctions.

Jilly rubbed a hand over her face, processing the shock. She was a terrible knitter. It brought out the impatient teenager in her, and that was never a good thing.

But here she was.

She'd have to find some way to occupy herself, but it wouldn't be anywhere near balls of yarn and pointy sticks. No blue-haired grannies, either.

Red called out to a woman in a bright

green and blue sweater that would have sold for a fortune at a trendy Aspen boutique. Jilly recognized the skill of the finished piece. The woman had a name tag and looked like she was in charge.

As she approached them, Jilly suddenly felt like a cornered animal. Piles of yarn waited to torment her with dropped stitches. Rooms of expert knitters would glare, studying her with pity and contempt.

"Sorry, Red, I, uh, just remembered. I have to return a call. A — business call."

"But you're supposed to be on vacation. And the retreat —"

"Better go." Jilly darted back up the path, ignoring the questioning looks of Red and his friend.

What was she supposed to do *now?*

Jilly couldn't imagine sitting calmly and chatting with a room full of strangers, all of whom were better knitters than she ever hoped to become. She would only manage to twist her stitches and drop whole rows.

She'd be a basket case inside an hour.

Jilly kicked a stone out of her path, frowning. If she hadn't gotten sick, she'd be back in Arizona perched on a sunny stool, overseeing produce deliveries and designing the next month's menu. She'd be busy and productive, thrilled to be alive.

She sank down on a little bench, aware of an alarming — and absolutely unfamiliar — urge to cry. She recognized that she had a good chance for a healthy future if she was careful. She knew that she was lucky to be alive.

But how did you pull yourself up and start all over? Where did people find the courage for that? It was terrifying.

She sighed, watching mist gather and then tumble over the mountains on its way down to the valley.

You didn't talk. You just did it.

Jilly squared her shoulders. No more whining or hand wringing. No more knitting angst, either. She was going out to find something fun to do. To heck with the yarnies and their cool projects.

Ten minutes later Jilly stalked up the steps to the main lodge.

The taxi service was unavailable. The hot tub was closed for maintenance. The tiny library didn't open until noon. And she hated spa treatments.

Meanwhile, the resort internet service cost twenty dollars an hour. Were they kidding?

Jilly thought longingly of Summer Island and the bustle of the narrow cobblestone streets, where she knew everyone. There were the repairs to Harbor House to discuss with her friends, part of their ongoing plan to create a chic café and yarn shop right at the foot of the harbor. And Jilly missed Duffy. She missed his warm body on her bed and his sloppy kisses in the morning.

She tried not to think about all the other things She should be doing, like check on her tottering business in Arizona.

Something glinted in the sunlight. A laughing couple pedaled past her on identical red bicycles.

Bicycles that said Lost Creek Resort.

Who needed a taxi?

She swung around and collared the first resort employee she could find. She could already smell the extra-large cappuccino she was going to buy in town.

So what if it was cheating?

The bicycle fit her perfectly. Its old-fashioned weight made Jilly feel safe and in control.

The wind combed through her hair as she turned onto the service drive and began to pick up speed downhill. How long had it been? Ten years? Fifteen?

Suddenly memories hit her, hard and fast. Her first bike.

Jilly was twelve when she'd been placed with her second foster family on Summer Island. She'd had pigtails and her own bedroom for the first time that she could remember. They'd tried to make her feel welcome, tried to show her the good points of the small, tightly knit community.

But she hadn't fit in. When the family had moved, Jilly had been placed again. And then again three months later. She'd never really fit in. Not until she met Grace and Caro and Olivia.

In the course of a week Jilly had discovered what it meant to belong. That summer had changed her life, allowing her to pull down the heavy walls she had built for protection after being shifted from foster home to foster home.

To cap the summer off, Caro's grandmother had given her a bike, bright green with a blue basket. At first Jilly had thought it was a mistake, that it was really meant for Caro. But when she saw that Caro had an identical Schwinn, right down to the blue basket and blue seat, Jilly was speechless at the generosity. She had tried to give the bike back, only to have Caro's grandmother frown and ask if she preferred a different color. Then Caro had gotten teary and said that if friends couldn't give gifts to friends, what good were they anyway.

That long, enchanted summer hung in her mind, clear as yesterday. She remembered every golden week of laughter, every shared secret. No complications, only lazy sunny days.

Then Caro's mother had checked out of her detox program and vanished.

Then Grace's grandmother had begun to show the ravages of lupus.

Then Olivia had revealed signs of panic attacks and stress at school. Through it all they had backed each other up completely. They had always known the best words to offer comfort and share pain.

Something burned at Jilly's eyes. She had amazing friends, but they were all moving on. Caro was married with a baby now, worrying about her marine husband in a hostile country. Grace was engaged, trying to juggle the demands of a long-distance relationship with a man she adored. A successful architect, Olivia was finally breaking free of her father's icy dominance and already planning a return trip to Europe.

It was all changing. They'd never be as close again. One day they might wake up and discover they had nothing at all left in common.

Jilly shuddered at the thought, unable to

bear the possibility of losing something so precious. She rounded a turn, the wind whipping at her hair. Something flashed at the middle of the road, and she yanked the handlebars, braking hard. Before her lay a bright red square that seemed to be a wool tote bag with leather handles, cables and big silver buttons.

She picked up the bag and glanced inside. Two pairs of knitting needles, one crochet hook, three balls of yarn and a cell phone. She looked back up the steep road and saw she'd come much farther than she'd thought. She'd never make it to town if she went back to the lodge now.

She rolled up the tote and slid it into the saddlebag on her bike. When she got back, she'd turn the bag in to the resort lost and found. But first she had a dream date with a gorgeous cup of cappuccino.

The town of Lost Creek looked like a backdrop for a ski commercial. The main drag held twenty shops where locals seemed to mingle amiably with tourists.

Jilly pedaled slowly, taking in the sunlight reflected on the neat windows. The town wasn't as small as she had first thought. There were nice shops and a cozy bookstore. Several of the restaurants looked promising.

Then all thoughts vanished in a rush of fragrance from a nearby door. Jilly careened to a stop and sniffed again.

Espresso. Dark roast.

Freshly ground.

Her brain short-circuited. She couldn't stop her feet. Leaving her bike on the curb and drifting on autopilot, she followed the smell of roasting beans. Before sanity returned, she was sitting in a wooden booth by the window holding an extra large steaming espresso and trying not to swoon.

For long, delicious moments she simply drank in the smell.

"Is something wrong?" A lanky young man with bright green eyes gestured at the cup. "I notice you haven't drunk your coffee. Is it okay?"

Jilly gave a guilty smile, painfully aware of the promise that she was about to break. "I'm having a transformational experience here. No point in rushing it."

"Cool." He smiled and pointed to the painted blackboard covered with local ads. "Mind if I go write that down for a testimonial?"

"Be my guest."

Jilly still didn't drink the coffee. She was pleased at her restraint. Waiting was good.

Meanwhile, a phone rang somewhere in a

back room. Two women in jogging pants came in, ordered lattes and left. More people came and went. Sunlight poured in a golden cloud over the narrow street. Jilly cradled the coffee between her hands, fighting an urge to drain the frothy cup in one greedy gulp.

But she closed her eyes, counted to five and then regretfully pushed the steaming cup away.

Another phone rang. Three more customers came in, ordered coffee to go and then wandered out. You could make a lot of money with a good business in a town like this. Both locals and visitors appeared to be spending money, and every parking spot on the street was taken. There were no For Rent signs or closed-up windows. And in ski season, with good staffing, a restaurant could —

Jilly shook her head. There she went, building another business empire.

"Would you like a refill?" the young man asked.

"No. I'm just fine."

"But . . . you haven't drunk any yet."

"Just taking my time."

The lanky worker hesitated. "In that case, if you aren't in a hurry, would you mind keeping an eye on things here for a few minutes? They just called me from the bank and I need to run over to sign some papers."

Jilly would have been more surprised at this trust afforded a stranger, but growing up in Summer Island she had seen the same easy manner. "I guess so. But are you sure —"

"I'd really appreciate it. Unlimited coffee on me as a thank you."

Great. Add torture to temptation, Jilly thought. "No need. I can stay for a while. Nothing special to do."

"That's cool. What did you say your name was?"

"Jilly. But —"

"Great. Thanks, Jilly. Just tell any customers that I'll be right back, okay?"

Jilly had barely managed a nod when he waved once and strode outside. The silence pulled at her, calming and deep. She studied her coffee, bemused.

The door opened. "Uh, is Jonathan around?" A small girl in a jean jacket glanced at Jilly, frowning. "I wanted to get a coffee."

"If Jonathan is the man with the red hair, he just left. He said he'd be right back. Something at the bank."

The girl looked anxiously out the window. "I have errands to finish. My brother will be waiting."

Jilly stood up. "What do you want? I can make it."

"I'd love a mocha latte, please. And some of Jonathan's hazelnut syrup. But I thought you were a customer."

Jilly walked around and checked out the serving area. "No problem. I can work the machines." After two summers working at a coffeehouse in Portland, she knew her way around an espresso machine and a steaming wand. "Have a seat while I make it."

She filled the silver coffee filter, pulled a shot and then went to work on the steamed milk, efficient and precise. The girl looked surprised at the frothy milk design that Jilly poured over the top of her drink.

"Wow, that looks great. You should teach Jonathan that. He always has problems with that new espresso machine." The girl pulled some froth onto her finger and licked it thoughtfully. "Wow," she said again.

The front doorbell chimed but Jilly barely noticed as she finished cleaning the small filter, rinsed the milk wand and leaned down to check the heat level on the boiler. Nothing ruined fresh beans faster than high heat or a bad grind.

She heard a man clear his throat. "Is anyone here? Jonathan?"

Jilly shoved back her hair. The air seemed dense, too heavy to breathe. She was painfully afraid that she was blushing as she turned and saw the tall man by the counter with the well-behaved brown dog right beside him.

CHAPTER NINE

Jilly rubbed a drop of milk from her hands and stood up slowly. "Walker, isn't it?" She hadn't blushed since she was nine. Why *now?*

"That's right. Is Jonathan around?"

She smoothed a dish towel on the counter, wondering if he looked a little tired. "Jonathan went across the street to the bank. Can I get you something?"

Some men would have made an off-color quip to an open question like that. Jilly suspected the thought would never enter this man's mind. He nodded and set a Thermos on the counter. "Coffee, if you don't mind."

"Any special kind?"

"Whatever you have, ma'am. I'm not particular."

"Jilly," she corrected. "And in that case I'll make you my specialty. Double shots of espresso with a nice amount of foam. Caffeine and froth happen to be my two favorite food groups."

"Don't tell that to the nutritionist's association." He watched as Jilly moved expertly along the work counter, making the espresso shots.

It felt like heaven to be back behind a counter, Jilly thought. Relaxing . . . in a busy sort of way. How could you ever explain that to a non-chef?

Walker glanced around the shop and raised an eyebrow. "I thought you were supposed to be on vacation."

"I'm just helping out."

She poured the espresso shots into a cup, then tipped in froth, studying the result. A little more foam, she decided. No Thermos. She wanted him to appreciate her artwork. "There you go." She pushed the cup over to Walker. "Tell me what you think."

He studied the cup warily. "I always take mine black. Nothing special."

"Try it. Just one sip." Jilly flipped a towel over her shoulder. "If you don't like it, I'll make you your nothing-special version."

Walker looked at the cup, shook his head and took a sip.

And then another.

He didn't move, staring at the sunshine on the counter. Slowly he turned to look at

Jilly. "That's nothing like the coffee Jonathan makes. Nothing like I ever had before."

"She's good, isn't she?" The girl from the booth held up her empty cup. "Mocha latte. She added some kind of design on the top, too. Best coffee I ever had. Really."

"Seems like you've got a magic touch," Walker murmured. "What's your secret?"

"Your friend Jonathan has great beans and an expensive machine here, but his grind setting was off. I also adjusted the overpressure valve for his machine. Nothing magical about that."

Walker took another thoughtful sip. "I'd say there's a lot of magic here. Jonathan better take notes when he gets back. This is really smooth. I like that dark undertone."

Jilly took a mock bow. "Put it down to two crazy summers working in a busy Stumptown branch in Portland. Caffeine boot camp, with lines from 7:00 a.m. to midnight. People there know every detail about coffee so you can't make mistakes. You got good or you got fired."

"Never had coffee like this at Camp Pendleton," Walker said dryly. "Probably would have started a riot. You're a dangerous person, Jilly O'Hara."

Jilly looked down quickly, feeling the blush flare up again, heating her face. "Glad you

108

like it. Finish that and I'll get you another. It's on the house." She peered over the counter. "And what about some jerky for your handsome friend? I found another piece last night and I happen to have it with me."

Walker grinned. "Yes to the drink. What do you say about some jerky, Winslow?"

The dog whined, banging his tail loudly on the polished wood floor.

"I'll take that for a yes. Kind of you, Jilly."

"Not a bit. They'd probably dry out before I got home anyway." She reached around the counter to offer Winslow his treat. Then she vanished back out of sight, hoping Walker wouldn't notice her flush.

"How about a refill on that mocha latte?" she called to Jonathan's young friend by the window. "I can make it a harmless on a leash if you need to go."

"Huh?" The girl sat up sharply. "Gosh, I'm going to be late. What's that mean, what you just said?"

Jilly moved smoothly, working as she talked. "Harmless is a decaf. Or in some places it means no-fat milk. Regional preference. On a leash means to go." She leaned over the counter and held up a to-go cup, smiling. "I made yours low-fat but full caffeine. You look like you could stand another shot."

"I'd better not. Sorry — Jilly, is it? I hope you're here the next time I come. But I'd better run. My brother gets mad if I'm late." With a shy smile, she strode outside, glancing up and down the street.

"Her brother sounds like a real jerk. Can't an adult female get a simple cup of coffee without looking over her shoulder in a panic?"

"It's not quite so simple." Walker rubbed his neck slowly. "Sara has epilepsy. Her parents are dead and her brother's very protective. She's taking a new medicine now, too."

"Small town. So you know all the gossip. That makes a lot more sense. I'm really sorry to hear that about her."

Walker nodded, staring at the street. "Bad break." Clouds were moving in from the north, and aspen leaves tossed and danced in the wind.

Walker turned the coffee cup slowly. "It's not much fun to be sick, or in pain. I think she's had her share of both."

Jilly propped her chin on one palm, studying Walker. "Sounds as if you have, too."

"Could be." He shrugged and turned away, clearly ready to drop the subject.

"What about that vacation your friends arranged? This doesn't look like time off."

"Any more relaxation and I might kill someone," Jill said wryly. "I need noise and bustle and work. It's the way I'm wired."

"So why are your friends convinced you need a rest?"

Jilly looked down, cleaning the counter carefully. "Because they're bossy," she muttered.

"And because they care about you," Walker corrected. "I'd say something happened to make them worry. Maybe something to do with that dizzy episode you had at the airport yesterday?"

"I survived, didn't I? And you'd better finish that coffee before I lose all my control, leap over this counter and wrestle it away."

"Swore off caffeine, did you?" Walker rubbed his jaw, trying to hide a smile. "Yeah, I've been there, too. You can have the rest of it." He measured the cup. "Shouldn't be enough to cause much trouble."

His eyes glinted with humor, deep blue drifting into rich gray. Jilly couldn't seem to look away, feeling as if she could study that face forever and still not know all its secrets. To distract herself, she pulled his cup around, smelled the excellent aroma and

111

then finished the last of his cappuccino with a sigh.

"Not bad, if I do say so myself. But no more for me. I promised my friends — and myself — that I wouldn't have *any* coffee." She saw a woman in a wool sweater walk by the shop, glance in and wave at Walker. Two men in worn jean jackets passed next. When they saw Walker they waved and nodded.

"Does *everybody* smile in this town? Or are you just Mr. Popularity?"

He gave a tight laugh that sounded almost like a cough. "People don't stand on ceremony much here. They can't afford to. If a blizzard dumps ten feet of snow in an hour and you need to be towed out, you'd better be on good terms with your neighbor who has the snow plow."

A uniformed police officer got out of his cruiser and stopped to speak to a woman with a baby. When he glanced over and saw Walker, he nodded, tipping his hat.

"Very friendly," Jilly murmured dryly. "Want to tell me what's really going on?"

Walker's eyes darkened. "I'd better get going."

Jonathan pushed open the front door, looking harried. "Sorry I took so long. New teller." He stopped when he saw Walker and broke into a smile. "Hey, Walker, good to

112

see you." Jonathan leaned down to scratch Winslow behind the ears. "How's it going up on the mountain, buddy?"

Winslow lifted one paw, which Jonathan shook gravely. Then he glanced behind the counter. "Wait, did you pull those shots, Jilly? And you ground new beans?"

"You were almost out. Plus the grind was off for your machine. A coarser grind works best on that model."

Jonathan scratched his head. "I could swear the rep told me to use fine."

"They changed that recommendation last month." Jilly had seen a memo on the subject.

"Don't tell me you're in the coffee business? Man, that's sweet." Jonathan looked at Walker's empty cup and smiled. "Fast worker, too. You didn't tell me you were a pro."

"Two summers do not a professional make," Jilly said. "But I remember the moves. And I use the same espresso machine in my restaurant. Or I did." She cleared her throat.

"You've got a restaurant? Of your *own?* That's awesome." Jonathan's voice rose so fast it broke with his excitement. "Where? How many can you seat? What kind of cuisine?"

"In Arizona. Forty max. And the theme is American organic and light fare specialties with a local produce base. That's just a talky way to say that I use whatever best produce is in season. Good produce is everything."

Was, she reminded herself. Painful memories hit her hard.

"Man, we really have to talk. I like this shop, but I've totally wanted to be a chef forever. I've got a few thousand questions to ask you." Jonathan set a bag with pastries and utensils beside Walker's Thermos.

"Thanks." Walker reached into his pocket. "How much do I —"

"Forget about it. It's on me."

"I don't want to forget about it." Walker frowned. "How much, Jonathan?"

The lanky shop owner crossed his arms and glared right back. Jilly was pretty sure they'd had this argument before. "I told you. It's on me."

Jilly raised an eyebrow. "Hey, are you two arguing? I was just about to name this The Friendliest Town in America."

Walker took the Thermos and the bag of pastries and put a ten-dollar bill on the counter. "It's not an argument. It's an ongoing . . . conversation," he said calmly. "Thanks for the coffee, Jonathan. By the way, have Jilly make you her specialty. It's a

114

— what did you call it?"

"Double espresso. With lots of foam," Jilly added with a cheeky smile.

"Right." Walker picked up his dusty cowboy hat from the table and scratched Winslow behind the head. "That cup could just about make a grown man weep." He walked to the door and patted his leg. Winslow raced to his side. "Don't work too hard, Jilly. You're supposed to be on vacation, remember? Maybe one of these days you'll tell me why."

He gave Jilly a long look and then pushed open the door for Winslow.

Two elderly ladies passed, smiling at him and calling him by name. Jilly thought that Walker looked uncomfortable at the attention.

What was going on here?

"Hold on." Jonathan leaned under the counter for a newspaper and some magazines. He shoved them into a big paper bag and headed to the door. "I keep the papers and a few magazines for Walker. He forgot them today. I wonder why?"

When he came back from his errand, Jonathan looked thoughtful. "So you know Walker? He doesn't say much to anyone. Just comes in once a week for coffee and some reading material, usually when he and

115

Winslow are headed out for a survival or training drill."

"What do you mean, he doesn't talk to people? He seems normal to me."

"Yeah, that's the funny part. He must like you a whole lot because he never hangs around. Not ever. Not," Jonathan said slowly, "until today."

"I'm sure you're mistaken." Jilly turned away, to hide a little buzz of pleasure. "He just liked the coffee." She couldn't help glancing outside. Walker was opening the door to a big green pickup. "I can help you with the machines, if you want."

"Great. Maybe you can take a look at my newest machine. It's been squirting espresso."

"Okay. Are you watching the shots as they fall? Are you stopping them when you see blonding? And you're changing your grind as the beans age?"

Jonathan looked confused. "Nobody told me to do that. I don't want to mess anything up."

"You'll be fine. I'll show you what to do." Outside Winslow jumped up on the passenger seat, turned around once and then settled at the window. Jilly watched Walker slide behind the wheel.

Two more people passed and waved at him.

"What is it with this town? It's starting to feel like *Stepford Wives.* Why does everyone smile at Walker and Winslow?"

Jonathan's face turned grave. "You don't know?"

"Know what? I just got here last night. What's the big secret?"

"He's a real hero, Jilly." Jonathan put his elbows on the counter, looking gravely after Walker's green truck. "He and Winslow saved a whole platoon over in Afghanistan. Nearly got themselves killed, too. Walker's still recovering. He's more than welcome anywhere in this town. In any home, shop or office, and he always *will* be," Jonathan said fiercely.

Something squeezed at Jilly's chest. "So that's why you wouldn't take his money."

"Damned straight, and you can bet he won't *ever* pay for anything in here as long as I own this place." Jonathan pulled open a drawer and dropped the ten-dollar bill in beside half a dozen others. "Once it reaches two hundred dollars, I'll deposit it in his account at the bank. Nobody gave those two a parade when they came home. Winslow was hurt pretty bad, and Walker got special therapy for the dog. More than he got for

117

himself, so I've heard. Walker's still got to pay off all those expenses. His family — well, that's a story for another day." Jonathan shook his head. "The postmaster's son was in his platoon. So was my cousin. And Walker's going to get help from us, whether he likes it or not. It's the least this town can do to say thank you to a hero."

CHAPTER TEN

Jilly couldn't speak as the dusty green truck drove away in the sunlight. "He didn't tell me," she murmured.

"No, he wouldn't." Silence stretched out. Jonathan leaned against the counter, watching clouds drift over the peaks to the north. He shoved his hands into his pockets. "I only wish I was half as brave and tough as Walker is."

He stopped, coughing to hide his embarrassment. He shifted some cups and pulled out a yellow pad. "If you don't mind, I'm ready to take notes. Let's start with those grind instructions." He glanced up the mountain and then checked his watch. "We're supposed to have rain later, and you don't want to be riding a bike back uphill in a storm. I'll close up early and drive you to the resort when we're done."

Jilly was a good teacher. Experience had

made her thorough and detailed. She didn't rush Jonathan, explaining how to time a shot of espresso for maximum flavor. After that, she worked on his steaming technique for milk.

All the time she worked, Walker kept invading her thoughts, along with images of war and the hammer of gunfire. Now she understood why he rubbed his right shoulder when he thought no one was looking. It also explained the almost tangible loyalty and intelligence that shone from Winslow's eyes and the protective way Walker stroked the dog's head, as if they were an inseparable team.

So Walker seldom stayed long in town? Didn't he miss being around people?

She had seen the curiosity in his eyes and the pleasure when he'd tasted her coffee. She knew there was interest. Maybe more than simple interest.

As Jonathan cleaned up, he continued to cross-examine her about his machines. Jilly promised to return the following afternoon for a refresher course.

"No way. I don't want to interfere with your vacation. You should chill."

Jilly gave a dry laugh. "Too much relaxation will kill you. Working today at your shop was the most fun I've had in weeks. I

120

love being busy."

"See? That's what I love about chefs. You're all driven. Totally nutty. But in the totally best way," he added quickly. "You know what you love and you just charge ahead. That's the way I want to be."

He sounded so young, Jilly thought. So innocent in his eagerness. Had she ever been that open and confiding? "Don't change, Jonathan. The cooking world can be brutal, with cutthroat competition and impossible hours. Sometimes the bravado is because we're scared."

"You?" Jonathan turned around slowly. "I don't think you're scared of anything."

"Yeah? Thanks for the compliment, but you're wrong."

"Could have fooled me." Jonathan locked up and then the two lifted Jilly's bicycle into the back of Jonathan's Jeep Wrangler. As they finished, Jilly felt something cold hit her cheek. Thunder rumbled in the distance.

"Better jump in. It's gonna open up any second."

"But it was sunny. Just a little wind —" The sharp hammer of rain made Jilly scramble inside the Jeep. In a matter of seconds the whole valley had darkened. "You were right about how fast the weather changes up here." Her teeth chattered as she rolled down the sleeves of her shirt.

"Grab a blanket from the back. They have a great log fire every night up at the resort. You can make your own s'mores. They serve amazing local wines, too. It's a cool tradition. Be sure not to miss it."

And what would happen after dinner? Would Jilly sink into bed, only to bolt awake at 3:00 a.m., unable to sleep any longer?

It was her usual pattern over the past months. All the herbal tea and yoga exercises in the world made no difference. In the months before her collapse she had worked until she was bone-tired, dropping into bed at 2:00 a.m. and praying she'd sleep through a normal night.

Usually dawn found her wide awake, staring at her bedroom ceiling, juggling details of a restaurant and two food lines. Every night sleeping got a little harder and dawn came a little sooner.

But last night she'd finally gotten some decent sleep. Jilly prayed that tonight would be the same. . . .

"I am *not* a coward." Jilly studied her reflection in the mirror of her room while she changed into a warmer sweater. "I am *not* running away from anything. If I *choose* to avoid the knitting area, it has nothing to do with fear."

The truth was that knitting intimidated her, bringing out the awkward rebellious teenager. Despite all of Caro's instruction over the years, Jilly couldn't seem to relax and stop fighting the process. She always dropped her needles, poked herself or twisted her yarn into a tangled mess.

So knitting was nowhere on her agenda. She was going to find a nice, quiet spot where she could relax and think.

As she finished dressing for dinner, she took a quick glance outside. More clouds poured over the mountains, covering the sky and the green slopes below. Digging in her carry-on bag, Jilly found a wool shawl that Caro had knitted for her. Soft and dense in a rich mix of reds and amber, the cabled shawl always made her feel like a Celtic princess.

But there was something inside the shawl.

Frowning, Jilly opened the folded wool and saw a bulky envelope with her name on it. Somehow, in her exhaustion, she had missed it the night before.

She recognized Grace's elegant handwriting instantly. When she tore open the envelope, a folded sheet of paper and two balls of cashmere yarn fell out, along with a small wrapped package.

Confused, Jilly sat down on the bed and began to read.

Dear Jilly,
So now you've found our gift. We debated hard about what to hide in your suitcase to surprise you.

George Clooney wouldn't fit. Neither would Daniel Craig. Really sorry but we tried.

But these things did fit — and before you make a face and start muttering, please hear us out. (Us because Livie and Caro are sitting beside me, helping me write this letter.)

We know you don't love knitting. You say it makes you crazy and you'll never be any good at it. But you never try long enough to get better!

Remember that summer when you were twelve? You were determined to learn how to make soufflés. You kept us going through eggs for weeks with awful results.

Did you give up then?

Of course not. You just tried new recipes. And by the end of the summer . . . Do you remember?

By the end of the summer Jilly had a blue

ribbon from the county fair for her chocolate soufflé. She'd forgotten about that.

She rubbed a hand over her eyes, remembering the lazy August day with all the sharing and the laughter. Could you ever have
better friends than this?

She went back to the letter.

Fast forward a few years.

You've had setbacks. You're worrying
about work, life, your future. Since we
can't change those things, we gave you
something almost as good.

We gave you time.

This is your week to relax. Throw away
your daily planner and your cell phone
and let yourself consider a new kind of
life. It's all in your hands now, Jilly.
Whatever you decide, we're totally behind you. That's without question or
limits. Always.

But take this week and slow down. For
once in your hectic life . . . be lazy. Let
someone else cook for you.

Sleep late.

Eat lots of chocolate.

Watch old movies.

Take a long bubble bath.

Eat more chocolate.

Watch the sunset and really see it.

And instead of sneaking out of the retreat (because we know you want to!) give the knitting classes a chance. You've got great teachers and a passionate group of knitters in residence there. You could have the time of your life.

If you just let yourself.

XOXOXOXO

Below the X's were three hand-drawn faces: Grace, Caro and Olivia.

Jilly sat very still, clutching the letter hard. She didn't have any family, but this was something far better. This was a family by choice rather than by a mere accident of blood. They were anchored and bound by hopes and laughter and occasional tears. Because they knew her inside and out, they wouldn't let her off the hook.

Jilly folded the letter carefully, returning it to the envelope. The balls of cashmere were light as angel wings, the perfect mix of reds and amber. Under the yarn she found a narrow package that felt heavy. When she opened it, a pair of vintage ivory knitting needles fell into her lap, burnished from age and careful use. At one end of each needle intricately carved lions growled above what might have once been tiny words.

Jilly took the needles in her hands, feeling

the weight of history and the joy of a lineage of skilled women. They had celebrated births, deaths and weddings with the work of these treasured old needles, probably for generations.

The right tools for the job had always been Jilly's motto. As the cool ivory rolled over her palm, Jilly felt an odd sense of anticipation. It was as if she had just been given a rare and unexpected gift, something that could take her places she could not imagine.

If she let it. If she stopped being anxious, opinionated and proud long enough to try something different.

She glanced outside, watching rain hammer at her patio. She couldn't skip out when this retreat meant so much to her friends. She'd have to make an effort to learn. If she was a failure, at least she could assure her friends that she'd honestly tried.

And Jilly was certain she would fail.

Walker looked at the packages on his desk and glanced at his watch. The request for updated maps with field schematics had come in barely twenty minutes after his return from town. He had finished those and packed them carefully. He had to post some signed medical forms, too.

He rubbed his shoulder, watching the sun

vanish behind the racing clouds. The rain had stopped, and it wouldn't be a bad drive back to town. He could drop everything off and be home for an early dinner with any luck. He had a good book, some new music and a nice stew in the freezer. It was his usual kind of evening here in the mountains.

But maybe he was getting into a rut. Maybe he needed to be a little more adventurous tonight.

Like Jilly O'Hara.

He was pretty sure *she* wouldn't sit at home with some reheated stew and a good book. No, she'd round up her friends and go cook on the beach. Or maybe they'd pile into her car and go line dancing at some smoky place down a dirt road where the drinks were cheap and the music too loud to talk.

Walker blew out an irritated breath. Why was he thinking about Jilly and her maddeningly husky laugh?

Because tonight his house was too quiet.

There were too many ghosts waiting for him.

So what are you afraid of? Go and find her.

Shaking his head, Walker gathered up his packages, tossed Winslow's leash in his bag and pulled on his coat.

■ ■ ■ ■

After dropping off his parcels at the little town post office, Walker turned to look at the night sky. The air was clean and stars sparkled across the dark velvet above his head. The quiet seeped in, rich and deep, and he leaned against the hood of his truck, drinking in the beauty.

Growing up in Washington, where his father had an office, there had never been silence or time to think. His parents had scheduled every minute of his life, demanding perfection in everything he did. For years Walker had thrived on the challenges and the pace of that life. And for years he had done all he could to make them proud.

To make them love him, the way a boy wanted his parents to love him.

But one day he realized that all the awards wouldn't be enough. There would always be another hoop to jump through and another test to prove himself.

Right about age fifteen Walker had decided he'd had enough of the hoops.

He hadn't seen eye to eye with his driven and demanding parents about a lot of things since then. The years had passed and they had become estranged. Now the calls were short and curt, if they happened at all.

Walker thought he should do something about that, but he wasn't going to go home bearing any olive branches. Too many harsh words had been thrown his way for that. Especially after he announced that he was joining the marines and was headed to Afghanistan.

Hell, why was he dredging all this up tonight?

He just wanted a little noise and some good food. Maybe some easy laughter and talk. No reason to make it into more than it was.

He was already in town. The resort wasn't too far.

He slid into the truck and whistled to Winslow, who was busy tracking a rabbit in the bushes. "Round 'em up, troops. Let's go find something to eat."

But he almost turned back three times on the way. Once he stopped to pick up some books he'd ordered at the library. Then he'd stopped at the hardware store.

What was the big deal? Couldn't he have dinner out once in a while?

As he stopped at a light, he saw Jonathan cross the street and wave.

"Back already, Walker? What did you forget?"

Walker rubbed his neck. "Nothing. I had some things to drop at the post office. Since I was here, I figured why not go up to the resort and have some dinner."

"Dinner? Up at the resort? Tonight?" Jonathan stood on the sidewalk and blinked at him.

"A man can't eat?"

"No. I mean — yes. Of course you can. But heck, Walker, you haven't been up there in weeks. Why did you decide to go tonight? Is there —" Jonathan stopped and cleared his throat. "Oh."

"Something wrong?"

"No. Not a thing." Jonathan glanced up the street and then ran around to the passenger side, smiling broadly. "Let's go see what Red has on the menu."

CHAPTER ELEVEN

A long line snaked toward the restaurant so Jilly went off in search of the lost and found. Following directions, she wound through the big, cheerful lodge past hand-forged sconces and fieldstone walls. Everything added to a sense of rustic luxury that Jilly was finding addictive.

At the end of the hall she followed the sound of laughter to a reception area where a tall, confident woman gave instructions for what appeared to be an intricate crescent scarf knit on tiny needles.

Crescent? Could you knit that shape? Jilly had only seen triangle scarves and they had never appealed to her practical nature. Decoration aside, how did you wear a triangle and keep it from falling off?

But a crescent scarf had definite possibilities.

"May I help you?"

"Uh — yes. I found a bag on the road

today and I think it may belong to someone here." When Jilly held out the wool bag, the woman gave a sigh of relief.

"It's Anna's bag. I'm so glad you found it. She was distraught because her cell phone was inside along with her knitting things. I believe she was offering a reward, too. If you'll leave your name and room information, I'll tell her."

"No need for any reward. I was happy to help out."

Jilly glanced into a large classroom as clapping filled the air. Excited knitters began to spill out into the hall. When a group approached the desk, Jilly slipped away, avoiding any more questions. She decided she wasn't ready to look into classes tonight.

She found a cozy table near the roaring fireplace and scanned the menu. She ordered the resort's specialty chili with a grilled corn and asparagus salad. Red wasn't breaking new culinary territory, but his choices looked imaginative and guaranteed to please a wide range of tastes. Healthy, too, Jilly noted. A whole section of the menu was devoted to salads using fresh local ingredients. Plus for Red.

"Sorry to bother you, ma'am, but I think we owe you a big thanks." A slender woman with elegantly cut silver hair stood with her arm around a younger, taller version of herself. Both women wore colorful sweaters that would have made Caro's or Grace's eyes fog over with envy.

Clearly knitters, Jilly decided. Likely mother and daughter.

"I'm Anna Jamieson. I think you turned in my knitting bag. Honestly, I had just about given up hope. I can't tell you what it means to me."

"Uh — no problem. I was glad to help out."

"Well, Andie and I had posted a reward. We want you to have it."

"No, really. There's no need to —"

The woman raised an eyebrow. "You don't want unlimited free desserts for a week? That was what we promised. If you can pass up one of Red's chocolate soufflés with fresh raspberries, you're a better woman than I am. By the way, I didn't get your name."

"Jilly O'Hara."

"Thanks a lot, Jilly." The daughter, Andie, reached out to shake Jilly's hand. "My mom was going bonkers. You just saved us a huge bar bill. So the desserts are definitely on us."

"You really don't have to."

"Oh, we insist." The younger woman

glanced at Jilly's tote bag. "Are you here for the knitter's retreat, too?"

Jilly didn't want to lie. As the two women waited expectantly for an answer, she realized she was being rude. "Uh, not exactly." *Great lie, O'Hara.* "Would you like to join me? Or have you already eaten?"

"Thanks, we'd love to, but we just finished our class. We need to go put away our notes and knitting stuff. How about we meet up for s'mores and wine later?" Anna Jamieson glanced at her watch. "About 8:30? And this is definitely our treat. You're not getting away so easy." She nodded happily to her daughter. "Andie was right. I would have gone nutters without my bag. So we insist, our treat."

"Sure. That sounds . . . very nice." Jilly managed a smile. As the two women vanished into a crowd of knitters, Jilly counted seven lace scarves, four multi-color vests and one glorious full-length coat knitted in crimson mohair.

Each garment was a work of art. And not a single blue-haired granny in sight.

Jilly felt guilty at how biased and uninformed she had been. This was a varied and inspired crowd. But she'd never fit in with experienced artists like these. Her fiber skills were a joke.

Fortunately her server appeared just then. One glimpse of the fresh corn, grilled asparagus and steaming bowl of chili made Jilly forget about her quandary.

She'd drown her worries in comfort food.

Red, the head chef, appeared ten minutes later. He greeted several guests, stopped to speak with the seating attendant, then spotted Jilly and made a beeline toward her table.

"Nice to see you again. I hear you had a full day — pulling espresso shots at Jonathan's coffee shop and then finding someone's lost bag." Red raised an eyebrow. "Not to mention a nice long visit with our local hero. You've been pretty busy."

Jilly felt her face heating. Why did she flush whenever Walker was mentioned? "Jonathan is very nice. I was glad to help him out with a little espresso tutorial."

"More than a little one from what I hear. And Anna and her daughter are over the moon about that missing bag. Don't even try to talk them out of your reward."

"If dessert is half as good as this chili was, I'll be thrilled." Jilly tapped the empty bowl. "Very nice mix of flavors here. Chipotle and cumin. And is that a hint of espresso for a smoky base?"

"You got it. I learned that from Mamie. She started the resort with her husband forty years ago. I try to keep at least one of her recipes on the menu. People have been coming here for decades and now they expect it."

"If it isn't broken," Jilly murmured. "Nice cornmeal muffins, too. That salsa you used was killer, by the way." Jilly gave a cheeky smile. "Who made that?"

Red snorted. "As if you didn't know. That was Jilly's Naturals — pineapple mango chipotle salsa. A great mix of flavors that really pops with the muffins. Not much could stand up to that chili, either, but your salsa line manages just fine." He looked thoughtfully at Jilly. "So how long have you known Walker?"

The sudden change of topic made Jilly blink. "I met him yesterday at the airport. We arrived at the same time and Winslow took a shine to me. More likely to the dried jerky treats in my pocket. As for me, I think it was love at first sight."

Red looked startled. "Does Walker know?"

"Know what?" Suddenly Jilly began to laugh. "No, I don't mean Walker, Red! I barely know the man. I meant his dog. Winslow is amazing."

"Oh. I get it. Sorry." Red hesitated. "The

truth is, we all look out for Walker here. He seems to have taken a serious interest in you, from what Jonathan says."

"It was just a simple conversation. I made him some coffee, and he liked it. End of story." Jilly toyed with her water glass. "Anyone would think you were trying to marry the poor man off."

"Of course we are," Red said flatly. "He deserves to be happy. It's high time he had a family in that beautiful house of his. He needs stability and roots. If we can give him a nudge in the right direction, you bet we'll do just that."

"Don't look at me." Jilly shifted uneasily. "I'm *never* getting tied down. I've got too many other important things to do with my life."

"Settling down is important, too. Frankly, I'm surprised that no one has scooped you up already." Red frowned. "You don't have anything against marriage, do you?"

Jilly laughed. "No, marriage is fine and beautiful — as long as it's someone else's."

"Now that's cynical. Don't give up on marriage quite yet. You've got your whole life ahead of you. And now I'll buzz off so you can look at the dessert menu. I suggest something chocolate. You'll have a whole lot to choose from," he added with a wide grin.

He moved off, stopping to chat at four different tables. Jilly saw that he was passionate about the resort. Most of the staff seemed to have the same enthusiasm, almost as if this place was a second home rather than simply a job.

And Red was definitely right about his desserts. Jilly counted six different chocolate fantasies, and they all looked over the top. Chocolate espresso cheesecake, flourless chocolate cake with raspberry sorbet, chocolate blood orange ice cream and double mocha chocolate brownies with whipped cream and coffee bean sprinkles — the list was impressive.

Jilly would have loved a small tasting menu instead of a full serving of any one. Families or friends eating together would enjoy sharing carefully plated desserts and arguing happily over favorites.

Maybe Red could serve them in espresso cups or shot glasses, Jilly mused. Or with a teapot and tray. Something quirky and unexpected would make a happy end to the evening. Red could also package dessert mixes as resort souvenirs. The brownies and chocolate espresso cheesecake would be a huge hit. Back in Scottsdale she had —

"Hey, Jilly." Jonathan loomed over the table, smiling. "We looked all over and they told us you were in here." Jonathan gestured to the empty chairs around the table. "You want some company?"

Jilly felt a wet nose nudge her hand. Winslow bumped her leg, tail thumping.

The sharp prick of awareness struck again, with a tension of skin and scent and heat. Jilly looked down, laughing as Winslow licked her face. Walker was somewhere close. She could feel that odd hum in her blood.

She cleared her throat. "That would be . . . nice."

Walker leaned down beside her, scratching the dog's head. "I think Winslow here wants more treats. Greedy is his middle name."

Jilly started to say she was sorry, no more treats. Then her eyes met Walker's. The interest was there all right, though he didn't smile. Maybe there was more than simple interest.

Her face felt warm, and she picked up her menu to hide her surprise at seeing Walker again.

"You haven't eaten dessert yet. Great." Without a pause Jonathan pulled out a chair. "We'll have whatever you have, but with seconds. Red's chocolate cheesecake is

140

stellar." He looked questioningly at Walker. "Take a load off, Walker."

CHAPTER TWELVE

Jilly shifted restlessly, frowning at Jonathan.

Had any matchmaking ever been so heavy-handed? Didn't Jonathan realize he was embarrassing both her and Walker?

Completely at ease, he stretched out his skinny legs and waved to a female staffer who blew him an air kiss. Grinning, Jonathan sent a kiss in return.

"Maybe Jilly wants some peace and quiet." Walker stood behind a chair, studying Jilly's face.

"Then why'd she come to a busy resort?"

"I guess that's her business, isn't it?"

Jilly's usual chatter had vanished beneath the almost painful awareness of Walker's leg only inches from her thigh. Why was everything so sharp, every sense so alert and filled with possibility when he was nearby?

Jonathan shrugged. "If she had a problem with it, I guess she'd tell us. I haven't heard any protests."

"That's just the point. She hasn't said anything at all."

Jilly cleared her scratchy throat and looked up at Walker. She was fascinated by his veiled expression and the sense of intensity and quiet control. Jilly wondered what it would take to pry away those barriers that always seemed in place.

The thought was dangerously appealing.

"No — I mean, it's fine. Pull out a chair and join me. Please. I'm here alone." Winslow nuzzled her leg, nosing around for more hidden jerky treats. "I'm sorry, honey, but all the treats are gone. Maybe Red can drum something up for you. Why don't I go ask —"

"Stay right where you are. I'll go find Red." Jonathan shot to his feet.

"Sure we aren't intruding?" Walker said quietly.

Jilly worked at sounding calm. "Not at all. I was just trying to pick out what I wanted for dessert. Unfortunately, I want everything." She realized that Walker was still watching her thoughtfully. "Well, go on. Sit down and order something. Gluttony loves company."

Walker slid into the chair beside her, then patted his leg. Instantly Winslow settled on the floor at his feet, calm and quiet despite the bustle and noise around them.

Jilly passed Walker a dessert menu. "People tell me that Red's chocolate selections are out of this world."

"They are. I've eaten here before." Walker scanned the menu, idly scratching Winslow's head. "I lived up here for a while before my cabin was finished, so I know how good Red's food is."

"So how long have you been in Lost Creek?"

"Almost two years." Walker shook his head. "Doesn't seem that long. I've still got a lot of work to do on the cabin. It's been in my family for years, and things were run down."

Another clue, Jilly thought. "So you're originally from this area?"

"My mother's grandfather was. She moved east as a girl."

"And you decided to go all Mountain Man here in Wyoming? Back to the land and all that?"

Walker's lips curved a little. "Not exactly."

"But your family has a tradition here. Ranching? Farming?"

"Not exactly," Walker repeated dryly. "We were never big on ranching."

"*Walker?* Is that you?" A frail woman in navy slacks and a bright red sweater crossed

144

to the table and frowned at him, hands on her hips. "Why didn't you come and say hello? It's been almost three months now."

Walker stood up and took the elderly woman's hand, squeezing it carefully. "Sorry, Mamie. I've been busy. First with work on the cabin. Then Winslow and I had some work out of town," he said quietly.

"And how *is* my favorite dog doing?" Mamie leaned over to scratch Winslow's head. When Walker spoke quietly, the dog rolled over, legs up in the air. Playing dead.

Mamie laughed and rubbed Winslow's soft stomach. "You're still a big ham, aren't you?" Mamie shot a measuring look at Walker. "Your job out of town went okay? No . . . problems?"

"Everything was fine. You should sit down, Mamie." Walker pulled out the chair next to Jilly. "Have you two met?"

"Not yet. And there is no need to go pulling out chairs and offering me your arm. I had a heart attack, sure, but I'm fine now. I hate people hovering. I'm old, but not feeble," the woman said fiercely.

Jilly liked the woman's directness. There was a nice glow in her cheeks, but she didn't look completely solid on her feet. One hand shook a little as she balanced it on the back of the chair.

"I wouldn't dream of calling you feeble, Mamie. You're still the most powerful person around. You lift one finger and heads roll," Walker said. "Everybody knows that."

"No flattery, either, young man." Mamie sat down slowly and studied Jilly. "I'd be delighted to meet your friend, Walker."

"Mamie Bridger, meet Jilly O'Hara. She's here for your knitting retreat. Jilly, Mamie owns the resort. She's the one to see if you have any complaints."

"Damned straight. You come right to me with any problems, Jilly."

"Nothing so far. It's lovely here, Mamie. Everyone has been wonderful."

The small woman looked pleased. "That's what I like to hear from our guests. Better than all the blood-pressure medication in the world." She glanced at their menus. "Have you ordered yet? Red's got some real crowd-pleasers there."

"We were just getting around to it. Jonathan went off to the kitchen a few minutes ago."

"Figures. That boy has always been cooking crazy. And whatever you order is free tonight. You never did let me pay you for all the work you did on Red's new oven and walk-in freezer, Walker."

"I'd say room and board was a fair enough

payment," Walker said quietly. He frowned a little. It was clear that he didn't want to pursue the subject.

Mamie smiled at Jilly. "So are you from Wyoming, Jilly? Do you ski? Our winters are one step short of paradise."

"No, I never learned. And I'm from Oregon."

"Never too late to start. A healthy young woman like you would be doing moguls in an afternoon."

"I doubt that. But your resort must be magical in the winter."

"So I've been told. We work hard at it. The weather doesn't always make it easy." She frowned. "It doesn't help when people don't keep to their plans, either."

"Is something wrong, Mamie?"

"I had some bad news earlier. We had a big wedding scheduled this weekend, but now it's off."

"Something happened?"

"The bride changed her mind. And the groom ran off with a bridesmaid." Mamie blew out a short breath. "I guess I like to believe in happy endings. I like when people do what they say they'll do." She sighed. "Probably that makes me a dinosaur." She nodded at Jilly. "You must be the woman who was helping Jonathan at the shop today.

I hear you brew a mean cappuccino."

"I think that story must get more exaggerated every time it's told," Jilly murmured. "It was fun to help out."

"My grandson can use all the help he can get. He's got passion and grit, but he's not always very organized."

"Jonathan is your grandson? I didn't know." Jilly considered this information. "He's got the beginnings of a wonderful shop there. With a little more experience he'll be able to compete with anyone."

"I hope so." A cloud crossed Mamie's face. Then she smiled as Jonathan appeared, carrying a metal bowl filled with water for Winslow.

"Hey, Grandma. You look great. Not working too hard, are you? You promised."

"I can rest when I'm dead, and that won't be for a long time yet, God willing. Now sit down and tell me all the things this nice young lady taught you today at the shop."

"No secrets in this town," Jonathan muttered. "Jilly walked me through some ways to improve my coffee settings. We worked on brewing and frothing techniques, too. She's got a great hand, Grandma. If you don't believe me, ask Walker."

Mamie smiled slowly. "What do you say, Walker? Is Jilly that good? If so, maybe we should find a way to keep her here."

Walker started to answer, then frowned as Winslow sat up slowly, growling low in his throat. "What is it, Win? What's wrong?"

The dog gave a low bark then raised his head, sniffing the air. Walker looked around the crowded room.

As far as Jilly could tell, nothing was wrong. Staff were carrying platters. Tables were full of diners laughing and talking, enjoying their food.

But Winslow was restless, sniffing the air and looking up at Walker.

Walker stood up. "Jonathan, why don't you stay here with Mamie and Jilly? Win and I are going to have a look around."

"But —"

Suddenly an alarm began to clang. All the talking stopped. Jilly glanced toward the kitchen and saw a dark cloud of smoke billow through the door. A waitress appeared, waving and looking distraught.

"Jonathan." Walker's voice was calm and very controlled, but the tone of command was unmistakable. "Take Jilly and Mamie outside. *Now.*"

CHAPTER THIRTEEN

Jonathan held out his arm to Mamie. "Come on, Grandma."

"But that's smoke." Mamie's face was pale, strained. "I have to —"

"Grandma, you heard Walker. We're going outside. You, too, Jilly."

At the nearest table, a frightened mother with two young children was trying to gather up her bag, bottles and a folded stroller.

Walker put a hand on Jilly's arm. "Jilly, why don't you help her outside? Her children look pretty frightened."

"Of course." Jilly glanced back at the growing cloud of smoke. "You'd better hurry." Her hand met his and she squeezed hard. "Be careful."

He nodded, touched Winslow's collar and walked away, stopping to point several anxious diners in the direction of the nearest exit.

Jilly quickly crossed to the lady juggling two crying children. "Can I help you with the stroller? You look like your hands are full."

"Oh, yes, please. My children are so upset by that siren." She shot an anxious glance back toward the kitchen. "So am I."

Diners poured toward the door, where they jostled and shoved to be the first outside. Jilly was proud of Jonathan as he stepped into the fray, holding Mamie's arm while he spoke calmly, directing people out in threes until the jostling ended.

A harried man raced up to Jilly, holding a baby in his arms. "What happened? Are the kids okay?"

"We're fine." The mother gestured toward Jilly. "Take the stroller, Dave. I need to get the kids outside and calm them down."

"Okay, honey." He swung the baby against his shoulder and took his wife's bag and the stroller from Jilly. "Thanks for the help. I'll take it from here."

When Jilly looked around, Jonathan and Mamie had vanished. There were only a dozen people left at the doorway.

Walker was talking on a cell phone at the kitchen. Then a billowing wave of smoke cut him off from view.

Jilly hesitated. As a chef, she was familiar

with kitchen accidents. She knew how to handle a fire as an outsider would not. And her decision was made in that second. She moved quickly toward the door, only to find her way blocked by a waiter in a resort uniform.

"Ma'am, you need to leave the building. We have an emergency in the kitchen."

"It's okay. Mamie sent me. I'm going to help Walker. Is it a grease fire?"

Jilly already knew the answer. Close to the kitchen the smell of acrid oil drifted out with every wave of smoke.

"Yeah. It's bad in there. You can't see for all the smoke and we can't find the fire extinguisher. Someone's gotten badly burned."

Jilly bit back questions, focused on the fastest way to tame a grease fire. Inexperienced workers usually went for water, which was the worst thing to do, sending boiling oil up in an explosion that would sear anyone in close range. And a grease fire could spread fast.

The answer was a fire extinguisher. Since that wasn't available . . .

She opened the door and immediately her eyes began to burn. She heard someone groaning and saw open flames near the far end of the kitchen. Red was digging in a nearby drawer, while giving orders to the staff nearby.

Walker was trying to wrestle a fire extinguisher from its hanger on the far wall, but it appeared to be stuck.

Jilly scanned the cooking area, saw a cast iron pot and grabbed the heavy lid. "Red, use this." When the worried cook turned, Jilly put the lid on the floor and shoved it hard over the tiles. Red dropped the cast iron lid on the smoking unit, and she heard the hiss of hot oil. Then the flames vanished.

"Stay back, everybody," Red called. "Any luck with that extinguisher, Walker?"

A metal bar pulled apart and crashed to the ground as Walker tugged the extinguisher free from its frame. "Right here. Let me get that oil."

But the flames were gone and no more smoke rose from the deep fat fryer. Walker kept his post watchfully just in case, while Red went to help the two wounded workers, who were hunched over the counter, clutching their arms.

"Ambulance is on its way," Red said. "I don't want to put anything on the burns until the medics arrive. Here's a chair, Nan. Sit down before you fall down." The siren stopped abruptly. "Thank heaven for that."

"It hurts like hell. I don't know what happened, Red." The cook's voice shook. "One second it was fine, and the next thing I knew the whole unit was on fire."

"We'll have it completely checked," Red said grimly. "Last week there was a short in the back refrigerator. Maybe it's the wiring. It's been too long since we've had this area overhauled." Red glanced back at Walker. "Everything okay over there?"

"Looks good. But I'm not moving."

The smoke was almost gone now and Jilly could see clearly. There were gray smudges on the back wall and burned oil stains on the surrounding steel counters.

But it could have been far worse, Jilly knew. She walked past Walker to examine the fire extinguisher housing. The metal frame had separated and half lay on the floor. Jilly picked up a twisted screw, studying it carefully.

"Rusted through. Maybe you had a water leak or the sprayers went off back here in the past. It looks like this piece got torqued out of alignment, so the unit wouldn't release when you needed it." She held out the screw to Walker. "In my restaurant I have the frames replaced every year." Jilly felt a pang at the thought that she would never have that kind of responsibility again.

"Good tip," Red said grimly. "I wish I'd

started doing that sooner." He looked out the window as the wail of sirens filled the air. "Thank heavens." He hovered near the burned workers. "They'll take good care of you. And you'll get full pay while you recover. You have my word on that."

A team of booted and uniformed firemen burst in from the back, followed closely by three EMS techs.

"Over here," Red called. "The fire was in the deep fat fryer. It seems to be controlled. We've got a lid on it, and an extinguisher ready if needed. We have two burned workers who need attention here, too."

Jilly backed out of the way of the emergency teams, who worked swiftly, assessing the fire and enclosing the fryer unit while the medics helped the burned workers.

She blinked as the floor spun and she put a hand against the wall, fighting a wave of dizziness. Her heart seemed to drum in her ears.

"Are you okay?"

Jilly felt a hand on her arm. Her heartbeat was getting louder, and the room was a little blurry. "Um, I'm not sure."

The grip on her arm tightened. There was a comfort in the strength of that touch, Jilly thought dimly. And that was very odd, because normally she hated being touched by people she didn't know well.

She blinked as Walker guided her a few feet forward and nudged her into a chair. "Sit. I want one of the EMS workers to check you out. Your face is white and you're breathing too fast."

He didn't wait for her to argue, simply motioning to the last of the med-techs, who trotted across the room.

"Need any help over here?"

"No." Jilly's voice was raw.

Walker just looked at her and frowned. "Yes, we do. My friend looks a little faint. Maybe you could run a test on her vitals."

"Can do."

Jilly opened her mouth to protest that she was just fine, maybe a little tired, but the fierce look in Walker's eyes cut her off. Then she realized her hands were shaking.

The tech moved smoothly, taking her blood pressure, pulse and temperature. Walker waited in silence, one shoulder against the wall, his gaze never leaving her face. Jilly was surprised at just how comforting it was to have him nearby. He didn't say much, but clearly he was a man who could be counted on. And she liked counting on him.

And when in the world had that begun?

The tech put away his stethoscope with a

snap. "Okay, BP a little elevated. Ditto for pulse. But it's nothing unusual, given a stressful event of this type. No signs of coughing or smoke inhalation. No burns, right, ma'am?"

Jilly shook her head. Her throat felt dry. "I am a little thirsty."

"Probably part of the problem, ma'am. You need to drink a whole lot of water today. And take it easy. No hiking or strenuous athletics. Any heart problems? Emphysema?"

Jilly just stared at him. She wasn't going to blurt out her whole medical history, not like this. As long as her pulse and vital signs were within expected range, there was no reason to make a big deal about this. "Nothing to speak of. Stressful life. Some bad working habits and too much caffeine. That's about it."

The tech nodded, grinning. "Tell me about it. There's a whole lot of that going around. Probably everything's fine. On the other hand, if your symptoms continue, or if they get worse — dizziness, nausea, any sudden chest or stomach pain — get yourself to an E.R. Better to be cautious." He nodded at Walker and then trotted off to join the last of his crew, who were pushing a gurney toward the side entrance, where an ambulance waited.

Jilly stood up carefully and smiled at Walker. "See? Everything's fine. I'm probably just dehydrated."

He didn't look convinced. "You're pale, Jilly. And your hands are still shaking. I don't like it."

"I don't like it, either, believe me. But I get this way sometimes when I get stirred up. It takes me a long time to relax. Once we had a robbery at the restaurant. I was swinging from the rafters for twenty-four hours after that."

Walker frowned. "Were you hurt?"

Jilly blinked at the rough emotion in his voice. "Only in the checkbook. He cleaned out the register, and it was a Saturday night, our biggest night of the month. The jerk probably knew that. We thought it might have been an inside job. But no one was hurt, thank goodness. He had a knife but he didn't use it."

"You need to be careful." Walker glared at her. "You don't work in the restaurant alone at night, do you? Because that would just be crazy in this day and age."

"No, I'm not alone there."

"Good." He held out a bottle of water. "Drink this," he ordered.

"Are you bossing me around?"

"Damn straight I am. Someone has to," Walker muttered.

"Okay." Jilly felt a little zinging sensation in her chest. She was pretty sure it had nothing to do with dehydration and everything to do with the way Walker's fingers suddenly slid up into her hair.

"Hold still," he said roughly.

All the noise in the room, all the bustle and distant sirens, seemed to fade. She was mesmerized by the intensity of Walker's eyes as he lifted a strand of hair from her neck. The brush of his calloused fingers along the nape of her neck made her feel disoriented. "Walker, what —"

"You've got something sooty on your neck," he said gruffly. "Don't move."

Jilly couldn't have moved if her life depended on it. She could smell the scent of his body, a mixture of wood smoke, some kind of pine soap and leather. His breath touched her hair as he leaned down and gently lifted something from her neck. Jilly hadn't known that a man could be this gentle, that calloused fingers could move with such slow care. "Did you —" She had to stop and clear her throat. "Is it gone?"

"There's one more piece. It probably happened when you grabbed that lid. It was reckless of you to come in here, Jilly." His hands stopped moving. Jilly felt his breath brush her cheek. "Brave, but reckless," he said softly. "Do you always charge at life like this?"

"Pretty much. My friends say that I have two speeds in my life. Fast forward and downright crazy." She frowned, remembering the fights that she, Grace, Caro and Olivia had had on this particular subject. "I happen to have a lot of energy. I also like to set goals and keep them. What's wrong with that?"

"There's a difference between setting goals and putting yourself in mortal danger." Walker's hand rose and Jilly saw that he was cupping a wisp of burned paper. Again she had the sense of a powerful man capable of patience and infinite care.

And Jilly didn't know what to make of that. Admittedly, her experience with men was limited. An orphan, she had grown up without a father, uncles or brothers. She had seen her friends' families and had learned how deep and unbreakable the bonds of blood could be. But it was always someone else's family. As for relationships, there hadn't been many. She'd always been too busy chasing her dream of a cooking empire. Her few involvements had been with fellow cooks; their time together had been fun and intense, but with no permanency.

Because Jilly wanted, suddenly, to move closer and smooth the frown lines from Walker's face, she forced herself to stop. She had to think clearly.

She took a step backward. There was no way she was going to fall apart over a man, especially a man she would never see again after her stay.

She took another step. The movement was harder than she had expected. "The emergency appears to be over, so I'll go back to my room."

She had to get away from Walker.

There was something about his calm control that knocked her usual equilibrium way off-kilter. For some reason, she was thinking about a relationship, digging into all the secrets hidden behind Walker's stoic exterior.

Jilly squared her shoulders, angry at herself for wanting to stay. She gave Winslow's head a scratch, took her bag from the table and headed to the door. "See you later, Walker."

Walker murmured to Winslow, who darted in front of her. Tail wagging, the big dog blocked her way.

"Sorry, Winslow. Gotta go. Calls to make

and rows to knit."

The dog's tail kept thumping. He didn't move.

With an irritated sigh Jilly turned back to Walker, who was still leaning calmly against the kitchen counter. "Do you mind asking your dog to get out of my way?"

"I do. You may develop symptoms of smoke inhalation. I figure I should keep an eye on you."

His expression was unreadable. Something about the darkness in his eyes made Jilly feel a little breathless. "Keep your eye on me *how?*" Great. Now her grammar was tanking along with her common sense.

"For starters, Win and I are going to walk you back to your room."

"I don't need —"

"No, probably not. But it's the right thing to do." Walker took Jilly's arm and guided her to the door. "As for what happens after that, we'll just have to see."

CHAPTER FOURTEEN

Jilly figured things should have been more chaotic. People should have been frightened or angry. But the staff had moved into full gear and announced impromptu dining on the outdoor patio behind the meeting rooms. Jilly could see Red and half-a-dozen kitchen staff working a barbecue, and it appeared that free drinks were being served.

As usual, Walker had been right. She *was* feeling effects of smoke inhalation. Her throat was raw, her eyes burned and she panted slightly as she walked up the path to her cabin. In the gathering dusk, she lost her footing and was relieved to feel Walker's arm slide under her elbow. When he pulled her closer against his side, Jilly had to work not to sigh in pleasure.

When had she felt so comfortable with a man? When had she felt so . . . protected?

One simple answer. Never.

They didn't talk. For some reason they

didn't need to.

The silence between them was very calm, wrapping Jilly in warm fingers.

Added to the feelings she was starting to think of as *the Walker Effect,* Jilly had to factor in the sheer pleasure of Winslow's presence. The dog explored every detail around him, and nothing got past him. The bond between man and dog was almost powerful enough to touch. It was clear that they had been through hardships together. Even if Jilly hadn't known the full story of Walker's heroism in the war, she would have sensed a history between the two.

Winslow bounded around her in happy circles, nudging her pockets, wagging his tail and shoving at her hand to be petted. Since Jilly was missing her own dog painfully, she was more than happy to oblige.

"If Winslow starts bothering you, just tell me. He seems to have taken a real shine to you," Walker said gruffly.

"What bother? He's fantastic. Plus, I have to admit that I'm missing my dog, Duffy, even though he's safe with my friends. You'd really like Duffy." She reached down, scratching the dog's head, laughing when he gave a little yowl of pleasure.

"I don't want him to be a nuisance." Walker studied her face in the gathering shadows. "There's something else, and I'll just go ahead and say it. I don't think you were telling that EMS worker the whole truth. When he asked about your medical history, you closed up. If there's something wrong, I need to know about it. I'll get you right to the hospital."

"Why do you care?" Jilly blurted out the question. "You barely know me."

Walker slid a hand into his hair, frowning. "I care. That's all."

"But *why?*"

Walker glared at her. "Damn, Jilly. Does it take a reason? People look out for people. If you're in trouble, I'd like to help."

Oh, now Jilly understood. So it wasn't personal. This odd attraction she was feeling for Walker was one-sided.

Ignoring her disappointment, she summoned a smile. "That's nice. I guess I'm a little prickly. Sorry."

"No need to apologize."

Jilly knew she couldn't hide from any mention of her condition. But talking about it wasn't easy. "There is more, Walker. It's — complicated. I'm still trying to sort it all out."

"Go ahead. I'm listening."

She watched the first star appear above the distant mountains, a pinpoint that

165

glowed against the purple sky. "Here's the gist of it. One night during dinner service I collapsed in the restaurant. Totally blacked out. I had a lot of tests in the hospital after that, and the consensus is that I have a long-standing heart defect. It appears to have caused some kind of cardiac event."

"You mean you had a heart attack?" Walker demanded, stopping to stare at her.

Jilly hated the words. She couldn't bear to think them, much less say them out loud. But she forced herself to nod. "Yes. A heart attack. A very small one, the doctors tell me." She took his hand and pulled him forward. "Let's keep walking. It makes this whole subject easier to bear." She cleared her throat when his fingers slid through hers and tightened. There was the heat again, sharp and insidious.

"So what happened then?"

"My doctors . . . Well, they want more tests. When I get back, I have to go for another stress analysis. As for my job, being a chef in a busy restaurant isn't an option. I have to slow down. I'm going to have to learn a new speed for my life. And I hate it," she said fiercely. "I worked so hard. Things were just starting to grow. I could see the future taking shape, and then every-thing went to hell." Her voice wavered. "I don't *want* to change," she said angrily.

"Nobody does. Change is hard." A small branch had fallen across the path, and Walker took her hand, helping her climb over it. Jilly closed her eyes, memorizing the smell of his skin and the clean feel of the wind on her face.

Since she was finally talking about her situation, she might as well blurt out the rest. "The truth is that so far I'm making a big mess of things. I can't face losing my restaurant, but it may happen unless I can find someone completely reliable to manage it with me. I've postponed detailed discussions with my suppliers. I've avoided straight explanations with my staff," she said quietly. "I've almost alienated my friends, who are just trying to help me do the right thing." She stopped abruptly and turned to stare at Walker. "Why am I telling you all this?"

He chuckled. "Simple. Because I'm a stranger. It doesn't matter. These other people? They're important."

Jilly wasn't so sure about that. The second part, yes. But she did value Walker's judgment. And she was finding it all too easy to walk next to him and talk about a subject that was very painful. It didn't make any sense.

Jilly was definitely going to have to consider the ramifications of that.

She frowned as they started back up the path. "You may be right. All I know is that I've made a general mess of things. Somehow it seems easier to face that mess when I'm up here, breathing this clear mountain air, a couple of states away from Oregon. And I still feel angry. I keep hoping I'll wake up to find it was all a bad dream. I mean, I'm barely twenty-seven. Who has a heart attack at twenty-seven?"

"You're right, it doesn't seem fair." Walker leaned down to scratch Winslow's head, using the steady, calm movements that Jilly had begun to recognize as a sign that he was thinking hard. And though the old Jilly would have begun to chatter, avoiding deeper truths, she didn't do that. She just kept walking beside him in the soft blue night, surprised that some of his calm had begun to rub off on her.

As more stars burned to life above the mountains, Jilly felt the hectic pace of her life slow down. It wasn't that all her questions were answered or she had become any less afraid of her future. But here and now she was able to wrap up those fears and slide them into a little box, pushing it out of sight for a short time while she found the strength to press on.

168

She ran her hand along Winslow's back, enjoying the feel of the smooth, warm fur. They came to the top of the hill, and Jilly reached into her pocket for the key to her room. When she opened the door, Winslow raced inside, sniffing the air, checking out every corner.

High energy, Jilly thought. She knew just how that felt. She had always had energy to burn, and no reason to throttle down her life.

Until now.

She turned slowly, seeing Walker's hard face half in shadow. Something made her raise her hand and touch his cheek. The slightest touch. But she couldn't seem to stop herself. "So . . . do you want to come in? I don't have wine, but I do have something in my suitcase that you might like."

He raised an eyebrow. "That underwear — I mean lingerie — that fell out at the airport?"

Jilly's face filled with heat. "*Forget* about my lingerie, Walker."

"Hard to do. Especially something as nice as that. It makes a man think . . ." Walker cleared his throat.

Jilly stood staring at him. "So you liked the lingerie."

"Maybe."

169

"And it got you just a little stirred up." She felt a sharp kick of excitement, thinking about what it would be like to wear a sheer piece of lace for Walker's appreciation. The thought made her pulse skip. "But you don't show it. You don't show much emotion at all."

Walker shrugged. "Kind of a habit . . ." He caught her hand when she tried to pull away. "Look, it did get me stirred up, Jilly. *You* get me stirred up," he said roughly. "Hell if I know why. We barely know each other."

Jilly didn't mind that he was staring and his voice was rough.

She realized that she *wanted* him to stare at her. And she liked the way his hand felt on hers, hard and strong, but gentle at the same time.

Her lips curved. "No, it's not the lingerie. It's the snack cakes. They happen to be excellent junk food."

Walker frowned. "Fancy chefs like junk food?"

"There's a time and place for everything. Comfort food can work miracles, just you remember that, pal." Jilly headed off in search of her suitcase. At the doorway, she stopped. "As for what comes after the junk food . . . We'll have to wait and see."

CHAPTER FIFTEEN

Something was *definitely* going on between them.

It felt like something man/woman. Something that shimmered with unspoken possibilities. Jilly didn't share her Tastykakes with anyone. Even her best friends had to whine a little before she shared. Yet here she was, opening her stash to a man she barely knew.

To a man nothing less than a hero.

She gathered up her hoard of sweets and dropped them in her tote to carry back out to the living room, shivering.

"Cold?"

When she nodded, Walker moved to the fireplace and flipped a switch. As gas flames bathed the room with a soft glow, Walker sat down in a chair next to the fire with Winslow nearby. "What's the big deal about these cakes of yours?"

"Not just any cakes. These little jewels are

the stars of the junk food universe. Let's get that straight." Jilly sat down on the arm of Walker's chair and dropped the stash of dessert cakes in his lap. She laughed when Winslow moved in, sniffing curiously, clearly hoping for a treat somewhere in the bag. "Not yet, honey. I'll find you something in a minute."

Walker picked up a plastic package. "Krimpet?"

"These things have been around since 1927. They're a Philadelphia product — even something of an institution. Krimpets are amazing. Light, and spongy, a cake with a butterscotch icing. They're perfectly moist with just the right amount of butterscotch flavor. In the spirit of generosity, I am going to share my stash with you." Jilly pulled another package from her bag, opened the plastic and held out a cake to Walker.

Winslow watched intently as Walker took a bite and then another. "Nice. I'm not generally big on desserts, but these aren't too sweet." He frowned. "Not that I'd call them healthy."

"There's a time and a place for healthy. Sometimes you just need a Tastykake. And you can make them healthy. They taste great with a glass of milk. Dip them in, swirl them around, and you've got two of the major food groups covered."

"And those two food groups would be refined sugar and carbohydrates?"

"Very funny. No, I meant protein from the milk and grain group from the pastry. Live a little, can't you, Walker?"

"Apparently not," he said dryly.

"We have to do something about that," Jilly said. "I had my first Tastykake at a food convention in Philadelphia. We had lots of samples during that week. I didn't understand all the excitement at first. By the time I left, I was a convert. You'll understand after you've tried a few. Seriously, these things melt in your mouth. But a friendly word of warning. If that was my last one in your hand, I'd wrestle you for it."

"I'll keep that in mind," Walker murmured.

Jilly was too fixated on the array of snacks to hear the rough edge in his voice. She charged right on. "And in the spirit of further discovery, I give you the Kandy Kake." Jilly pulled out another plastic-wrapped cake. "Just the right amount of peanut butter. Not too sweet, but a little shot in the arm when you need it."

Walker took a sample bite and then raised an eyebrow. "Not bad."

"Not bad?" Jilly frowned at him. "Would

173

you call the *Mona Lisa not bad?* These are the cream of the cream, Walker. I'm talking comfort food royalty. Is that all you have to say?"

He gave a slow grin, rubbing Winslow's head. "Let's try that again. They are better than not bad. Soft, moist, with a nice kind of texture thing. I don't know what you chefs call that."

"We call it crumb." Jilly crossed her arms, waiting for him to continue.

"They're not too sweet. They don't have an artificial taste. I can see why they're popular."

Jilly was somewhat mollified. "Fine. Just as long as you don't call them *not bad.*" She searched around in her bag and found another chocolate and peanut butter confection, which she handed to Walker. "Better enjoy it, pal. It's the last one I'm going to share." Smiling, she reached into her pocket. "And good news. I have one last wrapped piece of jerky that I saved for Winslow. I wish I had brought more. Maybe Red can remedy that situation. I have an amazing recipe for dog treats."

"Somehow that doesn't surprise me. I get the sense you love animals a whole lot."

"No question about it," Jilly said flatly. "From my experience animals are better behaved than most people, more honest, more loyal and worth more in the general scheme of things."

"And I thought I was cynical." Walker rubbed his jaw slowly. "Anyone in particular make you that way?"

"A whole lot of anyones." As Jilly watched Walker finish his cake, she had a sudden wave of inspiration. "Wait there. Right there. Don't move." She rummaged in her suitcase and pulled out a bag of corn chips, which she dumped into a large ceramic bowl near the tiny refrigerator. She scanned the two small glass jars on the counter and opened one. Then she carried everything back to the table beside Walker. "Close your eyes."

"I beg your pardon?"

"Just *do* it, Walker. Have a little faith, why don't you?" When he complied, with obvious reluctance, Jilly scooped up some salsa from the jar onto a chip and fed it to him. "What do you think?"

"Spicy. But there's fruit, too. Maybe mangos? More than one flavor, I think."

"Have another bite." Jilly loaded up another chip and slanted it toward his mouth.

Walker nodded slowly. "I wouldn't call this good."

Jilly blew out a breath. After all, there was no reason for his reaction to bother her this much.

"No, it's way beyond good. Maybe it's that sweet-and-spicy thing going on. Fruit with some kind of chili peppers. I've never tasted anything like it. Where did you buy it?"

He opened his eyes. Slowly Jilly turned the bottle around so he could read the label. She watched his brow furrow.

"Jilly's Naturals? Are you kidding? This is one of your products?"

She nodded, pleased beyond all reason by his praise. "I started my business with this salsa line. That fruit salsa was my very first product. You really like it?"

Walker scooped up another chip. "I could finish off this jar without any problem. Very impressive, Jilly. It must have taken a lot of work. No wonder your life's stressful."

Jilly shrugged. "It's not brain surgery, but it's the only thing I ever wanted to do." She opened a second jar. "This one's more traditional. Corn and tomatillos with two other chilies."

Walker finished that chip off in record time, too. "I could get seriously addicted to this stuff."

Jilly stood up and stretched. She was drifting in a pleasant little haze fueled by exhaustion and happiness, but the exhaustion was winning out. Yawning, she glanced at the clock on the dresser. "Ten o'clock already?"

"Winslow and I better hit the road."

Jilly realized he was holding the jars of salsa as he stood up. "Go ahead, take those with you." Hesitating, she listened to the silence, amping up her courage. "But . . . I have a favor to ask. And I'd appreciate it if you didn't laugh."

"You need something? More blankets?"

"Not that. I wondered if you would mind staying. Just for a little while. I . . . don't sleep very well. It's been going on for about a year now. If you and Winslow wouldn't mind, maybe you could stretch out on the couch. Only until I fall asleep."

Walker didn't move. "And you think our being here will help you sleep?" he said slowly.

Jilly nodded. "Having you two around makes me feel calm. Safe somehow. Grounded, I guess." She turned away, suddenly embarrassed. Why had she even brought this up? "It's a stupid thing to ask. And you're probably anxious to go. So never mind. You don't have to —"

"We'll stay, Jilly."

"Really?" She was surprised by the wave of relief she felt. "I mean, you don't have to if —"

177

She felt his hand slide under her chin and tilt her face up gently. "Of course we can stay, Jilly. You caught me by surprise, that's all." His eyes narrowed. "You've been having trouble sleeping for over a year now? Why didn't you do anything about it?"

"I tried the usual. Exercise. Meditation. It didn't help. After that came the prescriptions. But I didn't want to go that route."

"Yeah, I hear you there. It's got to be hard." His voice turned gruff. "Okay. You go get into bed, and I'll set the fire. Winslow and I will be right out here if you need us."

If you need us.

It was the strangest thing. The idea of the two camped out on her couch made Jilly's worries retreat. She yawned and headed off to put on her pajamas. "I really appreciate this," she called over her shoulder. "In fact, it could earn you a year's delivery of Jilly's Naturals."

She heard Walker chuckle. Then she heard the rustle of his jeans when he stretched out on the couch near the fire. Wood creaked. There was a thud as his boots hit the floor. When she looked back, Jilly saw Winslow turn around in a little circle, sniff the air and jump up on the couch right next to Walker.

As comfortable as if they had always been

178

there. And in that moment the sense of peace that surrounded Jilly was heavy and warm.

Jilly fell asleep the second her head hit the pillow. She fell into a golden dream of hot spices and elegant buttery French madeleine cookies. Winslow appeared, herding the dream cookies as if they were sheep. Suddenly the dog raced away, and Jilly heard a sound that might have been thunder or distant artillery fire. In her dream she felt the cold press of danger.

A shadow fell. Winslow dropped the cookie at Walker's feet, barking with excitement.

The thunder turned into gunfire and the air took on a bitter stink of gunpowder. Jilly tried to call out to Winslow, but neither the dog nor the man heard. Jilly had a sudden, terrible intuition of danger.

She heard a shattering explosion and ran toward Walker, tripping over boulders and bushes, afraid that she would be too late. . . .

Jilly shot awake, shuddering, her fingers digging at the blanket.

Something was wrong.

Fragments of her dream swirled through her mind. She remembered that Walker and

179

Winslow were nearby, sleeping outside on the couch. Had something happened to them?

She threw back the covers and lunged toward the living area.

Flames danced in the fireplace, casting golden light over the deep red rug. Jilly made out a long shape stretched on her coach. Walker was asleep, and Winslow's head was angled across his chest.

No danger here.

Jilly froze as Walker began to twist and mutter in his sleep. She didn't move when he began to speak. Winslow made a low growl in the back of his throat and moved closer to Walker.

"Have to move, Win." Walker's voice was low and raw. "A patrol over the ridge. Another one right behind us. We've got fifteen minutes. Twenty at most. Need more det cord."

He was still asleep, Jilly realized. And in his dreams, he was back in enemy terrain, reliving a mission with Winslow.

And she relived it right along with him, watching the memories unfold. On the couch, Winslow looked up, as if waiting for her to do something important. Jilly pulled a bright Pendleton wool blanket from a nearby chair and gently draped it over

Walker's sleeping body.

He didn't seem to notice. He rolled onto one side, lying stiffly as if hiding. "Over there, Win. Can you see them? I make out sixteen," he whispered. "More over that hill."

The big dog didn't move. His posture was rigid and protective.

What stories the dog could tell, Jilly thought. What terrible dangers had the two faced together?

She had a sudden urge to lean down beside Walker and slide the dark hair off his forehead. She wanted to wake him gently and tell him he was safe now, and everything would be fine.

She closed her eyes, listening to the hammer of her heart. She seemed to be standing in a stranger's body, full of new and powerfully unsettling emotions. And because Jilly had grown up with so little control over her life, she was afraid to do the thing that she most wanted.

She couldn't stay. She couldn't offer comfort. She didn't know how.

So she walked back to the safety of her bed, regretting it with every step.

CHAPTER SIXTEEN

Jilly woke to the sound of a branch tapping on her window. She stretched slowly, lulled by the scent of wood smoke and clear mountain air.

She glanced at the bedside clock and blinked in amazement. 6:05. Another decent night of sleep. Was this a product of the mountain air? Would it happen every night?

But of course there could be another explanation.

The Walker Effect.

Jilly sat up in a rush, frowning. She wasn't going to rely on Walker to relax. She couldn't rely on anyone. She had her life under control, and it was going to stay that way.

Peeking outside, she saw that the couch was empty. Walker's boots and coat were gone. The sudden sense of disappointment left her irritated.

So . . .

What she needed was a distraction.

It was too early to call her friends back in Oregon. And she figured they would be waiting to hear her fume and rant. Once it was a decent hour, she'd put them at ease. But first she wanted to check on the kitchen fire damage.

Shivering, she pulled a pair of wristlets out of her tote bag, glad for Grace's gift. In fact, wristlets seemed like a great idea for her first project here. Not that she was going to take any complicated classes. The last thing she needed was a demanding teacher to attack her knitting skills. Jilly figured the best idea was to find a pleasant knitter and ask for a little private help. She wanted to get something out of the week's program. Just a few rows of garter or a simple scarf to show her friends when she went back to Oregon.

Jilly frowned, hit with another idea. What about a blanket for Winslow? A thick, soft blanket to warm him and Walker during the long winter nights.

The more she thought about it, the more Jilly liked the idea. First she'd have to pick out a pattern. Then yarn. And she didn't have a clue about either.

Jilly wished she had Grace or Caro or Olivia close by for guidance.

She stretched and then padded across to the big picture window. There were no guests in evidence yet. Only one grounds-keeper was at work, trimming hedges. Then Jilly saw movement on the big patio at the conference and classroom area. Someone in a resort uniform was standing on a chair, cleaning windows. As Jilly came closer, she shook her head in disbelief.

Wasn't that the owner of the resort? The gray-haired lady kept right on working, stopping occasionally to catch her breath. The sight of that frail body working so hard made Jilly feel ashamed. Her friends had given her a lovely gift of time to relax and all she had done was grumble. Meanwhile, Mamie Bridger was barreling right ahead, doing hard physical work like a person half her age.

When Jilly crossed the patio, Mamie waved. There was dust on her face and her cheeks were bright with cold and exertion, but she smiled with pleasure when she saw Jilly. "You're up early. I hope you slept well."

"Excellent. There's something about this mountain air." Jilly moved over to the table and picked up a cleaning rag. "Why don't you let me do that?"

"I wouldn't hear of it. I've done this every week since the resort opened."

"I insist," Jilly said firmly. She reached out a hand, waiting to help the woman back down to a seat.

Mamie frowned. "I really don't mind."

"I don't mind cleaning, either. Just as long as it's not my *own* apartment," she said with a grin.

"I'll clean every window of the restaurant, but don't ask me to do it at home, either." Mamie slanted a measuring glance at Jilly as she climbed up onto the chair. "Red tells me I owe you a big debt of thanks, Ms. O'Hara. He said we were lucky you were there when the fire started yesterday. More people might have gotten hurt if you hadn't been so quick and decisive with that pan lid."

"I'm sure Red would have thought of it, too. Any experienced cook knows that trick. But he was busy helping the staff. I hope everyone is okay?"

"One worker has a bad burn, but she'll come through fine. We'll take care of her." Mamie shook her head. "We should have checked the fire extinguishers more often. Now I've ordered inspections every week in the restaurant and in every building across the resort. Frames will be changed every year. This is never going to happen again," Mamie said fiercely.

"That's what counts. By the way, Red is a spectacular cook. His chili last night was amazing." Jilly kept scrubbing at a greasy spot near one edge of the window. When Mamie didn't answer, Jilly turned around. She was startled to see the petite woman slumped over, one hand pressed to her stomach.

Jilly dropped her rag and darted toward Mamie, taking the old woman's hand. "What's wrong? Should I call Red or one of the staff?"

The elderly woman took a raw breath and straightened slowly. "No you should not. I'll be fine in a minute. I won't have everyone fussing over me. It's just a pain in the ribs. I did a little too much cleaning out here."

Jilly studied the woman's pale face with concern. "Are you sure? You want me to get you some water? A blanket?"

Mamie shook her head. "No need to fuss. While I catch my breath, why don't you sit down here and tell me about yourself? Red has been singing the praises of your salsa line for months, so I tried some. Great stuff. You must be an excellent knitter as well as a cook."

Jilly snorted. "Not even close. But my friends keep hoping I'll improve. The problem is, I have no patience. I drop stitches. I twist the yarn the wrong way. My rows are crooked because my tension is all over the place. I'm hopeless."

Mamie stared thoughtfully at the sun rising over the distant peaks. "I tried to knit once. It was a disaster. I've never been much good in the patience department, either." She raised an eyebrow, looking at Jilly. "I guess that gives us something in common. And since I owe you for your quick thinking in the kitchen, why don't I have Red make you one of his finest breakfasts? He's been nagging me to come down, too. Maybe this morning he'll get his wish."

Jilly frowned. "Are you sure you feel up to this, Mamie?"

"I'll have all the time I need to rest soon enough." Mamie stood up slowly and took Jilly's arm for support. "In the past few years I've lost too many of the things I love. I've lost friends. I lost my beloved husband, Jack. Now I'm losing my sight." She gave a husky laugh. "I haven't told anyone else about that. Growing old takes guts, honey." Mamie studied the broad patio, smiling with pride. "But all that loss has given me something priceless." Her frail hands tightened on Jilly's arm. "I've learned to live in the time that I have and make every minute count. I'm only sorry it took me this long.

So if I want to ask a brave and very helpful guest to breakfast, that's my right, isn't it?" Her piercing blue eyes narrowed with mischief. "You wouldn't disoblige an old woman, would you? Especially one who asks too many personal questions?"

"I wouldn't dream of it."

Mamie nodded. "That's the right answer. Now let's go find you a warm coat. I can see you're shivering. You're not used to our temperature changes up here in the mountains. You probably didn't pack a jacket."

"My friends packed for me. They seem to have omitted that. At least they remembered the junk food. God bless them for that."

"Something else we have in common." Mamie waved to two staff members who opened the big wooden doors. "While we eat, maybe you can tell me what miracle you worked with my grandson. He swears your coffee can make a stone weep. I wouldn't know, since I had to give up coffee last year." Mamie tapped a finger against her chest. "Heart problems, but I'm holding my own. There are too many things I need to finish before I die. So I do what my doctors tell me, even if I don't like it. A healthy young woman like you wouldn't know anything about that."

Jilly started to answer that Mamie was

wrong, but the frail old woman plunged right on. "That's the way it should be. Enjoy your life, Jilly. Don't waste a single moment." The woman's voice tightened. "Not for pride. Not for ego. Not even for stupidity. It's a terrible waste of time. Now I'm done being a busybody." She smiled as Red appeared at the door.

"Mamie, what are you doing up here? Did you need something?"

"A good breakfast, for a start. You've been nagging me to come for a month, so here I am. And I brought a friend. I think we'll take that nice little table at the back with the view of the stream where Jack and I built our first cabin. I think Jilly would like that." The old woman shot a look at Red. "Walker uses the cabin when he's helping us here at the resort. He's completely gutted the inside. New floors, new beams, everything. He's very skillful, that young man." Mamie frowned. "I think he needed to work with his hands after he came back from Afghanistan. He never speaks about it, even now." Mamie shook her head. "But enough of that. I'm hungry, Red. Let's eat."

Mamie kept up a steady stream of stories about the resort while they finished off a southwestern breakfast and Mexican-style hot chocolate flavored with cinnamon. For a small woman, Mamie had quite an appetite. Or maybe the explanation was that Mamie hadn't been eating enough for quite a long time.

Jilly was glad that she was eating now. A steady stream of resort staff stopped by to say hello to her.

It felt like a big extended family, except Jilly really didn't know what a family felt like. She felt the calm and peace, and that was enough. This was the mood she wanted to create at Harbor House back home in Oregon. She wanted grandparents, parents and their children to come back year after year, warmed by memories of chintz-covered chairs, unforgettable pastries and quiet sunny days on the beach.

Mamie had had that vision for her resort years before.

Jilly understood completely.

She turned around as Red brought another basket filled with freshly baked bread. "Not for me. I'm stuffed. It was wonderful, Red. I'm glad to see that you have everything cleaned up. I don't see a single sign of a fire. How did you manage that?"

"I borrowed a new piece of equipment from a friend in Denver. He drove it up himself last night. It's a special kind of machine that uses ozone to cut through odors from grease, smoke or mold. Amazing." He handed Mamie another chocolate-chip muffin and then refilled the women's cups with hot chocolate. "I better get going. There's an army of hungry knitters anxious to eat before their classes start." Red glanced at Jilly. "Say, aren't you supposed to be in one of those classes?"

Jilly rolled her shoulders, feeling a twinge of guilt. "Eventually. I have to work my way into it. Frankly, the whole idea intimidates me. I'm going to be surrounded by world-class talent out there."

"Everyone was a beginner once." Mamie patted her hand. "Finish your hot chocolate. Then I'll take you down to meet the women in charge. Believe me, they won't bite."

Jilly didn't make it to the classroom building.

She hadn't even reached the front steps when someone called her name. Jilly recognized her two friends from the night before, loaded down with bags full of yarn and needles.

"It's still too early for class. Let's sit here for a while." Anna, the mother whose bag Jilly had found, smiled and gestured to the empty armchair that overlooked the whole valley. "A little bird told me that you want to refresh your course in basic stitches, Jilly. We brought yarn, needles and all the help you want. Fire away."

It was impossible to say no in the face of so much enthusiasm and genuine goodwill, and Jilly soon found herself clutching a pair of bamboo needles and frowning her way through two rows of simple garter stitches. "It doesn't feel right," she muttered.

"It's right. You're doing great. Now knit another row."

To call her work great was a stretch, but it wasn't as awful as Jilly expected. At least she hadn't dropped any stitches. And as she knitted another row and then another, her fingers seemed to relax and find a rhythm. She was even able to join in the conversation without losing track of what she was doing.

At nearby tables other knitters sat chatting, working on socks or hats or intricate lace shawls. To her surprise, Jilly noticed she wasn't the only beginner present.

"Okay, I think I kind of understand the garter stitch. Now what was that other thing? The one you do with knits and purls? It starts with an *r*."

"Ribbing." Andie studied Jilly's work. "This time you knit two stitches and then slide the yarn in front and purl two stitches. It's easy. Watch and I'll show you."

Jilly wasn't so sure. She was pretty sure that Olivia and Caro had spent an unpleasant afternoon trying to teach her how to alternate knits and purls in a pattern, but she had never gotten it.

The old sense of incompetence hit.

"Try it this way instead." Anna leaned over Jilly's shoulders and readjusted the position of her hands. Now her left forefinger controlled the yarn in a new way that felt much better. "That's it. Yarn in front. Great work, Jilly. You've got it."

Her friend was right. She was actually doing ribs!

It wasn't nearly as bad as she remembered. She couldn't wait to tell Caro and Olivia.

Anna's daughter glanced at her watch. "Class starts in twenty minutes. Aren't you going, Jilly?"

Jilly hesitated. Making a fool of herself in front of a room of forty women was not high on her list of favorite things. "I have an errand to do for Red. But I'll check out the courses, I promise. And this afternoon I'll do . . . something."

"You'll like it, Jilly. I promise you."

As she watched her two friends wander off, talking with a group of knitters, Jilly pondered the strange, unrecognizable sense of contentment that was oozing through her. There was something to this camaraderie, with its laughter and joy in shared creativity. Jilly had never given herself time to create anything other than food. All her energy and drive had been focused on her cooking. Any time left after work had been earmarked for her beloved dog, her circle of friends and their ongoing renovation project at the Summer Island harbor. For as long as she could remember, those things had been enough.

But now, surrounded by excited women caught up in deep discussions of cast-ons, cables and short rows, Jilly finally understood the deep pleasure that her friends felt when they picked up their needles to knit together.

She gave a little jump as her cell phone rang.

It was a local number, but not one she recognized. "Hello?"

"Jilly? This is Jonathan. I — actually I've got a huge problem here at the coffee shop. I spoke to my grandmother and she said you could borrow one of the resort cars. I hate to ask but . . . do you think you could drive down here? I really need help."

"Right now?"

"Trust me — now would be a *very* good idea."

CHAPTER SEVENTEEN

Jilly's mind raced as she pulled onto the main street of Lost Creek. She was relieved to see that there was no smoke, no cluster of emergency vehicles and no other signs of a disaster in progress. What had Jonathan been talking about?

Then she saw the cars crawling past the coffee shop. A line of people stretched all the way down to the small post office. Probably sixty people were waiting to get inside the shop, Jilly realized. She had a glimpse of Jonathan and one assistant, looking harassed behind the long counter.

What was going on? Had he offered some kind of discount to local residents?

After ten minutes Jilly managed to find a parking spot.

Jonathan saw her inch through the crowded doorway and waved her over. "Am I glad to see you! It's been crazy like this all morning."

"Why?"

"Sara spoke to her friends, and they spoke to their friends. Someone told the mayor. Apparently, the word's out about your barista skills. I have your notes and they've helped a lot, but frankly, I can't keep up with this crush. I know you're supposed to be on vacation, but . . . would you mind awfully helping me for an hour or two? That's all I ask. Just until I get things under control."

"Sure I'll help." Jilly found an apron and flipped it expertly around her waist. As she smoothed the cloth, she assessed the best order to tackle the problem. It was the way she always worked in her kitchen. In life, she charged headlong at problems. In cooking, she was calm, ordering her priorities with the calculated logic of a seasoned soldier.

And more often than not a kitchen resembled a war zone, she thought.

While Jonathan took orders Jilly cleaned an overturned canister of coffee, tossed out an empty carton of half-and-half and brought more milk from the refrigerator. She washed the metal pitchers that were soaking in the sink. Finally, with all her weapons ready, she waved to Jonathan.

"Okay, I'll tackle the next thirty or so

orders. Just keep feeding them to me. Your assistant should go in the back and get more coffee cups, too. When I parked, there were probably sixty people waiting out there and the line snaked down to the post office."

"No kidding." Jonathan stabbed a hand through his hair, grinning. "I've never seen anything like this. It didn't even take a two-for-one sale."

Jilly went to work, juggling espressos, lattes and doppios with cool skill while Jonathan passed her the materials she needed. They made a good team, and within twenty minutes the line outside had begun to thin.

But it hadn't stopped.

"How are you set for coffee beans?" she whispered. "This could go on for a while, Jonathan."

"I'm in good shape. Thankfully, I had just placed a big order." He waved to Lost Creek's mayor, who was standing with her husband and daughter, chatting with a man in a police uniform. Behind them were two firefighters.

The ease and friendship reminded Jilly of Summer Island. Everyone seemed to know everyone and there was no sign of irritation about the delay. People were taking advantage of the time to catch up on town news and family gossip.

Nice, she thought. Just the way it should be.

She passed an iced mocha to Jonathan and cranked out two more orders. She could have used a nice espresso herself. The rich smell of fresh coffee was killing her.

"I'll have a mocha cappuccino, please. Make that your biggest size." The smoky, familiar voice made Jilly's head shoot up. Walker was wearing a sweater today. Its rich brown tweed wool was knitted in intricate cables and textured stitches. Jilly was no expert, but the sweater looked handmade — with a lot of love. It also looked as if it had been well worn. She noticed a small tear under his right elbow and two small holes near the neckline.

Walker seemed to feel the force of her gaze. His eyes darkened, moving over her face. "You slept okay?"

Jilly nodded, feeling a little embarrassed that she had had the nerve to ask him to stay.

"Glad to hear it. We tried to be quiet when we left." A muscle moved at his jaw. "You've got cinnamon on your cheek."

"The way things have been moving in here, I'm surprised I don't have whip cream in my hair. This is crazy."

Walker glanced around at the crowded

199

room. "Busier than I've ever seen it. What kind of promises did Jonathan make to get you back here? You're supposed to be on vacation, remember?"

Jilly looked down, already intent on finishing Walker's order. "I love doing this. I was glad to help out when he called, but I still don't understand what's drumming up all the business."

"My guess is your coffee." Walker nodded at the mayor as she walked past, savoring her latte. The chief of police patted Walker on the shoulder before he followed the mayor out. "Jonathan's coffee is okay, but yours is something to write home about. Some of these people have never had coffee like this." His voice fell. "Me included."

Jilly tucked a wisp of hair behind her ear and shrugged. "It's just coffee. I'm happy for Jonathan, but this is a little hard to believe." She poured in milk froth and then put a lid on Walker's coffee. As she pushed it toward him, she tried not to notice the way the sunlight glinted on his hair and how his broad shoulders moved beneath the lines of his sweater.

It was a losing battle. He seemed to fill the room with his presence, quiet and thoughtful. His strength was part of his character, but you had to look to see it. He was exactly the kind of man Jilly had never looked at twice before. Not that he was hard to look at. Just the opposite. But Jilly's prior involvements had been with quick-tempered, flamboyant and charming chefs with no interest in anything long-term.

Walker was none of those things. She was trying to figure out whether that was good or bad when Jonathan pushed a metal pitcher filled with steaming milk toward her. Suddenly Walker leaned forward.

His hand closed over her shoulder. "Hold still. Keep everything just where it is, Jilly."

Her eyes locked with his. She did what he said without thinking. She didn't reach for sugar or flavoring or the pitcher of hot milk.

"What's wrong?"

Something nudged her foot. Jilly looked down in surprise and saw a pair of wide blue eyes staring up at her. A toddler with bright red hair and a stuffed dinosaur shoved under one arm was inside the back work area, fascinated by the noise and the movement, oblivious to the dangers of boiling coffee and steaming milk.

Jilly cleared her throat. "Jonathan, we've got company. Maybe you should —"

Before Jonathan could move, Walker had stepped behind the counter. With the calm, easy movements that Jilly was coming to recognize, he scooped up the little boy, then picked up the stuffed dinosaur when it dropped next to Jilly. "Sorry, pal. This isn't a good place for dinosaurs. They don't like coffee very much."

The boy frowned. "No coffee?"

"I'm afraid not, Teddy. Your friend there is strictly a grass eater. Nuts, vegetables. Healthy stuff. You like those things, don't you?" Walker ruffled the boy's hair. "I bet you eat a lot of vegetables."

"Sometimes. I like candy better."

"Don't we all," Walker muttered.

The boy studied Walker's face. "Where's doggy? Winnow."

"Outside in the car. It was too crowded to bring him in today. You want to go see Winslow, buddy?"

Teddy nodded vigorously. "Wanna go out there now."

"First we have to find your mother, Teddy. She'll be worrying. Plus it's not safe to be on this side of the counter. That dinosaur of yours might eat something that makes him sick. You might even get burned back here. You wouldn't want that."

The little boy shook his head. "Want my mom. Where is she?"

"Let's go find out." Walker carried the boy carefully around the counter, then turned and latched the door, which had swung open from the crush of people standing in line. He shot a glance at Jonathan and then pointed to the latch. "Might want to have a look at that."

"You bet I will," Jonathan called out. "Has anybody seen Maryanne? We have Teddy over here."

A harried-looking woman with the same bright blue eyes as her son elbowed through the line of waiting customers. She sighed with relief when she saw her son safe in Walker's arms. "I was looking for him everywhere. I don't know how he got over here so fast. I'm sorry, Jonathan. I won't bring him with me again. Thanks for watching out for him, Walker."

"No hurry. We're just having a little chat about dinosaurs eating their vegetables, right, Teddy?"

The boy kept a careful eye on his mother. "Wanna go see Winnow. Out in the car."

His mother shook her head. "We're going straight home, Teddy. That was very bad. You could have been hurt or lost your dinosaur in this crowd. You know the rule. You *have* to hold Mommy's hand." The emotion in her voice made the toddler's mouth quiver. The next thing Jilly knew, tears streamed down his face. His chubby fingers tightened on Walker's sweater.

"Don't wanna lose Dino. Don't wanna be lost."

"Then you have to remember. Hold Mommy's hand. Always." Now tears glistered in Maryanne's eyes. She glanced up at Walker and shook her head. "I'll take him now. There's no need for him to be crying all over your nice sweater."

"He's welcome to come see Winslow in the truck. I'm sure Teddy's going to pay close attention to what you've told him. And he's going to hold your hand in the future, aren't you, Teddy?"

The boy nodded dutifully.

"And you're going to eat all your vegetables, too, right?"

This time the boy wasn't so sure. After considerable thought, he finally nodded. "Wanna see Winnow," he insisted.

Walker chuckled. "Whenever you want. But first, what's that thing in your ear?"

The boy burst into laughter as Walker pulled a quarter out of the air next to Teddy's face. "Would you look at that? I guess you never know what you're going to find in an ear."

"A quarter!"

"We better go home, Teddy. We'll go see Winslow another day." Maryanne lifted her arms and Walker carefully handed the boy over to her. Teddy waved his dinosaur and his bright new quarter wildly at Walker as his mother carried him outside.

Jilly didn't move, struck by the certainty that Walker would be an amazing father. He would lavish all that calm strength on a family and never let them down. No children would ever be more loved.

Walker's easy smile and watchful glance on the child told her that he wanted a family.

The thought was a dash of icy water. Jilly couldn't face the emotions that churned up and flooded over her. Blindly she yanked off her apron and grabbed her purse. "It looks like the emergency is over, Jonathan. I'd better go. Glad I could help."

"Wait. At least let me pay you, Jilly. I couldn't have managed without you today."

"No need." She swept up her sweater, careful to avoid Walker's eyes. "See you around." And she rushed through the crowd past Walker without looking back.

Jonathan scratched his head, staring after Jilly.

"Did I miss something?"

"If you missed it, so did I."

Walker stared after Jilly's stiff shoulders.

Something had upset her, and he didn't think it was the crowd. She was a real expert behind the counter, and she liked people. She had kept up an easy flow of conversation all the time she worked, and nothing had flustered her. No, something else had left her white, looking as if a horse had kicked her in the chest.

Walker had a hunch it had something to do with the boy. When Jilly had looked at Teddy, wriggling in Walker's arms, she had rubbed her chest as if it hurt. Then her eyes had filled with longing — followed by raw dismay. Walker had wanted to reach out and smooth away that longing. He had wanted to touch her hair and kiss her until she sank into his arms with a husky sigh.

It had taken all his willpower not to do any of those things.

Then without warning she had bolted. He had to find out why.

Walker swept up his battered cowboy hat and laid a five-dollar bill on the counter. Jonathan was so distracted that he didn't argue for once.

"See if you can find out what's wrong," Jonathan called after him. "Apologize for me if it was my fault."

"I don't think it was anything you did, Jonathan."

"You don't?" Jonathan shook his head. "Then what happened?"

"I don't know." Walker stared out after Jilly. "But I'm going to find out."

The mayor of Lost Creek blew on her steaming cup of coffee, studying the crowded street. "Something's going on there, mark my words."

"Aw, Shirley, you say that about every new woman in town." The chief of police took a last bite of his pecan pie and eyed the mayor's untouched dessert. To his credit he didn't ask for part of it. "You said it about that visiting nurse from Canada last month. A few weeks before that, you were convinced he and that blonde vet from L.A. were going to get hooked up. Didn't happen. I doubt Walker's the marrying kind."

"Nonsense. Anyone with eyes can see that he's ready to settle down. He's just waiting for the right woman."

The chief of police pushed back, balanced on the back two legs of his chair. He moved a toothpick from one side of his mouth to the other. "And you think that she's the one? Too flighty. Jumpy like a young colt. Heck, Shirley, she'll be gone at the end of the week. She's just visiting up at the resort."

"I know that. Doesn't mean they wouldn't suit." The mayor continued to sip her coffee. She sat up straighter as Walker emerged from the coffee shop and followed Jilly to her car. She gave a soft laugh. "What did I tell you? The man deserves a good woman beside him. And you know as well as I do that that's what had everyone lined up at Jonathan's place today. It wasn't for the coffee, no sir. People were hoping to get a look at this woman who's brought Walker out of his shell. And I like her, skittish or not."

Her old friend cleared his throat. "That may well be, but take a look at them now. If that isn't an argument, I don't know what is."

"Can't you stop being so pessimistic, Tom?" The mayor clicked her tongue. "That's a discussion, that's what it is. Walker is a man who knows what he wants. When he sees it, he'll go after it. Just for the record, my money's on the marine."

CHAPTER EIGHTEEN

Jilly's heart was pounding.

She was pretty sure it wasn't because of altitude or dehydration or anything to do with her medical problem. It was the cursed *Walker Effect.* All he had to do was lean close and talk in that slow, careful way of his and Jilly forgot every careful plan in her life. Like right now.

She didn't want kids. She didn't know *anything* about kids. She had no idea how a family worked. And she wasn't cut out to be a mother anyway. She was too impatient, too critical. She'd never know how to soothe a frightened boy or doctor a scraped knee.

Having a family had never made it into her day planner.

And then Walker had picked up that toddler and ruffled his hair and Jilly's heart had twisted in circles. For a moment, just a moment, she had wondered what if she *could* have a family?

And *that* was insane.

Muttering, she shoved the key into the ignition. Once she got back to the resort she was going to dive into a knitting class — any knitting class — to stop this total insanity and fixation with Walker.

She heard a tap at her window. Her heart took another quick twist when she saw Walker leaning down. He made a little circular gesture for her to roll down her window, and Jilly was tempted to ignore him, but she wasn't that far gone.

She had her pride, after all.

She rolled the window down a crack. "Something wrong?"

"I was going to ask you the same thing. You ran out of there so fast that Jonathan is convinced he said something to offend you."

"What? No — it's nothing Jonathan said. You can tell him that."

Walker rested one hand on the glass. "Then maybe it was something I said."

"It wasn't anything that either of you said."

Walker turned his battered cowboy hat, smoothing the brim with his long fingers. Jilly was fascinated by those slow, careful movements.

"So you're not angry?"

Jilly sighed. "I can't explain it, okay?"

"Why don't you try?" Walker said quietly.

Jilly swallowed hard. She didn't want to be rude or abrupt, but she didn't want to dissect what felt like an open wound. She was still trying to figure out all these new feelings. "I got edgy. Too many people crammed in that small space. And then I saw that boy. I could have spilled hot coffee on him, Walker. I could have jostled that pitcher of steamed milk and he would have gotten badly burned. What if —"

"Don't." Walker reached in the window and rested his hand on Jilly's. "None of that happened. I may have seen him first, but you would have noticed. You're sharp that way."

"Am I?" Jilly didn't think so. When Walker was around, her senses dimmed to a tunnel focused completely on him. "You're good with kids. Teddy loved your magic trick."

"My sister's got four boys. I like kids." He turned the hat slowly. "What about you?"

"I couldn't say." Carefully Jilly drew her hand away from his. "I was an only child." She didn't know if it was true. She had no idea *what* she was. But why was she discussing this anyway?

"Look, I'm sorry if I was abrupt." She stared off at the distant glistering mountains. "I'll call Jonathan later and explain, but everything's fine. It's the way I am." Jilly shrugged. "I get edgy."

"You're sure that's all it was? You aren't feeling chest pains or a racing pulse?"

She shot a quick glance at Walker and saw the concern in his eyes. "It wasn't physical, not heart problems or anything like that. I just felt . . . a little claustrophobic." Jilly studied her short, stubby nails and the sprinkling of scars from old cooking burns. There was a deeper scar at her wrist from cooking school, when another student had dropped his heavy butcher's knife on her hand. Jilly had never really thought of her work as being dangerous, but she realized other people would think so.

Yet she'd take the risk of a few lacerations or grease burns over this deep, gnawing sense of need. If she kept staring into Walker's blue eyes, she might get so lost that she never came back to reality. "You probably have a busy day ahead of you," she muttered. "I don't want to keep you."

She couldn't stay here talking. Because Jilly knew this well. If you *wanted* things too much, you got hurt. And she wasn't going to get hurt again.

"I'm glad there's nothing wrong. I didn't say anything to Jonathan, but I thought maybe you were having some symptoms. If it happens, you should tell me."

Of course she should. The man would be a rock of stability, calm in any crisis. She, on the other hand, went into adrenaline overdrive. She could tackle hard challenges, but she had a tendency to become a lunatic, yelling and screaming. People ended up avoiding her afterward.

Were two people ever more different?

"Can we drop this subject? I'm *fine,* Walker."

"Then why haven't you looked at me for more than two seconds in a row?"

Because she *wanted* to look at him too much. She wanted to look at him all day and all night. He had already become too important to her, and she needed to get away before she said something really stupid.

Like the truth.

"Gee, it's almost noon. If I don't hurry, I'm going to miss the afternoon knitting classes," she said brightly. "So unless there's something else . . ."

Walker cleared his throat. "Actually, there is. I had a question for you. A favor, really. Feel free to tell me to shove off, but it's about Winslow. Something's come up."

Jilly shot him a worried look. "There's nothing wrong with Winslow, is there? He's not sick or anything?"

"He's doing great. The thing is, I got a call this morning. I have to go out of town for forty-eight hours. It's last minute, and I don't want to put Winslow through the stress of a long plane ride. There are other people I could ask, but he likes you a lot, Jilly." Walker turned his hat slowly. "So I was wondering if you would consider . . ."

"You want to leave him with me? I'd love that!" Jilly frowned. What did he mean about taking Winslow with him on the plane? "It's none of my business, Walker, but do you always travel with Winslow?"

Walker's eyes were unreadable. "Sometimes he goes with me. It's work, Jilly."

"What kind of work?"

Walker kept turning the cowboy hat. "Can't talk about it."

"Does this have something to do with the military? I know that you and Winslow worked together." Jilly took a deep breath. "Back in Afghanistan."

"There's a connection," Walker said quietly. "But I can't say more. The fact is, Winslow got pretty banged up over there on our last tour." Walker's voice was rough. "I almost lost him. But that boy is tough, and we got him through it. All the same, I don't like to put him through the strain of long-distance travel in a crate if I don't have to."

"And you trust me to take care of him?" Jilly said softly. "Anybody in this town would watch Winslow for you, Walker. They wouldn't think twice about saying yes."

"Well, I'm not asking anyone in town. I'm asking you, Jilly. You got a special way with animals. And Winslow is more than halfway in love with you." Walker gave a dry laugh. "Did I tell you that he won't eat the jerky treat you gave him? No, ma'am. He takes it to his doggy bed every night and curls up with it. He goes to sleep with his head right on top of it." Walker rubbed his jaw. "That's a doggy crush if I ever saw one."

Jilly couldn't think of an answer. The truth was, she was already half in love with Winslow herself. "I'd love to have him stay with me, Walker. You'd bring all his stuff? I mean, every dog has a favorite blanket and toy." Jilly frowned. "I wish I had more jerky. I'll talk to Red. I can make a bunch of snacks and leave them with you. The dog's supposed to eat them, not sleep with them," she said, laughing.

"You're sure he wouldn't be a bother? First Jonathan puts you on emergency coffee duty. Now I'm sweet-talking you into taking care of my dog. And you're *supposed* to be here on vacation."

215

Jilly saw the uncertainty in his eyes. He wouldn't ask for more than she wanted to give. The man had a solid code of honor that would touch every corner of his life. "Of course he won't be a bother. It would be a total hoot to take him along with me to knitting class. I think he would be quite a sensation. I might even knit him a little scarf to wear. Unless you think that's too girly?"

Walker gave a crooked grin. "Knit away. Winslow will love anything you make for him."

Wind swirled up the street, tossing leaves around the car. Neither one spoke for long moments. The line in front of the coffee shop was thinning, but not much. Jilly looked down, picking at her nail. "So . . . when are you leaving?"

"Tomorrow morning. If it's okay, I can bring him by the resort. He has full certification as a service dog, so you can take him anywhere, even a classroom."

"It doesn't surprise me. Anyone with eyes can see that Winslow is very special."

"There's one other thing. It would mean a lot to Winslow. To me, too." Walker's eyes darkened. "We were hoping . . . that is, we were wondering if you'd like to have dinner tonight."

The force of her response made Jilly

freeze, panicked. "I'm not sure that's a good idea," she said quietly.

"I see. If you don't want to, I won't ask again."

"No." Jilly reached out and tugged the hat from his fingers. She wanted his full attention when she came to this part. "I *do* want to, Walker. That's the problem. I want to talk with you. I want to look at you and I want to watch those slow, careful movements you make when you're turning that hat and thinking something over. Don't you see? It's getting personal here, and I'm no good at *personal.* Personal scares me to death. I'm great at transient. Some people would even say I'm excellent at *irresponsible.*"

"You're not irresponsible." Walker looked up, his eyes shifting with emotions that Jilly couldn't read. "You don't strike me as someone who is afraid of a challenge, either. And personal could be . . . interesting. So what do you say? Dinner at eight, at my place. I'm cooking."

"I — I don't know."

Walker's lips curved. "Admit it. You're itching to know what I'm going to cook, but the only way you'll know is by saying yes."

Jilly closed her eyes. Personal was so dangerous. So messy. Where would this end?

"Fine. Eight o'clock. You better make something wonderful."

"Count on it."

Somehow, despite all Jilly's best intentions, she found herself smiling back at him, enjoying the glint of heat that filled his eyes.

Even though she was *certain* they were both going to regret this.

"That's right, a knitting class. I'm in line right now." Jilly held the phone closer, trying to be heard against the chatter around her. "Which class? Cables. At least I think that's what it was. The picture in the catalog looked nice."

"That's wonderful, Jilly." Caro sounded delighted. "I'm sorry we tricked you. It seemed the only way at the time. It looks like a beautiful place."

"Totally beautiful. Mountains in every direction. Clear, cool air. I admit I was mad at first. You know how I hate when anyone lies to me. Now I'm actually enjoying myself. I learned some basic knitting skills this morning, and I think I'll use those cables on the blanket I'm making."

Caro cleared her throat. "So this man you mentioned last time we spoke — he's a visitor at the resort?"

"No, he's a local. Ex-marine. Actually,

218

he's invited me for dinner tonight, and I said yes. It must be this mountain air."

"You do sound different. More relaxed. But this man, how well do you know him, Jilly?"

"Sorry, Caro, I have to go. Class is starting, and it's a madhouse. Don't worry, I'll call you tomorrow. Every detail. The full nine yards."

"But this man that you —"

A bell rang. Immediately Jilly was engulfed in a wave of eager knitters. "Talk to you tomorrow, Caro. And stop worrying, will you? Everything's fine here."

CHAPTER NINETEEN

Walker finished scrubbing down the counter and then studied the kitchen. His chili was ready in the refrigerator. The salad was set to toss. The floor was freshly mopped and he put out the set of handwoven place mats his sister had sent him for his last birthday.

Maybe he should call Darrah.

Walker frowned. Maybe not. The last time they'd spoken, they'd both gotten angry. They never would agree about the direction Walker had chosen for his life.

He shoved away thoughts of his family before they could ruin his mood. One piece of good news was clear. Winslow's hip seemed to be doing better. With any luck their last field action in Afghanistan would fade from the dog's mind, too.

As if he had picked up Walker's thoughts, Winslow trotted in from the living room, tail wagging.

And darned if he wasn't carrying that old

piece of jerky Jilly had given him at the airport. Walker reached down and ruffled the dog's fur. "Well, buddy, the house looks as good as it's going to get. And you look ready for a guest shot on *Animal Planet*. What about me?" Walker rubbed his jaw, glancing at his reflection in the mirror near the door. Hearing the pensive sound of his owner's voice, Winslow pressed closer to Walker's leg. "Yeah, I know. It's not like a major date or anything. If I get dressed up, it would probably scare her off. I've never seen anyone more ticklish than Jilly O'Hara." Walker glanced down at the threadbare cuffs of his old plaid shirt and frowned. "Maybe it's time you and I did some shopping. You could use a new leash, and those old boots of mine have a hole in the sole. I've had them repaired three times. Probably time to get a new pair. Nothing fancy, mind you. Black, like I always wear. But maybe a little stitching on the toes." Walker ran his hand over Winslow's back and nodded. "Not that it's a big, official date or anything," he muttered.

He glanced at the clock on the wall and then reached for Winslow's leash.

"I figure we just have enough time to make two stops on the way to get Jilly."

■ ■ ■ ■

Jilly didn't know where the afternoon went. She hadn't dreamed there was so much to learn about knitting — or that she would have so much fun learning it. She had mastered three new ways to cast on and she now understood the importance of knitting a gauge swatch, to make certain a project actually fit. Come to think of it, she had heard Grace complaining about fit. Now she could understand them and even carry on a conversation about knitting, Jilly thought smugly.

But best of all was the camaraderie she had found with the other knitters in her class. Even the teacher was friendly and approachable. Jilly liked the way people encouraged each other in their projects, offering suggestions without making a big fuss about it.

As Jilly carried her tote bag back to her cabin, she wondered if rain was predicted. That thought brought her around to Walker and what she was going to wear.

And whether she was going to go at all.

Twice she had started to call him with some excuse to cancel their dinner. Each time she had stopped herself. Backing out would have been unbelievably wimpy as well as rude. Jilly had never considered herself either of those things.

So the date — if it really *was* a date — was still on.

She stopped outside her door and rubbed her chest. She was *not* going to get flustered about this whole thing. She would never understand makeup and perfume and jewelry. She was lucky if her socks matched. On a rare occasion when she had a formal event to attend, she relied on fashion advice from Olivia and Grace, who always looked beautifully put together.

Besides, it wasn't *really* a date. It was just dinner. Food. Talk. Laughter.

Then home. Her hormones were *not* going to take control. Nothing . . . major was going to happen tonight.

But Walker had been right about one thing.

Jilly was crazy curious about what he was going to cook for her.

The mountains were purple in the gathering twilight when Jilly heard a knock at her door. She took a deep breath and stood up quickly.

Too quickly. She grabbed the back of her chair and waited, unsteady in a slight wave of dizziness.

Probably because she hadn't eaten any lunch. And she hadn't been drinking enough water, Jilly thought. She swept up a bottle from the table and took a long drink, relieved when the dizziness passed.

There was another knock.

When she swung open the door, Winslow shot over the threshold, bounded through the room and then raced back to Walker's side.

Jilly laughed when she saw a bright blue bandanna tied around the dog's neck. "Well, someone is all dressed up." Jilly reached down to ruffle Winslow's fur. "How are you doing, gorgeous?"

The dog barked twice and spun in a happy circle.

Jilly looked up at Walker in the doorway. There it was again, a wave of heat that snaked straight up her spine. This was decidedly new territory. Jilly felt too open, her skin too sensitive.

Walker, on the other hand, looked totally at ease. Faded blue jeans met a plain white shirt. He wore a blue wool sweater and a simple belt with just a hint of silver at the buckle. He looked rugged, all man. Delicious enough to eat.

The blasted *Walker Effect* left Jilly's throat dry.

Jilly coughed, wishing she had put a little more effort in dressing. Not that it would have helped much.

"All ready," she said with forced casualness. "Let me get my jacket."

Without a sound Walker was behind her, helping her into her red fringed suede jacket. It was a little flamboyant, but Jilly loved it dearly. It was the first thing she had purchased with her own money, earned washing dishes after school at the long since closed Summer Island Steak 'N Suds. Jilly could still remember that breezy November afternoon, and the way pride had welled up inside her when she placed a row of crisp dollar bills on the counter for her purchase.

"Nice boots." She pointed to the shining tips of the boots under Walker's well-worn jeans. "Are they new?"

He rolled his shoulders, flushing a little. "My old ones had holes. Winslow needed a leash. While we were there, the salesperson talked us into a bandanna. A little bit of a splurge, but we haven't been shopping for a while."

"Everything looks great."

Walker leaned down and toyed with a row of fringe on Jilly's cuff. "Nice coat. Not many women could carry it off, but you can."

"So you're saying that I'm flamboyant?"

He frowned. "I'm saying that you're an original. Like Jilly's Naturals. No point in looking for criticism where none was meant."

"Just checking. Now I don't have to pummel you to the ground." She grabbed her bag from the table. "So where is this cabin of yours?"

"At the top of a mountain. Winslow and I like our solitude, don't we, boy?"

The top of a mountain?

This is going to be good, Jilly thought.

He hadn't been kidding about the solitude.

They climbed for twenty minutes and had passed the last house long before that. Jilly was sorry that she couldn't get a better view of the rugged terrain in the darkness. She was certain it was spectacular.

As they drove, neither one spoke, but it was a comfortable kind of silence. Winslow was right behind her seat, with his head on her shoulder, looking very alert.

"I spoke to Red about those jerky treats. You'll be glad to know that a new batch is in the works. I wanted to make them myself, but Red wouldn't hear of it. He keeps insisting that he owes me for the kitchen fire. Stubborn man."

"Almost as stubborn as someone else I know," Walker murmured.

"I heard that."

They rounded a curve. The car lights lit a row of weathered boulders. Stone steps rose, vanishing in the darkness.

"Hold on." Walker reached into his pocket and flicked some kind of remote. Instantly the driveway was blanketed in light. And above the stairs, like a jewel glinting above the pine and spruce trees, Jilly saw a three-story house composed entirely of redwood and glass.

She could only blink. She had seen some grand houses in Scottsdale, but nothing like this. It wasn't a mansion-size building. It was the thoughtful placement of each level that caught her eye. She didn't have to look out the windows to know that the view would be perfect from every room.

"It takes my breath away, Walker. Who's your architect?"

He didn't answer.

Jilly turned around, staring at him. "No way. Do *not* tell me what I'm thinking."

He shrugged. "Before I joined the marines, I toyed with becoming an architect. I had a few years of school. It wasn't so hard

227

to brush up on building codes and weight-bearing walls." He sat in silence, studying the light glinting off the windows. Then he slowly released a breath. "I love this place. The site has called to me since the first time I saw it. My family has a house on the other side of the mountain. But this . . . this is mine. It was in bad shape when I started working on it. I dreamed the house in my mind, fully formed, the second time I saw this ridge." Winslow heard something in his voice and pushed between the seats, nudging Walker's shoulder.

The bond between the two was as tight as ever, Jilly saw.

"We've been happy here. Haven't we, pal?"

"Isn't it a little lonely?"

"Quiet. Not lonely. There's a difference." Walker scratched Winslow's head and then turned off the motor. "Ready for your mystery meal?"

Winslow pressed his body against Jilly's leg as they climbed the steps to the front door. Far away to her right she saw the faint lights of Lost Creek, down at the bottom of the mountain. Then she understood just how far away from the rest of the world Walker's home was. Mountains and sky ringed them on every side.

Walker scraped his boots and ran a hand lovingly over the carved front door.

"Don't tell me you made the door, too?"

"No, a friend carved it. I did the rest of the work here on-site. When I got here it was late February and we had about seven feet of snow, so it wasn't the best of working conditions. But it was a good distraction. I needed a distraction back then," he said quietly.

All her other questions vanished as soon as Walker pushed open the front door. Jilly stood spellbound at the threshold. Her first impression was of glowing wood from wall to wall and floor to ceiling. Neat window seats framed the tall glass that overlooked the valley, and more warmth came from the hand-woven Oaxacan rugs scattered across the floor. A crimson rug hung above the distressed wood mantel that capped a river rock fireplace. Each detail was impressive, yet thoughtful. Power without ostentation.

It was a tricky mix, Jilly thought. And the mix suited Walker perfectly. She turned slowly, taking in the beautiful room. "All I can say is the world of architecture lost someone special when you decided to change careers. I've never seen anything like this house." On an impulse, she rose to plant a quick kiss on his cheek. "You've made a very special place."

A muscle moved at his jaw. His hand slid along her hair. Then he leaned down and kissed her back, but this kiss was not nearly so quick. Walker lingered, teased. When her breath caught, he cleared his throat and released her.

"Welcome to my house. This place has stayed with me during some hard times. It probably saved my life once or twice."

He didn't explain. Jilly watched his hand move over the carved wood mantel and the worn stones of the fireplace. She wanted to ask more, but it felt too intrusive.

"Why don't you have a look around? In the meantime, I'll get things set for dinner. If you find dust balls, don't tell me."

Jilly took her time, poking in the corners. She didn't find any dust balls, but she found beautiful examples of handcrafted furniture and polished beams everywhere. She understood why Walker had run his hand over the stones of the fireplace and the top of the rugged mantel. She found herself doing the same thing.

Pans rattled in the kitchen and amazing smells drifted her way. Jilly tried to think of the last time anyone had cooked for her, other than her friends, and gave up.

There had only been work. Only other chefs who had dropped in to share a new recipe with her.

It felt decadent to let someone else cook, she discovered. And her curiosity was killing her. "Are you done yet?"

"Close enough. You can come sit down."

Jilly followed the sound of Walker's voice to a cozy room with windows on three sides. Each of the chairs around the big wooden table was slightly different, with hand-carved backs and seats.

Jilly closed her eyes and took a deep breath. "I smell chipotle chilies. Tomatoes, of course. What else? Cumin and coriander and caramelized onions. You've been a very busy man, Walker."

"I figured you'd be a tough judge. The recipe is my sister's so I can't claim credit for it." He set a bottle of wine on the table and turned the label to face Jilly. "I thought you might be game for a glass or two." When she nodded, he worked on the cork.

It was a red wine, a California vintage that Jilly had always thought underrated. Clearly, the man had good taste in wine, too. Jilly's doctors had warned her not to have alcohol, but just for tonight, she would indulge in one glass.

The chili was spicy and perfect. Jilly

vowed to work the recipe out of him before the night was over. When she felt Winslow brush against her leg and curl up at her feet, she breathed a little sigh of contentment.

And somehow between the wine, the food and the good conversation, she let go. She forgot to worry about her health, her restaurant, her future or anything else. They argued about music and movies and the best way to cook broccoli. They laughed and they were silent.

Through it all Jilly simply sat and enjoyed being alive.

And that had *never* happened to her before.

"I don't believe you. That's just a tall tale." Jilly finished her second bowl of chili and turned it over to prove there was nothing left. "Great recipe. I want it, no matter the price."

"I'll keep that in mind."

"But seriously, Walker. Winslow in Hollywood? Does somebody actually think you would waste him in a reality TV series? He's got far too much self-respect for that. So do you."

"I didn't put it that bluntly when I told them no. I figured it was a good idea to be diplomatic. But no way is Winslow going to work on a reality TV show," Walker said gruffly. "Me, either." Walker stood up and began to clear the table. As he moved, Jilly saw him rub his right shoulder. He had made the same small movements before, and she wondered how much the pain bothered him.

When he finished, she followed him into the tidy kitchen. "How long has your shoulder been bothering you?" she asked quietly.

Walker continued stacking dishes in the sink. "What makes you ask that?"

"I have eyes, Walker. You rub the top of your right shoulder. Sometimes you cup your elbow, too. Working in a busy kitchen, I have a little experience with shoulder pain. Want to tell me about it?"

He glanced out the window, into the unbroken darkness of night. "Not really." He took a deep breath. "But you're right. My shoulder gets stiff. I have some pain, too, mostly when the weather is about to change." He stretched a little, rolling his shoulders carefully. "I've been told it's something that I'll have to live with. So I will."

Jilly crossed her arms. "Let me tell you a story. I have a friend back in Arizona who's a fanatic regular at my restaurant. One night I did something to my arm, and I was doubled over in pain. He tracked me down in the back room, explained that he did deep tissue work of some kind, and then proceeded to do some movements on my back. After he was done he told me to sit down and have a cup of tea. By the time I finished, I could move my shoulder again. Most of the pain was gone. Crazy, but true. After that, we had a deal. He taught me a few tricks of the trade and I gave him a free dinner once a month."

Walker leaned against the counter, rubbing his shoulder. "And?"

"And," Jilly continued slowly, "I may be able to help you. I'm no professional, but I strain my arms fairly regularly. It goes with the territory. Why don't you let me try a few things to help you?" She read the wariness in his face and moved closer. "Don't go all silent and macho on me, Walker. What have you got to lose?"

"That's nice of you to offer, Jilly. But I don't think —"

"See? You're doing it again, cupping your right elbow. You don't even know it." Jilly moved next to him, taking his arm before he could move away. "It won't hurt. I won't hammer at you, if that's what you're worried about. Let me show you."

He took a husky breath as she gently

234

traced his shoulder, finding tension spots that she knew from personal experience would hurt the worst. She made little circling movements and moved slowly around to his shoulder blade.

Watching his face, Jilly made two more small, strumming movements.

His shoulder twitched. "What did you just do?"

"That didn't hurt you, did it? The movements are gentle. They're not supposed to hurt."

"It didn't hurt." Walker's voice was tense. "But I'm not sure this is a good idea."

"Why? Are you afraid I'll make it worse?"

"No."

"Then what? I'm trying to help you here, Walker. Can't you see that?"

"I can see it. I can feel it, too." Walker didn't move. "The problem is, if you keep on touching me, it's going to be impossible to keep my hands off you any longer."

CHAPTER TWENTY

Jilly just stared at him. "You're saying . . . that you think something's going on here. Between us."

"I'm saying."

"Oh." Jilly was seldom at a loss for words. Okay, she was never at a loss for words. But now she could only take short, husky breaths while she got lost in the darkness of his eyes.

"That big of a surprise, is it?" Walker stared at the carton of double chocolate fudge ice cream and shrugged. "It's not like I'm going to jump you or anything. It's just dinner. I meant that. You can trust me, Jilly."

"I know I can trust you, Walker." Strangely enough, it was true. Jilly didn't feel uncomfortable or anxious. The only problem was whether she could trust herself. Right now she was mesmerized by the sadness that darkened his eyes when he stared over the mountains toward the lights in the valley.

She was caught by the pain that he worked so hard to hide. He would never complain and Jilly doubted that he would ever ask a favor willingly. That was the kind of man he was.

Which meant that he was like *no* man she had ever met before.

She cleared her throat. "Now we know where things stand. So why don't I deal with your shoulder first? Then we'll decide about the rest."

Walker put one hand against the counter, wincing a little at the movement. "So things might go . . . somewhere?"

Jilly felt the insidious wave of heat snake up to her chest. Suddenly she wanted things to go somewhere. She wanted to trust herself to this man's careful, strong hands, even if they only had a night or a week together.

Right here, right now Walker was alive and offering her something she knew they'd never forget.

One step at a time.

"Let's have a closer look at your shoulder. Sit down in that chair and then take off your sweater. The shirt, too. It's hard to work through bulky fabric."

His eyebrow rose. "What else?"

Jilly felt heat swirl through her face. "You

can leave on your T-shirt. I'm not sure I could handle the whole enchilada," she muttered.

He reached for the bottom of his sweater. "I heard that. The nicest thing anyone's ever said to me." The sweater came off, and then his crisp white shirt.

Jilly nodded. "Now get comfortable. We'll start with your good side." When he was settled, she rested her hand on the back of his neck, the way she remembered her therapist friend always beginning her treatment. She felt the tension in Walker's muscles and opened her hands slowly, tracing the tendons and the trigger points that always bothered her.

Slowly she worked her way down his neck and then lower, making small movements as if she was playing a stringed instrument, plucking gently.

Walker's breath drew in sharply. His shoulder twitched. "I don't know what the heck you're doing, but —" He shifted in the chair and eased out a long breath. "Whatever it is, don't stop."

Jilly knew just how good release of tension in sore, tight muscles could feel. In Arizona, the winter was her busiest time, especially in December, when families gathered for the holidays. Sometimes she had seen her friend twice a week. The results had always been instant and almost miraculous.

She moved again, lifting Walker's arm carefully. "If anything hurts, tell me." She started at the outside of his arm, making the same small circular movements down his arm, taking time to work near his elbow and then moving to the outside of his wrist. She felt him twitch twice, but he never complained. His muscles tightened when she came to the inside of his elbow.

"Now turn around. I'm going to do a little maneuver on your arm." She cupped his arm with one hand the way her friend had shown her, just above and below the elbow.

Jilly had to smile when she felt Walker shift and give a rough sigh. His body seemed to slide back against the chair, suddenly relaxed.

She knew exactly how that felt.

"Now let me do the other side, the one that really bothers you." He raised his right arm slowly, and Jilly saw a long silver scar running up the inside of his arm. She could only imagine the violence that had put it there.

Slowly she repeated the gentle movements, watching for signs of a response. He was far more relaxed now and his breath came slow and even.

Jilly finished his elbow, avoiding the scar, and then stepped back. "Well, what do you think?"

Walker moved his right shoulder, lifting it up and down slowly. He opened and closed his right hand.

Then he smiled. "I won't say that the pain is all gone. But something seems different, like the muscles have shifted. My arm feels lighter, too. I've been to a lot of physical therapists, and none of those visits was as pleasant as that, Jilly. Thank you."

"My pleasure." Her voice seemed odd and husky. She was touched by his simple thanks. To cover up her sudden emotion, she turned around.

Walker was right behind her.

"Thank you, Jilly. I mean it. I can feel a difference already." He turned smoothly and his hands slid along her cheek. His thumb traced her lips. "I would have been a lot faster going to therapy if you'd been there."

Jilly was still having trouble facing him. She had to get herself under control. "So . . . what about that dessert you promised me?"

They sat out on Walker's porch wrapped in fleece blankets, overlooking a view that went on for fifty miles. Jilly could see the lights of Lost Creek off in the distance, twinkling like calm, remembered dreams.

All of which was very odd, because calm was simply *not* her style. Manic energy and driven behavior fit her usual character profile.

It was all very confusing.

"About that thing you did on my shoulder," Walker began gruffly. "Do you think you could teach it to me? Or maybe tell me more about it, so I can find someone in practice around here?"

"Of course. I'll call my friend and ask him to recommend a therapist." Jilly crossed her legs, wriggling deeper under the blanket. "So it really helped? I mean, your muscles seemed more relaxed afterward, but it's hard to know."

"It helped. And I'll take any help that doesn't involve major surgery and long-term drugs," he said flatly.

"Amen to that." Jilly smiled, holding up her bowl. "How about a refill?"

"Another bowl of double chocolate fudge, coming right up." When Walker started through the door, Winslow rose from the spot he had claimed at Jilly's feet. Walker shook his head. "No need to go inside, Win. Stay out here and keep an eye on Jilly."

The dog almost seemed to understand, turning to look at Jilly and then settling back down on the rug that Walker had spread over the cold cement. Jilly saw that Winslow moved a little slower and it seemed to take him longer to settle into a comfortable position.

She reached down, stroking his head, pretty sure that Winslow, just like his taciturn owner, would rarely reveal any signs of pain.

Walker came back, carrying the wine from dinner. "How about a refill on your glass?"

Jilly shook her head. Tonight had already gone to her head. The clear air, the good companionship and his amazing chili were working their way deep into her defenses. She wasn't about to add more wine to that heady mix. "A girl needs to keep a clear head around you, my friend." When she reached out for the bowl of ice cream, their hands met. His thumb stroked her palm, just for a moment.

A moment was all it took to shatter years of defenses, Jilly discovered. An instant was all you needed to find yourself playing a game of what if, perched on the dangerous edge of possibilities that you had never before considered.

Yet Jilly had never been one to sugarcoat the truth or console herself with empty promises. She looked down at their hands, one big and capable, the other small, yet equally capable. There was next to no chance that they had a future together. There was next to no possibility that she would even stay in touch with him after this week ended.

She forced her eyes up to his. "You're a very good man, Walker. I wish I had met you years ago. But right now . . . you could say that my future's murky. And even if it weren't, I'm not a good prospect in the relationship area."

He didn't move, studying their hands, so close together. "I think I know how you're feeling right now. I understand about pain and illness, how they can worm right into your head and strip you bare if you let them. So don't. Because if there's one thing I learned in Afghanistan, it's this. *One boot in front of the other. Eyes ahead.* If you keep looking back, it will kill you."

Jilly traced a line of condensation running down her bowl. "Oh, I'm trying to wear the happy face, Walker. But sometimes around three o'clock in the morning, the smile gets a little shaky." She studied his face closely. "But then you know all about that, don't you? Even though you never complain."

Walker seemed to choose his next words carefully. "Yeah, I know all about the graveyard hours. At three in the morning the memories can walk. Most of the time they're the bad ones. The words you wish you hadn't said. The faces you wish you could have saved. Three o'clock is their time, no mistake about it. I figure they're not going away anytime soon so the only thing to do is compromise. I give myself fifteen minutes a day to worry. That's when I pour out all the dark stuff. I let it go full tilt, believe me." His jaw hardened. "And then I put it away. Back it goes, right into a little metal box and it stays there until the next night."

"I don't know." Walker's eyes turned a little distant, so she reached out, gripping his hand hard. "If you're strong, I can see how it would work. The problem is, these days I'm not always feeling so strong. When I try to shove the dark things back into their box, most of them escape."

"Give it time, honey." He gripped her hand back, and Jilly felt the strength in the calluses. She felt all the support, freely given.

"So far I'm holding on. Bad times or not, my friends help me."

"You never talk about your family. You must have someone you can rely on."

Jilly felt the old burst of regret and anger. These, too, belonged with the three o'clock memories. "Nope, no family. An orphan and glad to be one. From all I can see, families are a major screwup. I'm better off without them."

"Sorry to hear it. And you're right about families," Walker said dryly. "They can be a royal pain. I'm glad you've got good friends back in Oregon. What was the name of that town again?"

"Summer Island. You and Winslow should come visit sometime. It's best in the summer, with the harbor full of boats and sunsets that never end. But any month is pretty great."

"I'll keep that in mind." Walker cleared his throat. "Jilly, I won't beat around the bush. Something's going on here. I feel it whenever you're around." He gave a dry laugh. "Or maybe it's all one-sided."

"It's not one-sided." Jilly forced out the words. "The old me, the person that I was before all the medical problems began, would have jumped without a second thought. I'm attracted, Walker, and that's why I'm determined to be thoughtful about this. I want to be smart and grown-up. To do the right thing." She opened her hand over his and felt his muscles tighten. "I'm counting on you to help me," she said softly.

"Counting on me might not be the best

245

thing right now. I've come back from a dark place, Jilly. It's taken me time and more work than I ever thought possible. You're the first woman I've looked at twice in a very long time." He reached up slowly; his palm cupped her cheek. "So I'll give you a word of warning. I've wanted you since the first moment I saw you in that airport." A muscle moved at his jaw. "And I want you right now."

Suddenly Jilly wanted him to press her, and she wanted to press him back. She had a strong hunch if he kissed her right now, slow and thorough and careful the way he did everything else, her head might just unscrew and go spinning off into space and there would be no going back. And where did that fit in with her new plan to be responsible and grown-up?

Leaning her head against his shoulder, she closed her eyes, fighting a fresh wave of longing. "I'm not used to being careful, Walker. Reckless and impulsive is more my style. So don't give up. Don't let me give up, either." Driven by an impulse she couldn't control, Jilly leaned closer and brushed a slow kiss across his mouth. The contact made her body sing. She did it again and sighed with husky pleasure.

"I thought we were going to be smart."

Walker's fingers threaded through hers. "On the other hand, everyone should be impulsive sometimes."

He cupped her chin and angled her face up. Slowly their lips met.

It was heat and speed, wild danger and perfect calm all at the same time. Jilly wiggled closer and slid her arms around his neck, tracing the rigid line of his shoulders. When she brought her mouth hungrily over his, he muttered her name. His hands slid around her waist and tightened, bringing their bodies together.

She felt his heat and need. She felt the effort he was making to control both.

Jilly had never been wanted this way. She had never thought about relationships that could be measured in years instead of days. She had never wanted more than laughter and an occasional night of heat and need.

But now . . . she wanted everything. She wanted these strong hands to touch her. She wanted those dark, thoughtful eyes next to hers when she woke up in the morning. She wanted Walker, and heaven help them both.

His hands slid slowly to her hips, urging their bodies even closer.

Whispering her name, he stood up and lifted her against him. With the blanket still wrapped around her, he carried her through the silent rooms to the living room. Her hands slid around his shoulders as he kissed her, and his tongue brushed hers.

When Walker sat her down on the thick rug in front of the fire, her hands dug under his T-shirt. Clumsy with eagerness, she sighed when her palms met the heat of his chest.

"Jilly, wait," Walker said roughly. "I want you. I want *this*. But . . . we could both walk away right now and no harm done."

"I don't want to walk away." Jilly's voice trembled. She tugged the T-shirt over his shoulders and marveled at the powerful line of his body in the firelight. "I think I wanted you from the first second I saw you in the airport. Even if it *was* Winslow I fell in love with first," she said, with a shaky laugh.

"Winslow's pretty hard not to love. And you knocked me right off my feet. You were like some kind of irresistible force." His hands slid deep into her hair and he pulled her down onto his chest, kissing a line up her neck. "I've always been a sucker for a strong woman. You blow with gale force winds, but I can deal with that."

"I think there's a compliment hiding in there." Jilly struggled to pull off her jacket and sighed when Walker finished the job for her. Dimly she realized she was losing control and logic fast.

Down the hall a phone rang. Walker frowned.

"Do you have to get it?" Jilly whispered.

"No," he said raggedly. "It can wait."

And then another chime sounded, this time from his cell phone, hidden in the back pocket of his jeans. He glanced down at the screen and his eyes hardened. "Give me a minute, Jilly. It's my family."

"Oh. Sure . . . take your time."

Walker's eyebrows narrowed. "Don't worry. It won't take long," he said harshly. "It never does."

That didn't sound good at all. Jilly decided it confirmed her long-held belief that families were something you did much better without.

She heard him speaking tersely from the kitchen. Short questions and long silences.

He was only gone for two minutes. His face was unreadable as he walked back, sliding his cell phone into his pocket. "Sorry about that."

"Is everything okay?"

"Sure. As good as it ever is with them."

He frowned, and Jilly reached up and pulled him down beside her. "Forget about them. Think about this instead." She pinned him to the rug, kissing the hollow just beneath his throat. And then the curve of his shoulder. "I think this was where we stopped. And it was feeling pretty wonderful, believe me."

Walker's eyes closed. His hands slid around Jilly's waist as she began to kiss her way lower.

She felt the tension in his body. She felt the desire that raced through him. She gloried in her ability to trigger that swift, masculine response.

Her hand opened slowly over the waistband of his jeans. She licked her lip and looked up, her eyes searching his. She didn't know what she was looking for, but somehow Jilly knew she'd found it. She felt heat and trust and belonging. She saw tenderness flicker in that blazing desire.

Her toes dug into the rug. She nipped at his mouth and then yanked at his belt, hungry to touch him and be touched. The pleasure they shared would be unforgettable.

His phone chimed again.

"Hell. What do they want *now?*" He blew out a breath and rolled over, pulling out the phone a second time.

Then Walker went still, scanning the screen. "Jilly, I need to take this." He rose to one knee. "It's important. It's about . . .

a job. That's the only thing that would make me stop right now. Do you understand?"

The rasp of his voice touched her like a kiss. "Go on. Do what you have to do. Just don't take too long."

Walker touched her face gently. "I'm sorry."

"It's fine." With effort, she pulled her T-shirt back into place, wriggling away to sit up on the rug. She felt Walker slip a blanket around her shoulders.

Then he stood up and walked to the kitchen.

"Walker here. Yes, I'm leaving tomorrow. That's what we planned." There was a silence and Jilly heard him bite off an oath. "No, Winslow is *not* coming. I told you, no trips less than a week. It's too hard on him."

Another silence.

Jilly thought he had had this conversation before. She turned away, trying not to eavesdrop, but it was impossible not to hear.

"Fine. Pass it all the way up the chain of command. Take it to the President while you're at it. That rule doesn't change. Those were my terms when I agreed to help you. Winslow stays. And I'll be there tomorrow."

He stopped, listening. "What did you say? When? Where are they being held?"

Held?

251

"Are they still alive? Did they issue any demands yet?"

Jilly sat frozen, picturing a scene that left her cold. Walker walked away down the hall, so she couldn't hear anything else. She realized now that he had never really left that world. His terms of service had changed, but he was still a hero.

And Jilly was pretty sure that she had never loved anyone more than she did this strong, quiet man.

Winslow looked up from his comfortable spot on the couch and whined. She sat down next to him and scratched his head. "It's okay, honey. Everything is going to be fine. You're coming to stay with me tomorrow, and Red has a whole batch of jerky for you. You can have as many as you want."

She heard Walker's footsteps circle through the kitchen. Drawers opened and then closed. "Send me all the information you have. I'll go over it during the flight."

He walked back into the room, putting away the phone, and then stood staring out the window. Jilly could feel the waves of concentration flowing off him. Winslow noticed, too. The dog sat up and whined low in his throat.

"Is everything okay?"

"No." His voice was rough. "I've got to go

earlier than expected, Jilly." Walker's gaze softened as he pulled her into his arms. "Maybe it's better this way," he said harshly. "If that call hadn't come when it did, we'd be on that rug naked right now, halfway to paradise. I'm not sure I would have been able to stop once we got started."

"I wouldn't have wanted you to stop," Jilly whispered.

Walker blew out a breath. His hands tightened. Yet his grip was gentle, as if she was the most precious thing in his world and he wanted to remember this moment.

"Hell." He stroked the line of her neck downward, stopping just above the swell of her breast. "How am I going to walk away from you?" Slowly the leashed hunger in his eyes became wry humor. "Some mess, isn't it?"

"There will be other nights."

"Is that a promise?"

Jilly nodded, certain that the gift they had nearly shared would be worth waiting for.

Walker raised her face up to meet his and brushed a hair off her forehead. "You don't mind taking Winslow a little early?"

"I'd pay you for the chance. He's a dream. Let's round up his doggy bed and blanket, or any other special items. I don't want him missing you in the middle of the night."

But Jilly realized that *she* would be the one missing Walker. And no blanket or bed was going to make her wanting any easier.

CHAPTER TWENTY-ONE

They didn't talk much on the way to the resort.

Walker had stowed a big duffel bag in the back of the truck, and Winslow's bed, blanket and toys were stacked in the backseat. Jilly's skin still seemed to tingle, painfully alive after their encounter. She didn't have to wonder what might have happened if those phone calls hadn't come.

She knew.

And she couldn't bring herself to regret where her heart had led her, throwing caution to the wind.

She slanted a glance at Walker. His face was shadowed in the darkness, lit only by the beams of a passing car. "So where are you headed?"

He cleared his throat. "I can't tell you that."

"Will it be dangerous?"

The minute the words were out, Jilly

regretted them. Of course it would be dangerous. The rough urgency in Walker's voice while he'd spoken on the phone had made that clear.

"I don't know all the details yet, Jilly."

"But you'll be careful. Just . . . promise me that."

Without taking his eyes from the road Walker reached across and gripped her hand. "Always."

Jilly realized she would have to be content with that, though her head was buzzing with questions. Even Winslow seemed uncomfortable, standing up often and shifting restlessly in the backseat.

When they turned up the driveway at the resort, Jilly saw clusters of women moving up the path to the main lodge. She recognized some of them from her class that morning.

"I forgot to ask. How is the knitting going?"

"Better than I thought. And it can be relaxing, once I stop fighting with the needles."

"I'm glad it's working out. Mamie is proud of the classes here. She checks out all the groups very carefully. The teachers have to be the very best." He parked directly below Jilly's room and then reached back for Winslow's bed. "Jilly, about tonight —"

"There's nothing to say, Walker. I meant what I said. I'm not a good candidate in the relationship department. And it's clear that you have a lot of things going on in your life right now."

He crossed his arms slowly. "Which means?"

Jilly frowned. "It means . . . on the off chance that there could be something permanent hiding here, I want to do this right. So go off wherever it is you have to go. Do whatever it is you have to do. And then come back here so we can figure out what happens next. Winslow and I will be waiting."

And because her throat felt raw, burning with unshed tears, she yanked open the door and jumped out.

"Wait." Walker caught her at the bottom of the steps. Winslow danced around their feet, barking happily, certain that this was a new kind of game.

Jilly was frightened by the emotions that crested over her, watching Walker kneel down next to Winslow. "You're going to have to stay, buddy. Jilly will take good care of you. Don't be a pain in the neck, okay?" Walker grimaced as he got a mouthful of Winslow's wagging tail. He scratched the excited dog behind both ears and then stood up, holding out a piece of paper to Jilly. "That's got my cell phone number on it. Call me if you need anything. I may not be able to answer right away, but leave a message. I'll get back to you as soon as I can."

Somehow she managed to bite back her questions. She moved beside him and traced the hard line of his jaw. "One thing this illness has taught me is that life is too short to play games. You're too good for that. And I'm finally starting to realize that I'm too good for that, too." She blew out a little breath. "I can't believe how long it's taken me to see that." She rose onto her toes and slowly kissed him, a light touch that quickly grew raw with need.

Jilly took a step back, watching his face. "I can take these things inside. I saw you glancing at your watch. Go on. Winslow will be safe with me."

"I know he will." He smiled, tracing the fringe of her suede coat.

Then his shoulders straightened. His expression slowly turned distant. When he looked down at Winslow and patted his leg, the dog trotted across to him in an instant response. "Stay with her," Walker said in what was a clear command. "Take care of her, Winslow. That's your job." The dog's body quivered with eagerness and the desire to please. "Good boy."

Walker looked back at Jilly. "I'll be thinking about you. And about us." His cell phone chimed from his pocket and he frowned. "Jilly, I have to —"

"Take your call." She gathered up Winslow's bed and blanket from the backseat of the truck. "We'll be fine. Now get moving."

She forced herself not to look back as his truck drove away. Once she was inside the cabin, she filled the dog's bowl with water, set up his dog bed and blanket near the couch and yawned as the day finally began to catch up with her. After a quick shower, she changed and slid into bed, smiling to see Winslow watching every move she made.

Protecting her. Just the way Walker had ordered.

"Go to sleep. Everything's fine, honey."

Jilly turned out the light and yawned again. And though she braced herself for a typical night of tossing and turning and insomnia, she was asleep within minutes.

The moon was just rising over the mountain when a sound woke Jilly. She sat up, shivering in the darkness.

It took a moment to realize that there was a weight draped over her feet. A big warm body curled next to her on the bed, dark eyes studying her restlessly.

When had Winslow gotten up on the bed?

A wet nose nudged her arm and then burrowed under the blanket. Jilly laughed. "Blanket hog, are you? I'll have to remember that." She thought about Walker, somewhere in the night. Fighting the dark in ways that he could never discuss. "Be careful," she whispered.

Her hand slid through Winslow's fur and Jilly felt the dog relax, resting his head on her hip.

As if he'd always been there.

As if he always would.

It's going to be all right, she thought. Somehow they would figure this out.

She smiled a little in the darkness. "After all, Winslow, I'm a force of nature."

The sun was just rising. Pink light brushed the snow on the distant mountains as Mamie poured fresh orange juice for Jonathan, who was sitting at her kitchen table. He had slept there the night before, concerned about her health. Though she had meant to be tough and strong and send him home, somehow Mamie hadn't had the will.

Because she was frightened. Next week she was scheduled for more tests. Her breathing problems were worse. So was her erratic pulse.

It was hell growing old, Mamie thought.

But her smile never wavered as she filled Jonathan's plate with his favorite chocolate-chip French toast, added butter and then poured on a healthy dose of the organic maple syrup she kept in the pantry just for her favorite grandson. Then she sat down, simply enjoying the sight of his healthy appetite. It was so exactly like her beloved Jackson.

Jonathan brushed maple syrup from his chin and frowned. "Grandma, why aren't you eating? You don't eat enough."

"I had an egg an hour ago, before you got up. And Red sent over some of that nice oatmeal that I like so much. Stop worrying about me and finish your French toast." Mamie looked down the hill toward the curve of cottages strung out between the meeting rooms and the main lodge. "I hear that Jilly had a date with Walker last night."

"It wasn't exactly a date." Jonathan frowned at his plate. "At least according to Red. He said Walker and Jilly didn't look romantic or anything. Red made a point of watching them drive away."

Mamie stirred sugar into her herbal tea and drummed her fingers on the table. "But Walker might be interested? And Jilly might be interested back?"

"He wouldn't thank you for meddling," Jonathan said quietly.

"Then I guess he'd better never find out." Mamie blew at her tea and then sighed. "It's been too long since we've had a wedding here on the mountain. And believe it or not, I can remember back when we used to have weddings here all the time. Those were the days."

Mamie stood up and wandered through the kitchen into the living room. She straightened a pile of magazines she wouldn't read, plumped up a set of pillows on the couch she didn't use and then moved to the table at the big picture window. With gentle fingers she traced an assortment of framed photographs. This was what mattered. These smiling faces and the rich, warm glow of precious memories kept her heart moving. She remembered every photograph as if it had been taken yesterday. Funny, how the brain worked, Mamie thought. Some days she could barely remember what she'd eaten for lunch.

And yet these photographs were as clear as the Waterford crystal she loved.

She picked up the last picture in the row and studied a girl hiking up a mountain, hair flying, eyes radiant. Her heart tugged as it always did. The weight of loss left her suffocating for a moment. And then Mamie's fingers tightened.

It was long ago. Too long ago to be dwelling on the sadness.

"You still miss her, don't you, Grandma?" Jonathan stood beside her, looking at the bar of sunlight brushing the girl's smiling face.

Mamie reached over to pat his hand. "No, I don't. Because she's still here. Right now, beside me. I can hear her laugh ring through the air. Sometimes at night, I can swear that she's right back there in the kitchen, pulling milk out of the refrigerator the way she always did. Don't worry about me, honey."

"But I do worry." Jonathan took a sharp breath. "And I worry about those tests you're going to have next week. I hope —"

Gently Mamie put a finger across his mouth and shook her head. "Today we're not going to worry. Not about anything. I thought we agreed on that." With gentle care she rested the photograph amid all the others, the pieces of a life well lived. "Now you and I have work to do in the attic, remember? I'm finally going to throw out all those years of junk up there." Her eyes crinkled. "Since you get to do the heavy work, I suggest you go back in there and finish off that last piece of French toast. You're going to need it."

"I'm not exactly sure. I haven't done a lot of knitting." Jilly stared at the pile of yarn on the counter of the knitting shop set up temporarily at the resort.

The color range was overwhelming. Which shade would Walker like best for a blanket? Green? Red? Blue?

And what weight? She hadn't expected there would be so many choices.

The woman in the shop must have seen her distress because she looked down at the jumble of yarn Jilly had assembled and quietly pulled all but four out of the group. "I think these would be good. You said you were just starting to knit?"

Jilly nodded. "But I want it to be good. Nice and warm. A blanket for a winter night."

"We can do that. This is beautiful merino from Uruguay, hand spun and hand dyed. No wool allergies of any sort, I take it?"

Jilly didn't think so, but frankly she wasn't sure. Then she remembered all the wool hangings and wool rugs in Walker's cabin, not to mention the sweaters she'd seen him wear, and shook her head.

"Next is the color. It's for a man, right?"

"A man and his dog. And I think that teal blue is good. He has a blue shirt he likes. A blue sweater, too. Yes, the teal."

"It just happens that I have two bags' worth of that same color. That should be enough for a nice-size blanket. Now let's get you set up with some needles. Since you're just starting, I think you should make a swatch."

Jilly racked her brains and then remembered what the word meant. "Swatch. That's a small sample knit, something you do to test your needle size and how loose you knit."

"Correct. For this yarn, I'm thinking you should start with a size eight needle. Are you a loose or a tight knitter?"

Jilly didn't have a clue.

But the calm, expert woman at the counter only laughed and put two sets of needles down next to Jilly. "Start with the eights. See how it looks." She pushed one ball of the glowing teal yarn over to Jilly. "You can start with this."

When Jilly reached into her tote bag for her credit card to charge the yarn, the woman shook her head firmly. "You're Jilly

O'Hara, right? The woman who managed to put out that fire in the kitchen? No way are you allowed to pay. Mamie gave strict orders. Whatever you choose is on the house."

Jilly blinked. "I can't do that. She doesn't owe me anything. I just happened to be in the right place at the right time."

"Better take it up with Mamie. I have my orders." The woman looked wistfully at the wall of yarn and shook her head. "I only wish someone would offer *me* free rein in here. Good yarn is expensive."

As Jilly started to protest, three excited students gathered around the desk. Gathering up her needles and yarn, she found a seat by the window and sat down with the one-page stitch pattern the woman had helped her choose. It had lots of texture, but it was still supposed to be easy.

Looking at the chart, Jilly felt her confidence waver. There were so many stitches. So much to remember.

But for Walker and Winslow, she would give her best effort. They would have a blanket even if it killed her.

She looked down at Winslow, dashing in his blue bandanna. "Just so you appreciate the effort here. I'm way out of my comfort zone with this project."

Winslow yawned.

"Yeah, I didn't think you'd be impressed."

The big dog wriggled closer to Jilly, resting his head on her knee.

"But this stays our secret, right? Just you and me. It's going to be worth it to see Walker's face when I'm done."

Three hours later Jilly sat on the patio sipping a hot chocolate, bathed in a glow of pride. With the help of several knitters and her mother and daughter friends from the day before, she had completed four inches of the blanket.

Not that it had been easy. She had to think about each stitch, frowning over the chart that the woman in the yarn shop had given her. But already the textures popped, sharp and beautiful as they rose against the soft teal yarn.

Jilly O'Hara, knitting. Who would have thought it?

"So here you are." Red walked across the patio carrying a big plastic carton. "I have a little surprise for you."

Jilly knew what it was. She could smell it before he even opened the lid.

"You finished the treats for Winslow. That's wonderful, Red."

"Only the best for Winslow." With a flourish, he pulled out a treat and knelt down next to the dog, offering the smoked and dried beef. Winslow sniffed the length of Red's fingers, gently took the morsel and trotted off to eat.

"I'd say that was a success," Jilly said. "Five stars, if dog language says anything."

"Yeah, well I had a great recipe to work from. I loved how thorough you were. Every detail was spelled out. I think you could have a side business selling upscale dog treats, Jilly."

"Don't get me started. The last thing I need is another business."

One of the women at a nearby chair got up to leave and Jilly motioned for Red to sit down. They watched Winslow savor his treat, oblivious to everything going on around him.

Red cleared his throat. "So how long do you expect to have Walker's dog with you?"

"Not sure. Originally he said two days. But when he left he didn't know how long he'd be away."

"A job?"

"I guess." Jilly shrugged. "He didn't say much. I gather that he's not supposed to talk about what he does."

Red nodded. "Yeah, something very hush-hush, no doubt. Jonathan usually watches

Winslow if Walker has to go out of town. I guess this means that you and Walker are . . ." Red cleared his throat again. "Pretty friendly."

Jilly's eyebrow rose. "I'm just doing a favor for a friend, Red. Don't read a whole lot into this."

"No, of course not. You're just friends. Absolutely. The only thing . . ." He leaned down, studying Winslow, who was drooling over the jerky. "Walker isn't one to make friends easily. In fact, he's been an actual recluse up on that mountain for most of the time that I've known him. Between Mamie and Jonathan, they get him down to town once a week, at most. Then you turn up." Red's eyebrows rose. "And now we see him in town or here at the resort most every day. So . . . I'm not sure I would call it friendship." He raised a hand in mock surrender as Jilly started to argue. "No need to argue. What goes on between the two of you is your business. But I've been thinking about something. I've been thinking about it a lot." Red stood up abruptly, pacing in a circle around Jilly's chair.

"What have you been thinking about?"

He stopped, dug a broad, beefy hand through his hair and shook his head. "Never mind. It doesn't matter." He set the plastic carton of beef jerky down on the table next to Jilly. "Here you go. Don't let him eat them all in one sitting." Then he strode off toward the kitchen, leaving Jilly more confused than ever.

To her surprise, Jilly actually began to enjoy herself.

The teal blanket was growing, and she was now into her third ball of yarn. Walker had called her once on the phone in her cabin, speaking tersely, asking about Winslow. He hadn't volunteered information about where he was or when he would be back.

Jilly thought he sounded tired.

Over the following day she learned more stitches and made more samples with big and small needles. That afternoon she spread her knitting tools on the patio outside her cabin, pulled a warm fleece blanket around her and went to work on her knitting, while Winslow curled up beside her.

A beep sounded from her cell phone. Glancing down, Jilly saw a text message from an unknown number.

How's the knitting? Have you stabbed anyone with a needle yet?

Jilly realized this was the mobile number Walker had given her. She smiled and began to type.

Only one person. Myself. I was terrible at first, but I'm starting to get the knack.

Of course you are. You'd be great at whatever you try. How's Winslow?

Wonderful. Red made a batch of beef jerky for him. He's been in dog heaven ever since.

Lucky dog. Thank Red for me, will you?

Already did. By the way, you didn't tell me that Winslow was a blanket hog. Or that he was going to sleep in bed with me every night.

No kidding? I guess he really does have a thing for you. I guess now it's official. I think I'm a little bit jealous.

Jilly smiled, and then reached down to scratch Winslow under the chin. She looked up and blinked as something white drifted down across the patio. Seconds passed before she realized what it was.

A snowflake.

The first snowflake of the year.

She laughed as more flakes appeared. Pulling the blanket closer around her, she began to type.

Can you believe it? It's snowing here. Just a little, but that's definitely the white stuff.

That's early, even for Lost Creek.

Jilly watched more snowflakes drift across the patio. She'd never realized how beautiful snow could be. She never saw it back in Arizona. Even in their part of Oregon snowstorms were scarce. She looked down as her phone chimed with another text message.

Looks like we're finishing up here. With luck I should be back sometime tomorrow. Thanks again for everything.

My pleasure. In fact, you may have to fight to take Winslow back. It's going to be hard sleeping alone after this.

The minute Jilly sent the message, she felt her face burn. Why had she said that? Fuming, she scanned the screen, waiting for his answer.

I might have a remedy for that particular problem . . .

Jilly read the words a second time. There was no mistake about what he was implying. And she liked the image of Walker stretched out beneath a blanket, sharing her bed.

Sharing her life, too.

In his absence everything seemed to be clearer. She could accept her longing to be close and to open up, without worry for the risks. . . .

Up the hill the trees grew dim, curtained by the falling snow. Jilly watched the branches change and fade. She closed her eyes, rubbing her face hard. *Share her life?* Who was she kidding?

It was a fantasy, a lovely image with no chance of permanency.

She was caught in the middle of a dream about heirloom tomatoes and fresh mango salsa when she felt a pressure at her chest. For a moment Jilly froze, afraid that her cardiac symptoms had returned.

Soft fur met her hand. She realized the weight at her chest was Winslow, crawling across her to the edge of the bed.

"What's wrong, honey? Did you hear a

273

dog outside? Maybe a coyote?"

But the next sound Jilly heard was the tap of boots out on the sidewalk beyond the front door. Winslow shot across the room, whining and scratching at the door. Jilly knew only one person who could cause that excited response.

Walker.

He was home.

CHAPTER TWENTY-TWO

He looked like he had been to hell and back.

There were shadows in his eyes and lines of stubble across his jaw. He leaned against the doorway with a heavy duffel bag over one shoulder and Jilly could see it was an effort for him to smile.

"Walker! Come inside. I didn't expect you back yet."

"We wrapped things up faster than I thought. I managed to jump a flight right out. But I don't think I'd better come in. I'm pretty tired. Why don't I take Winslow and head home?"

"Now? It's 3:00 a.m. Are you crazy? Get yourself in here and sit down. You're not going anywhere."

Walker didn't move, one arm against the doorway, his body tense. Jilly could see that he was processing what to do next. He definitely wasn't used to being given orders.

Well, too bad. The man was a fool if he

thought he was going to drive up that twisting mountain road in the middle of the night, with a fresh layer of snow on the ground. Especially when he looked as if he might keel over from exhaustion.

Jilly didn't give him more time to come up with excuses. She grabbed his heavy duffel, nearly staggering beneath the weight of it, and then pulled him inside. Winslow was bounding around his feet, barking in excitement. As the light struck Walker's face, Jilly could see that he was in even worse shape than she'd thought.

"Go inside and get a shower. You'll feel better. I'll put some fresh towels out and make you something to eat. It won't be much, but I have a microwave. Then you're going to sleep. Winslow will keep you company. I'll take the couch."

His jaw tightened. He caught her arm as she walked past. "Jilly, I'll be fine. It's better if I go," he said roughly. "I'm not in the best frame of mind right now."

She saw his eyes then and couldn't even imagine what had put that kind of pain into them. "Just for the record, I happen to like taking care of basket cases. Red brought me extra food tonight, so I happen to be very well equipped. I have to tell you, that man has been acting very strange. He starts conversations and then drops them, but he won't explain." She gave a mock scowl. "Don't fight me on this, pal. Right now I think I could take you. You're dead on your feet. Get into the shower and then come sit down. Your food will be ready by then."

He muttered something under his breath. Jilly was pretty sure it sounded like *can't get a word in edgewise.*

"I heard that. Bite him, Winslow." She walked out of the bathroom carrying a towel and flipped Walker across the backside, laughing. "Now get moving. Unless you want me to undress you myself, because I will."

He looked at her, his eyes dark. Heat flared. "Would you?"

Jilly cleared her throat. "You're too tired to find out. Now move."

When he emerged ten minutes later, Walker looked somewhat revived. His dark hair glistened from the shower and Jilly noticed that the emotion in his eyes had been pushed deep. She pointed to the little desk and chair by the window that overlooked the patio. "Have a seat. I reheated some of Red's excellent chili. There are two pieces of corn bread that I filched at lunch. If you're very good, you'll get a Tastykake for dessert. Now eat."

Walker sniffed the air and shook his head. "I'm too hungry to argue with you." He slid into the chair, took a deep breath and then began to eat. Winslow stayed right beside him, pressed against his leg, and Jilly saw the careful way that Walker smoothed the dog's fur.

"I hope he wasn't any trouble?"

"Other than stealing the blankets, he was great. But we worked things out, didn't we, Winslow? We made a compromise."

"What kind?"

"He got to keep one of the covers as long as I got to sleep an extra twenty minutes in the morning. It was a good trade-off." Jilly pushed fresh chips and a bowl of salsa toward Walker. Then she nudged the unfinished blanket back into her knitting bag.

"What was that blue thing? Some kind of knitting?"

"That?" Jilly rolled her shoulders. "Just a project for my class tomorrow. Nothing that would interest you."

"I hope you've had some time to yourself. Has Jonathan asked you to go back to the coffee shop?"

"Only once, just for an hour." Jilly enjoyed watching him eat, and when he finished the chili she dished him out a second helping.

Walker finished it in record time, but he was looking sleepier by the minute. He sat back and stifled a yawn, then stood up, with Winslow right at his feet. "I appreciate this, Jilly, plus the good care you took of Winslow. But I really think we need to be going."

"I already told you. You're going nowhere. I made up the couch while you were in the shower, and the bed is ready." She gave him a little shove toward the bedroom. "Get going."

"Why is it that you give me orders?" His eyes narrowed. "No one else gives me orders."

Jilly pushed him toward the bedroom. "Get used to it. It's something I learned from my friends. When you like someone, you take care of them, even if they don't want you to. And in my book, taking care of people means telling them what to do. So get into bed and go to sleep." Jilly turned back the covers and then stood, hands on her hips.

She saw the moment he gave in. He walked slowly to the bed and sat down, exhaustion filling his eyes again. His hands opened and closed.

Jilly tossed him a pillow. "Hello? Sleep."

"I guess I am too tired to drive back up to the cabin tonight." He looked up at her and

279

his eyes darkened. "You win." He took her hand in his. Slowly he brought their fingers together, and his tightened around hers.

Jilly's pulse spiked. What if he pulled her down against him? What if he kissed her the way he had in his cabin?

No. He needed to rest. And if this went on any longer, he wouldn't be in that bed alone.

She took a deep breath and pulled away. "Go to sleep."

"Right." Walker pulled off his turtleneck and Jilly felt a sharp tug of heat at the sight of his lean, muscled chest.

She spread a blanket out over the foot of the bed and then reached down to turn off the bedside light. Winslow was already crawling onto the bed and draping his warm body across Walker's legs.

It wasn't the best couch in the world, but it wasn't the worst. The problem was that her insomnia was back. In fact, it was back even worse than before.

Jilly tossed and turned for almost an hour, thinking about recipes and knitting stitches and the array of tests that were waiting for her when she returned to Arizona. The more she thought, the more hectic and complicated her thoughts became.

And with everything else on her mind, now there was Walker. She hadn't planned on meeting him, and she definitely didn't need more complications in her life. But she couldn't ignore the way she felt around him. Fate had brought her the one thing she had always wanted but hadn't realized before.

Jilly glanced down at the worn duffel bag next to her door and shook her head. She picked up Walker's dusty boots and leaned them near the bag. Giving up on sleep, she pulled out her knitting bag and then dug inside it for her cell phone.

With luck one of her friends would be up. Caro didn't sleep so well these days, now that her husband was back in Afghanistan. They had often shared laughter and late-night worries via cell phone messages in the last few months.

Caro, are you up?

The answer shot back almost instantly.

Unfortunately. I was hoping to hear from Gage, but no message yet. What's up with you? You said you've been sleeping better up in the mountains.

Tonight appears to be a throwback. Have you heard from Grace? Everything okay with Noah?

Fantastic. They are in San Francisco. You know Grace. She managed to find a Ukrainian restaurant. Noah was in heaven. She'll be back home in a few days. Then Noah has to drive up north on some family business.

Jilly frowned and then began to type.

Something to do with his brother's widow and Noah's little niece? Didn't they move up north?

Right. Noah's family is determined to get visitation rights. Sounds like the widow is a bit of a . . . well, bitch comes to mind.

Jilly smiled. Caro was always generous and kind. She seldom cursed, so the woman must be a real piece of work. Jilly remembered hearing about how Noah's sister-in-law wanted to move far away with his niece in tow. Noah's family was very close, and now they were struggling to keep the little girl from being torn out of their lives.

Noah's family deserves better than that. I know some good lawyers in Scottsdale, if they want a name or two.

I'm already on it. Gage has an old friend from high school who is going to represent them. He's a real shark, and that's fine with me.

Jilly was about to reply when a new message came through.

But Noah worries. He's trying to protect his mother from any more pain. So he wants to go see the widow by himself and try to sort things out amiably. Grace says he's trying to protect the people that he loves.

Jilly cradled the phone as another message came through.

Hold on. Baby's crying. Be right back.

She waited anxiously, hoping it was nothing more than a bit of late-night colic or teething pains.

Her phone chimed.

Okay, wet diaper dispensed with. So spill. Knitting camp going well?

Way better than I thought. I learned how to knit cables today. And I'm working on a blanket.

That is so great. And you have been relaxing?

Trying to . . .

So you'll be back this weekend?

Jilly hesitated. She thought about the plan
that had been taking shape in her mind.
Then she began to type.

No, I'm going to stay on for a few days. I've
been helping the chef here work on his menu.
And I'd like a little more time to finish this
blanket.

There was a long delay. Jilly could almost
feel the force of her friend's thoughts and
worry at the other end of the phone. Caro
would always back her up in any choice she
made, but she wouldn't give Jilly a free pass
if she thought she was making a bad decision.

Don't suppose this has anything to do with
that man you mentioned? The one with the
dog.

Could be. You'll have to wait for the rest until I
get home. Talk to you in a few days. Give love
to Grace and Noah. And sloppy kisses to
Duffy . . .

Jilly smiled as she put her phone away.

That should keep her friends buzzing with curiosity. And that would serve them right.

She glanced through the door to the bedroom and saw Walker's pillow on the floor next to the bed. He looked lost in the world, with one arm spread out to cradle his head and the other on Winslow's back. As if aware of her gaze, Winslow's head rose. The dog studied her in the darkness and then rested his head protectively back on Walker's leg and gave a long contented sigh.

This was what belonging meant, Jilly realized. The emotional bond between the two felt like a physical presence, and Jilly wondered what it would be like to have that kind of anchor in her life. She had always thought having close friends and a job she loved was enough. But right now, watching Winslow guard Walker as he slept, Jilly knew that friendship wasn't enough.

She wanted more, even if it frightened her to want so much. Thanks to Walker, her life had changed.

She had changed. She had begun to want things she had never considered before.

She was in uncertain territory but she couldn't go back.

No matter how it ended.

■ ■ ■ ■

She drifted off to sleep an hour later.

The unfinished afghan fell to her feet in a blue pool.

Jilly didn't see Winslow wake up and prowl the room, checking on the two people he had come to love with fierce loyalty. She didn't notice the dog rest his head on her hand and study her face in the darkness.

But the contentment reached out to Jilly. Deep and real, it stole through her dreams to offer the comfort and belonging that had always eluded her.

Jilly sat up in a rush, blinking.

A big wet tongue swept her face and she looked into Winslow's excited eyes. Yawning, she sat up. "What's up, honey? Something wrong?"

The dog ran in a little circle, tail wagging. Then he ran to the door and scratched on the wood.

Jilly knew what *that* meant. She had had dogs long enough to know when an emergency visit outside was necessary.

Laughing, she stood up and tugged on her jacket. Walker was still sound asleep as she tiptoed across the room for her shoes and pants, grabbed her cell phone and then let Winslow outside.

Pink light touched the mountains in the distance. Snowflakes drifted down over the resort with an ethereal beauty that made Jilly feel as if she had walked into a movie. Winslow bounded around her feet, running up the hill and then racing back, the picture of canine excitement. Just watching him made Jilly feel ten years younger and a whole lot healthier.

She followed him up the hill, glad to have the resort to herself at this early hour. The peace of the silent mountainside felt like a blanket that she wrapped close. She needed the quiet, needed the space to think. Jilly knew she couldn't go on the way she had before. She couldn't be reckless and driven, a loner and a workaholic.

She wanted more.

She was certain that she wanted Walker in her life.

And that vulnerability scared her. What was she going to do?

When Winslow finished his business, she turned back down the hill. She didn't want to leave until Walker woke. He was going to need good food and a lot of rest to drive the shadows from his eyes. And Jilly was going to give him both.

Winslow shot off, tail wagging. Through the snow Jilly saw someone sitting on her patio. She recognized Jonathan, his shoulders slumped.

She walked up the little path and sat down next to him. "You're up early. You don't look like you slept much."

"I haven't. My grandmother and I just finished cleaning up her attic."

"At *this* hour?"

"I'm afraid so. When you get old, you get up early. I mean really early." Jonathan glanced into the distance and rubbed his neck. "She's not doing well, Jilly. She won't talk about it, but she's had more breathing problems. She goes in for tests in a few days. If they find anything, they'll —" He hesitated and took a deep breath. "They'll take her straight into surgery. And surgery is risky. I can't bear to think of losing her," he said hoarsely.

Jilly reached over and squeezed his shoulder. "She's a wonderful lady. She's also a very tough lady. She'll pull through this, Jonathan. You have to stay positive. That's for her as much as for you."

"I keep telling myself that. I do a pretty decent job most of the time until I see her medical forms and all the medicines she has to take. But she needs to stay positive, too.

She's having a hard time, with all the changes around here. She wants things the way they used to be." He cleared his throat. "Red brought something up. He and I — well, we've been talking it over. He told me I should come here and ask you for a favor. A really *big* favor."

Winslow raced down the hill, spun sideways in the snow and then ran back up again. "I'm happy to help in any way I can. Tell me what I can do."

He cleared his throat again, looking uncomfortable but determined to finish. "It's a favor of Walker, too, actually. Red and I have worked it all out. It would be the perfect morale booster for Mamie. It may seem crazy, but it's exactly what she needs before she goes into the hospital."

Jilly stared at him, totally confused. "Do you want me to bake something for her? Give her a recipe for the resort? I still have some of my salsa products left. I can make up a gift basket for her, if that's what you want."

"It's not food." Jonathan stood up slowly and shoved his hands into his pockets. He looked down and kicked at the snow. "No, what we're asking for is a wedding here at the resort."

"And you want me to cook?"

Jonathan gave a dry laugh. "I want you to *be* there, not cook. Red and I have everything set up. All you and Walker have to do is agree to get married. We'll do all the rest."

Jilly could only stare at him. Winslow bounded up the hill and shoved his face against her chest, licking her face in canine ecstasy. Jilly frowned as snow flew off his fur. "You want Walker and me to get married?"

"Yeah, I do. Not for real, of course. But for now. For Mamie. We can arrange everything."

Jilly didn't move. What was he suggesting? Didn't Jonathan see that it was completely crazy? After all, you didn't *pretend* to get married. Marriage wasn't a joke or a performance.

"It's out of the question." She made an impatient sound and stood up. "And you're *not* going to ask Walker, because he needs to rest. He came back exhausted from wherever he was. He's going to sleep until noon, and then I'm going to make him my best pecan pancakes slathered with butter and organic maple syrup. Nobody, and I mean nobody, is going to bother him until after that. As for this crazy idea of yours — I sympathize with you, but it's nuts. I wouldn't dream of doing it. Neither would

Walker."

Jonathan didn't answer.

Jilly heard the rasp of the patio door sliding open. Winslow began to bark loudly.

Walker leaned in the opened doorway, his hair rumpled, his eyes still dark with sleep. "I could hear you two arguing all the way from the bedroom. What's going on? And what is it that Jilly and I wouldn't dream of doing?"

CHAPTER TWENTY-THREE

Just perfect. *He'd heard them arguing.*

Jilly shot an irritated glance at Jonathan. "Nothing. We were just arguing about baseball scores, right, Jonathan?"

But he didn't answer her, and Jilly saw the raw entreaty in his eyes. But there was no way she was going there. Arranging a fake marriage would be reckless, irresponsible and manipulative.

Walker stepped outside. He looked from Jilly to Jonathan. "Baseball scores. I didn't know you were such a fan, Jonathan." He walked across the patio and sank down into a chair overlooking the valley. "Maybe you should explain."

"You should be asleep," Jilly said.

"I can sleep later. Something tells me this is important." Walker pulled the blanket over his shoulders and raised an eyebrow. "Now one of you needs to explain, because we all know you weren't arguing about baseball."

Jilly was determined to cut off the discussion, but Jonathan was faster. He sat down in a chair next to Walker and studied his hands. "Red and I have been discussing something. We have a favor to ask of you and Jilly. It's a big one, okay? But it's for Mamie, and we'd do anything for her."

Walker frowned. "Is something wrong? She hasn't had another heart attack, has she?"

"She's had more symptoms of cardiac problems. Breathing problems also, with swelling in her legs and fluid buildup. She has to go in for tests on Tuesday. She's feeling really bad now. That's why Red and I decided she needed something to raise her spirits." Jonathan cleared his throat. "She was up in the attic with me, going through old boxes. She found pictures of her daughter — my aunt, who died years ago. Seeing those photos really tore her up. It was as if it had happened all over again. She's going to need a big distraction, Walker. And there's only one distraction that works for her." He looked up, facing Jilly defiantly. "A wedding. *Your* wedding, that's what would be better than any doctor's visit. Better than medicine or any kind of surgery. You know that she's been trying to get you married for months, Walker. I can't think of a better time." He looked at Jilly and gave a crooked smile. "Or a better person."

And then, when Jilly began to sputter an answer, he raised his hands in surrender. "I know it wouldn't be real and permanent. I'm not asking for the impossible. We just want you to go through with the ceremony and a small reception afterward. Jilly will be leaving soon anyway, so it's not like you'll be bumping into each other every day. After a few months, you can have everything quietly annulled. I've already checked with my friend, who's a lawyer in Denver. We have the paperwork ready. You can leave everything else up to us. The wedding wouldn't even have to be legally binding, except I just know Mamie will want her own minister to officiate and he wouldn't stand for —"

"Hold. Halt. *Stop.*" Jilly stalked across the patio. "You aren't seriously thinking we would do this, are you? It's an insult to your grandmother, Jonathan." She glanced at Walker. "You agree with me, right?"

Walker nodded slowly. "I'm afraid so. It would be an empty trick, Jonathan. Sooner or later Mamie would realize the truth, and that would tear her up inside. I know your intentions are good, but this isn't the way to make her feel better."

"But —"

Walker shook his head. "Jilly's right. It's a bad idea. And frankly, even if it was a good idea, your grandmother is nobody's fool. Do you really think you could pass this over on her as a real wedding?" He slanted a thoughtful glance at Jilly. "Jilly and I have some chemistry between us, but I haven't known her for a week. She's not the kind of woman who would throw logic to the wind and get herself hitched to a stranger."

Was there a question in his eyes? And why did Jilly, for one blind moment, wish she was that impulsive kind of woman, one who could trust her heart wherever it led her?

Jonathan scuffed his toe through the snow at the edge of the patio. "It's not all that crazy. Heck, everybody knows there's something going on between the two of you. When you're in the same room, it feels like an electric storm about to hit. It wouldn't be hard to convince Grandma." He gave a dry laugh. "I'm halfway convinced myself." He waited hopefully, and when neither of them answered, he gave a stiff shrug. "Fine. You've got a right to say no. It would be inconvenient and take a few days out of your life. Sorry I asked." His voice was tight with disappointment. "Believe me, if it wasn't for Mamie, I would never have bothered you." He turned around, striding to the path that led to the street.

Snow drifted down. Neither Jilly nor Walker spoke.

She realized her heart was pounding. Was Jonathan right? Would this crazy plan really give Mamie the moral support to get through the difficult weeks to come?

Jilly sat down on the chair next to Walker and crossed her arms. When he didn't speak, she turned to face him. "You can say something. Anytime now would be good."

"Not a whole lot to say. You did most of the talking for us."

Jilly felt her face burn. "I only said what was logical. You have to admit, it's a crazy scheme."

"Absolutely."

"And it could all backfire. If Mamie found out that we lied, it would break her heart, good intentions or not."

"She would hate being lied to."

"Besides, you don't scoff at a serious thing like marriage. It's not a game."

"Couldn't agree more."

Jilly glared at him. "Will you stop agreeing with me? I'm trying to be reasonable here."

"Reasonable is good." Walker frowned,

watching Jonathan's truck speed away down the road to town. "You and I, we're both reasonable adults. Something like this is way outside our comfort zone. Even if it could make a wonderful lady very, very happy," he said quietly.

Jilly closed her eyes. "I can't believe I'm hearing you say this, Walker. You know it's wrong."

Walker watched the snowflakes swirl over the patio. Then he reached out and snagged Jilly's waist, pulling her down onto his lap. "Anybody ever tell you that you're gorgeous when you're spitting bullets?"

Jilly sputtered. No one in the world made her sputter, but Walker had managed it. He had twisted her up into tiny knots and then scattered sunlight gently into the dark places she worked so hard to ignore. He was the best man she had ever met, a far better person than she was. He deserved a woman who was smarter, kinder, more patient. A woman with a future.

But the thought of Walker with any other woman was unbearable. "So you're really considering this? You think it's possible to pull it off without Mamie realizing the truth?"

"Only with a lot of help. Everyone would have to be in on it." He reached up and traced Jilly's cheek. "Especially you. And it would probably be impossible for you to pretend to be in love with someone like me. A loner who's pretty much given up on the world," Walker said harshly.

Jilly's breath caught. "It wouldn't be hard. It wouldn't be hard at all. I'm . . . well, I'm halfway in love with you already."

There, she had said it. The admission terrified her, yet left her feeling strangely liberated.

"I'm great at food but lousy at relationships, Walker." She felt her eyes burn with sudden tears. "And I may look like a reckless rule breaker but marriage means something to me. I don't like pretending."

Walker drew her head down onto his shoulder. "This is because of the way you grew up, without a family or the things that most of us take for granted. So to you these things matter."

Jilly just nodded. He was reading her again. It frightened her how easily he did that.

"No doubt about it, families are tricky. Generally a pain in the ass, but I guess they have their moments." He pulled her closer, draping the big blanket over them both. Snowflakes drifted down, whispering over Jilly's face. She breathed a slow sigh, feeling the heat of his chest warm her body.

"You're right," he continued, "it's a crazy scheme. I wouldn't think twice about it." He smiled a little sadly. "Except that now it's my turn to tell you a story. When I got back from Afghanistan, I was pretty much a shell. But Mamie was there. She never gave up on me. She made the drive up to my cabin twice a week in that old truck of hers. She brought me food and magazines and DVDs. She made me eat every bit of the food she brought while she told me all the local gossip, even when I didn't want to hear it. I was a hard case, too. It took her six months, but she brought me back. Without Mamie, I might not have made it, Jilly. My own family gave up on me. There were issues between us even before I left. They never wanted me to join the marines, and they made it painfully clear. When I got back, they wanted to pretend nothing had changed. They didn't understand the way war changes a person, but Mamie knew. She'd been through it once when her husband came back from Vietnam. She did all the right things." Walker's voice was husky. "Without Mamie, I might still be up in the cabin, fighting my way through bad memories. The walking dead."

Jilly lifted his hand, tracing the scars

around his elbow. His story had shaken her to her very soul. She realized that Walker was still fighting his personal war against dark memories. This was part of the sadness she had seen in his eyes when he had come home that morning. "Then I owe her, too," Jilly said slowly. "Not many people would have had that kind of determination."

She slid her hand under Walker's chin and studied that hard face, filled with so much strength and honesty. "You're a difficult man to say no to, Walker. You don't shout and push. You just stand there, strong and patient, letting the rest of the world come around to your way of thinking. You don't care how long it takes." Jilly shook her head a little sadly. "Me, I'm a shouter. I jump in headfirst and don't count the odds."

"Brave," he murmured.

"Stupid, more like it." She opened her hand and wove her fingers between his. Her voice was husky. "So when do we get this show on the road?"

They tracked Red down in his office. He looked guilty at first. Then as he studied their faces, he smiled hopefully.

"I guess Jonathan spoke to you. I'm surprised you're not coming after me with a hunting knife, Walker." He waved them into the cramped space and poured them coffee. "And before you say anything, I want this clear. We never would have concocted this scheme if Mamie wasn't facing some serious hospital time next week. All we want to do is stack the deck so she can be upbeat and happy when she faces those tests." He propped a hand on the windowsill and looked out at the snow. "I owe her for giving me roots and a sense of family when I was drifting. I might have gone the other way, running with a bad crowd, if Mamie hadn't grabbed me by the scruff of the neck and turned me around." He gave them a rueful smile. "So that's my confession. Now let's cut to the chase. What did you two decide? Am I planning a wedding or not?"

By the time Jonathan charged into the kitchen following Red's call, they were deep in plans for the wedding. Jilly felt queasy as she listened to the excited arrangements. Heaven help her if her friends found out. If Caro, Grace and Olivia knew, Jilly was a dead woman. End of story.

"Something wrong?" Walker leaned across the table and took her hand. "Is the bride getting cold feet?"

"I'm just thinking about what my friends will say if they find out. They'll kill me for

301

not inviting them." She gave a little shrug. "But it's not the real thing, so it doesn't count, right? What happens next?"

"We visit Mamie and share our good news. Jonathan wants us to go as soon as possible."

Jilly nodded, forcing a smile. "But after we do that, it's back to bed with you." She gave a little laugh. "A bride wants a man who isn't going to keel over in exhaustion on their wedding night."

"Thanks for the vote of confidence," Walker murmured. "I'll try to do a reasonable job so the bride has no complaints."

They rehearsed their stories with Winslow curled up at Jilly's feet.

Head over heels at first sight. Just want a small ceremony without any fuss.

No reason to wait.

All the details about their future and where they would live could wait.

Jilly shot Walker a searching look. "You're sure we're doing the right thing?"

"It feels right to me. But it's not too late. You can still back out." He raised an eyebrow. "I wouldn't be the first man jilted at the altar."

Jilly studied the tall windows of the main lodge, veiled with a light coat of snow. "Very funny. And for the record, I'm in." She reached down and retied Winslow's bandanna as it began to slip. "I still don't understand how Jonathan and Red are going to get all the details worked out. And I can't exactly get married in cooking clogs and blue jeans."

Walker rubbed his jaw. "I don't think I have a suit here." He smiled slowly. "But I wouldn't reject blue jeans so fast. That tight pair you're wearing now fits you like a dream. They make me wonder what you'll wear for the wedding night."

"Walker, we need to be on the same page with this. It's not a *real* wedding. And as far as a wedding night —"

He gave a deep laugh. "Yeah, I know. I just couldn't resist watching your face get all flushed. The groom won't be taking liberties." His eyes darkened. "Not unless the bride asks him to."

Jilly cleared her throat. She wasn't ready to come up with an answer for that.

Walker looked over Jilly's shoulder and his eyes narrowed. "Better brace for impact. Jonathan is up there with Mamie. I'd say it's show time."

Mamie insisted that they all come to her house and have lunch. She had a thick beef stew cooking in a crockpot and some of Red's corn bread in her oven.

"I couldn't believe it when Red told me. It's so sudden. But I watched the two of you together, and I knew there was something special going on."

The small woman took Walker's arm and patted it. "I always knew you would meet someone wonderful. And you did." Her eyes were bright with excitement. "Now for the details. I spoke with one of the teachers at the knitting camp, Jilly. She has a few thoughts about a veil. As for a dress, it would give me great pleasure if you would consider wearing the dress I was saving for my daughter. She never got to wear it. But maybe that would bother you?"

"No," Jilly said quickly. "I mean, that would be lovely, Mamie." Jilly took Walker's arm and managed a carefree smile. "We were wondering what would happen if I got married in blue jeans and kitchen clogs, weren't we, honey?"

Walker brushed a strand of hair from Jilly's face. She could have sworn his smile was real when he drew her fingers through his. "You look wonderful in jeans or anything else. But the dress sounds nice."

"Then it's settled," Mamie said firmly. "Now then, all of you sit down while I get the stew. I have an *amazing* appetite all of a sudden. After lunch I'll show you the gown, Jilly."

When she vanished into the kitchen, Jonathan gave Jilly a quick high five. "Man, you two deserve Oscars." Jonathan's eyebrows rose. "Except . . . I keep wondering. When did you both become such great actors? Or maybe it isn't an act at all," he said quietly.

After lunch, Jilly climbed to the big, sunny attic and stared at the beautiful wedding dress made of layer after layer of silk and antique lace. She had never seen a dress as elegant as this one.

"Are you sure it will fit me? I don't know anything about wedding dresses, but it looks a little short."

"It will be fine. You're very tall, but as long as you don't wear four-inch heels we should be fine."

Jilly laughed. "You won't see me in four-inch heels. I'm clumsy enough in kitchen clogs." She reached out and squeezed Mamie's fragile fingers. "Thank you for letting me borrow the dress. It's lovely."

Mamie reached onto a shelf and pulled down a framed picture of a laughing young woman with wild black hair. "Lindsay would have liked you. She and her friend

Raven both loved to cook. They traveled through Europe for six months and she wrote me the most wonderful letters about the meals they had in Italy and France. They hoped to start a restaurant here one day." Her voice quivered. "But that never happened."

Jilly waited for Mamie to go on.

"There was an accident in upstate New York. A driver asleep at the wheel let his van veer out of his lane on a small country road. Two other cars were hit. Everyone else walked away without a scratch, but Lindsay was killed instantly." Mamie cradled the photograph for a moment, looking lost. Then she squared her shoulders. "That was ages ago. I've tried to put it behind me. But sometimes late at night I can almost hear Lindsay's laughter from the kitchen. I know she would be honored to have you wear her dress." Mamie took the gown from its bag and held it out to Jilly. "Wear it. Wear it and be very, very happy." She gave a low laugh. "Although with a man like Walker, I can't imagine that you'd be anything else."

By the time Walker and Jilly got back to her room, Jilly was feeling overwhelmed.

Even Walker had begun to look tired.

But what they were doing felt right. "She

306

was so happy she glowed. Jonathan knows her too well. This is just what she needed." Jilly glanced back at the big cardboard carton that held the wedding dress. "Mamie has a friend who will make a few alterations, but she is convinced it won't take much. What a sad story about her daughter."

"She's had her share of pain." Walker was quiet for a long time. "Thank you for doing this, Jilly. We'll work out the details. We'll keep everything simple. I was thinking about coming to visit you in Oregon anyway. What do you think of the idea?"

"I'd like that." Jilly found it hard to imagine that she would be going home in a few days. How had her life changed so much so fast?

Yet one thing continued to bother her. "Walker, this morning you said something about your family. You mentioned that things were rocky between you. It's none of my business, but I have to say this, just once. I don't have a family. I'll probably never know who my mother is and I'll never know why she gave me up the way she did. But I'm good with that. The point is, you *do* have a family. You've got people who know you the way no one else does. So my advice? Ignore the shouting and the snide comments. Do whatever it takes to make it right. Because you only get one family." Jilly took a deep breath and smiled. "There, I said it. Just my two cents' worth." She stopped, suddenly embarrassed.

Walker nodded slowly. "I'll remember that. It's good advice. On the other hand," he continued dryly, "you've never met my family."

When he yawned, Jilly pointed toward the bedroom. "Off to bed with you. The bride has work to do." She looked down and smiled at Winslow. "Don't ask me what it is. Winslow and I have to have some secrets, don't we?"

She waited until Walker was asleep before pulling out the bag with her knitting.

The textured wool bandanna she'd decided to make to match the blanket was nearly done. The cables were complete and the panels continued in a line from one corner to the other. "Come over here, Winslow. Let's see if this thing fits as well as your other bandanna." The dog sat restlessly as Jilly tied the wool in place at his neck.

It was a perfect fit. The color was ideal for him.

Jilly sighed. "Nobody is going to look at me. You'll be the real star of the show,

Winslow."

Winslow pranced in a happy circle, showing off his new accessory. When the quickly tied knot came free, Jilly leaned over and grabbed the bandanna.

A sharp pressure burned through the center of her chest. The room seemed to sway.

She sat back slowly, fighting a wave of dizziness.

Not again. Not now.

Winslow bumped against her leg and began to whine. Blinking hard, Jilly leaned against the excited dog, dragging in air. Long minutes passed. Slowly the dizziness faded, and she began to feel a little better.

But it would be unforgivably stupid to ignore the episode.

Jilly pulled on her coat, one eye on the bedroom door where Walker was sleeping. Quietly she reached for her cell phone. Then she opened the door to the patio, walking through the snow to the little rise near the fence. At this distance Walker wouldn't hear her talking.

As Winslow shot up the hill, Jilly looked up the number of her doctor back in Arizona.

CHAPTER TWENTY-FOUR

"Has anyone seen Jilly?"

Walker scanned the group of people in the meeting room at the resort, but his bride-to-be seemed to have vanished.

She had been looking a little queasy earlier, and Walker knew exactly how she felt. Fake or not, a wedding was a big, elaborate undertaking. Right now all he wanted to do was head back to the cabin and sleep for three days.

His short rest had helped. But when he awoke, Jilly was gone. Walker had checked the cabin and then gone up to the main lodge, hoping to find her. He had found Winslow, but so far he'd had no luck with Jilly.

After the screwups on the mission he'd just returned from, it was hard to find energy to be optimistic about anything. He had felt helpless watching the cascade of failure from the hostage standoff. Their rescue effort had been doomed from the start, thanks to bad intel from Afghanistan and allies who had wavered under attack. An outpost that was supposed to be a rural hospital turned out to be a well camouflaged weapons cache.

As more field reports came back, while Walker was still en route, the news had gone from bad to terrible.

Five men had died. Two more wounded.

Walker's fists clenched. He had offered three rescue scenarios involving snipers and trained dogs, but there was only so much he could do. He had to remember that.

He slipped out of the noisy room, still searching for Jilly. Where had she gone?

He felt Winslow press against his leg, whining softly. As usual, the dog was a tuning fork, picking up the emotions of those he loved. The big dog bounded up the path in front of him, and then turned back expectantly.

"We're going to make it through this just fine, Win. After all, a wedding is just another kind of field mission, right?"

Winslow kept whining. He nipped the bottom of Walker's jeans and tugged him firmly up the hill.

It was a clear command.

"Who's giving the orders here?" Walker

muttered. But he followed the big dog up the hill, past women with knitting needles who waved at him in excitement. It seemed like everybody in town knew about this wedding, he thought grimly. One of the dangers of living in a small town.

Winslow shot up the slope toward Jilly's room. Was she inside? Walker stopped at her door, frowning when he heard the muffled sound of her voice inside. He couldn't pick up the words, only what sounded like anxious questions. He knocked twice, trying to calm Winslow, who was scratching hard at the door.

"It's Walker, Jilly. Is everything okay?"

He heard what sounded like a chair falling over. Alarmed when she didn't answer, he grabbed the doorknob and shoved hard. The unlocked door burst open.

Jilly was in the middle of the room, looking pale, her cell phone gripped at her chest. Walker saw the guarded look in her eyes.

"I thought you'd gone out."

She didn't answer, her body rigid.

"What's going on, Jilly?"

"I — I'd like to be alone."

The cold distance in her voice was unmistakable. Walker saw she wouldn't meet his gaze. "Why?"

"Does it matter?" She turned, her arms

tight at her chest. "Look, would you just go? I — I haven't had a moment to myself since this stupid wedding business began. I need a little space."

"Space." Walker crossed the room, seeing the way her hands trembled. Seeing the way color washed over her pale cheeks. "And that's why you're standing here, glaring at me. Because you want to be alone?"

"That's right." Her voice was firm, her shoulders stiff. But she was lying.

Fighting irritation, Walker tossed his coat on a chair. "Nothing else you want to tell me?"

"No." She spun around, one hand on the counter, the phone pressed against her chest. "Now would you please leave?"

He took a deep breath, fighting the anger — and the fear that kicked him hard. "Like hell I will. Not until I get some answers. What's going on here, Jilly? And don't tell me it's about *space,* because that's the most miserable lie I've ever heard."

"Go away."

Angry, Walker caught her shoulders. "Stop hiding." His fingers tightened. "I thought we had something, Jilly. I was willing to give it time. But there has to be trust, damn it."

She shoved at his hands and made a little broken sound. "Oh, go away. Please."

"Not until you talk to me." He shook his head, pulling her against his chest. "Something's happened. Why didn't you come and tell me?"

"N-nothing's happened."

"No? Then why are you white?"

"Okay, I got dizzy. I felt nauseous —"

"Sit down." Walker felt anger plunge into panic. *"Now."* He guided her to a chair and sank to his knee beside her. "You didn't black out or anything."

"No. Nothing like that." She closed her eyes and rubbed her face. "I — it passed, Walker. I had a bad moment, but it passed."

"When were you going to tell me? Next week? Or never?"

She reached out blindly and gripped his hand. "I don't know. Nothing makes sense right now. I just want my dignity back. I want to feel whole again. I want things the way they used to be. But I'll never have that, will I?" The catch in her throat broke Walker's heart, but he knew she would never want pity.

"I wish I could help you, but you have doctors for that. You called them, right?"

Jilly ran a hand through her hair. "Of course. They told me to rest and call them immediately if the symptoms returned."

Some of Walker's panic ebbed. "Okay.

That's a plan."

"Look . . . I'm sorry. I should have told you. I guess I'm not used to asking for help."

Walker sensed that this was a big admission for her. It soothed some of his anger at being cut out of something that could have been life-threatening. "Then *start* asking, Jilly. If you can't open up to me, then there's nothing and no point. You might as well walk out that door and go back to Oregon right now. Is that what you want?"

He was pushing her because he had to. He had to know if she would leave without a backward glance. If so, better for them both to find out now.

She looked down at their entwined fingers. "No. It's the last thing I want," she whispered. "But it's never been like this for me before, Walker. I've never trusted or wanted enough to let a man this close. I'm . . . frightened."

He slid his arms around her and whispered her name in exasperation. "I'm frightened, too. I want this to work out, Jilly. So let's take it one step at a time and stop screwing it up." Walker frowned. "I'm sorry if I was rough on you."

"Don't apologize. You had a right to be."

"I'm not so sure about that. And frankly, I'd rather you rip into me," Walker said

315

grimly. "I deserve it." He tilted her face up to meet his. "How do you feel now? Are you still sick?"

"Just tired. The dizziness has gone."

"But you were scared." Walker saw the weariness in her slumped shoulders. "I want the truth, Jilly."

"Yes. Scared out of my mind." She managed a faint smile. "But it passed."

"Next time come and find me. Tell me so I can help you." It was an order, not a suggestion.

Jilly blew out a breath and nodded. "I will."

"Okay. Now we have that settled." Walker sat down and pulled her onto his lap. His fingers moved over her wrist.

"You're taking my pulse, aren't you?" She frowned. "Is it high?"

"You're within normal range. That's a good sign."

When she moved restlessly on his lap, Walker fought down a vicious kick of lust. Angry at himself for rotten timing, he stood up, lifting her in his arms. "You need to rest. I'll sleep out here. I was going to drive back to the cabin, but now I'm staying."

Jilly didn't argue. There were dark shadows beneath her eyes as she nodded. Walker shook his head and carried her to the bed, muttering with every step.

"You don't have to carry me."

"The hell I don't. And if I don't like how you look in five minutes, I'm hauling you straight off to the emergency room. Now stop arguing." He set her down gently on the bed. "I'll call Mamie and tell her to cancel whatever she planned next for today. I'll be on the couch if you need me. And I warn you, I'll be checking on you. If I see something I don't like, we're out of here."

She frowned at him. "I'm not good at taking orders."

"Tell me about it," Walker snapped. The exhaustion was catching up with him. So was his uneasiness about Jilly. If he saw the first sign of any problem, he was taking her to the hospital.

He spread a blanket across the bed. "Go to sleep."

Jilly took a deep breath. "What about you? That couch isn't very comfortable."

"A lot better than other places I've slept."

Jilly cleared her throat. "We could . . . share the bed."

Walker forced down a hot wave of desire at the thought of Jilly's slim body pressed against his. He managed a crooked smile. "That's a nice offer, but with Winslow, there would be three of us. And you know Winslow would be part of the deal."

He was relieved to see her smile. More color came into her face. She finished the water bottle he handed her and then lay back on the pillow. "He does take up a lot of room, that dog of yours. But I don't mind." She yawned. "Sorry, Walker. I — I can't seem to keep my eyes open. There are fresh sheets and a pillow in the little closet. If you want me to make the bed —"

"You're staying right where you are, Iron Chef. I can wrangle a few sheets without your help." He glanced at Winslow, standing uneasily next to the bed. "Come on, big guy. She's fine. And don't think you're going to sleep on the bed, because you're not. We're bunking on the couch."

"Night." Jilly snuggled into her pillow, muttering something that Walker couldn't hear, and then her eyes closed.

It didn't happen that way, of course.

Ten minutes later Winslow was stretched across Jilly's bed while she slept. All Walker's gestures and gentle pushing seemed to have no effect. The dog simply wasn't moving. His big dark eyes studied Walker's face, radiating loyalty, protectiveness and sheer, uncomplicated joy.

The dog's head rested on Jilly's shoulder,

only inches from the curve of her breast.

Smart dog, Walker thought. Since Jilly had come into their life, Winslow had become more active. He had always been sociable, but now more than ever.

He also showed fewer signs of pain at night. He didn't wake up as often, prowling restlessly as if expecting danger.

Then Walker frowned.

What would happen to Winslow when Jilly went back to Oregon? The dog had become so closely attached to her in such a short time. But Walker knew she would have to go home before long. She had a life waiting for her back in Oregon. She had friends and work and plans to make. How could he convince her to stay here?

When she left, where was that going to leave Winslow?

And where was it going to leave *him?*

CHAPTER TWENTY-FIVE

Jilly felt something warm touch her neck. She gave a little sigh, stretching in her sleep. One hand reached out. In her dreams, she combed her fingers through Walker's hair and traced the hard angle of his jaw.

She gave a sharp gasp when a warm tongue licked her cheek.

Her eyes flashed opened. Winslow was draped over the bed, eyes glinting with happiness, tail wagging.

Jilly was sorry it hadn't been Winslow's silent, strong owner stretched out beside her on the bed. She didn't take orders from anyone, but when Walker had taken charge and ordered her to go rest, Jilly had found herself complying. He had been right to be angry at her for holding back the truth. Jilly was relieved that he knew the truth. She had seen that his anger came from his worry, so she let him take charge. In the process she discovered it could be surprisingly comforting to let a strong man take care of you.

Just once or twice.

She wouldn't make a habit of it, of course. Life had tossed Jilly around enough to teach her that you couldn't ever rely on anyone else. So she wouldn't get too comfortable accepting Walker's help, because it wouldn't last.

Bare feet scuffed over cool tile floor in the neighboring room. She looked up and saw Walker, delicious enough to eat, his long frame poured into worn blue jeans — and nothing else. His muscled chest left Jilly giddy.

Down, girl. A rapid pulse is bad for your health, remember?

"You're up." He leaned against the doorway, studying her appreciatively. That slow, thorough look was another thing Jilly decided she could get dangerously accustomed to.

"Everything hit me at once. I felt dizzy with exhaustion. I think that triggered . . . whatever happened." She ran a hand through her hair. "But I'm a little worried about this dressed-up stuff. I warn you, it is just not my thing. My friends could tell you stories."

"So you never did the whole prom night

extravaganza? No stretch limousine and four-inch heels?" Walker nodded slowly and smiled. "No, I'd say you and your friends boycotted the prom. You held an alternative prom of your own. You went to the beach and roasted hot dogs."

He was channeling her secrets again, Jilly thought wryly. How did he keep doing that? "Not the beach. We climbed the hill above my friend's house. At sunset we pitched a little tent, took out our favorite books and a lot of chocolate, along with our flashlights and sleeping bags. I guarantee you we had a whole lot more fun than the unfortunates down at the high school."

"I wish I could have seen that."

Jilly wished that he had been there, too. If she had had someone like Walker in her life back then . . . but you couldn't go back. And there was no point in brooding about what might have been.

"It was a good night. In fact, we're going to do it again one of these days — sleeping bags and flashlights. Chocolate and all our favorite books. We're going to camp out and stay up until dawn comes streaking over the cove, just like we did in high school. Everybody should camp out once in a while, don't you think?"

Walker didn't answer, his eyes unreadable.

"Something wrong?"

"Just the opposite. I was thinking that you and your friends must be pretty amazing when you get together. I know I wouldn't want to get in your way."

"Darned right. But you may get to meet them one of these days. If so, *don't* bring up this wedding, even though it's a sham. They'll have my hide. Yours, too."

"Warning noted." Walker turned around as the couch creaked. Winslow whined from the far end. "The big guy wants company. I just got up for some water. Want some?"

Jilly stretched slowly. "I'll get it. I've been lazy long enough. Hard to believe that I slept for two whole hours." She swept back the covers but took her time standing up, relieved when her dizziness did not return.

"You look good. Your color is back. I was pretty worried about you."

Jilly shrugged. "Sleep cures all."

When she started to walk past, Walker reached out and snagged her wrists. His hand moved slowly up her shoulder and across the top of her thin cotton nightshirt. "Forget the water," he said in a husky voice. "It can wait. This can't." His fingers opened on her cheek. Slowly, slowly he pulled her closer. She felt the muscles tighten at his chest as their bodies met.

Instantly the heat shot to life. There was no escaping the sensations that coiled into need. Walker's eyes glinted with desire and the slow, appreciative way he studied her body left no doubt that he liked what he saw — and that he would enjoy seeing a whole lot more.

He kissed the curve of her shoulder and his hands circled her waist. "I wanted to do this ever since I got here last night." He kissed the hollow beyond her ear and stroked the sensitive skin with his tongue. "You've got great ears. I don't think I've ever noticed a woman's ears before." He shook his head. "And then there's your neck. And your shoulders. Everything about you turns me on . . ." He kissed his way lower, tracing the hollows and curves.

Jilly closed her eyes in a haze of desire. It had never been slow and gentle before. No man had ever taken his time this way. She had never felt half as special, half as vulnerable as she did now.

The practical, logical part of her brain warned that being vulnerable was dangerous. This was not a man she could walk away from easily. Being touched this way would change things forever. Maybe even break her heart.

"You're a dangerous man, Walker."

"I'll never hurt you, Jilly."

"See? That's exactly why you're so danger-ous. Because you say things like that — and I believe you." She opened her hands, skim-ming his warm chest. "You make it feel too easy. You make me think that this could last and that it matters."

"If it doesn't matter, there's no point in touching and being touched. It's empty," he said roughly. "But empty is the last thing I feel right now."

Somehow her arms climbed up, twining behind his neck. He was tall, so she rose to meet him, urgent to claim his mouth and feel the hot brush of his tongue.

In an instant, the kiss changed. No longer slow and careful, Walker lifted her against him, his body tense. Jilly felt his hunger and the force of his control. When she opened her lips beneath his, he whispered her name in a groan.

Jilly tried to tell him to stop, but the words wouldn't come. She had waited too long to be treasured this way. Just once, she told herself.

Just once to last her through the cold nights after she went back to Oregon to pick up the threads of her life and he was gone.

She felt his hands tighten and gasped as

he swung her up against his chest. "Walker —"

"I want to feel you. That shirt you are wearing is driving me crazy, honey."

Dimly, Jilly realized he was carrying her to the couch, not to the bed. Walker read the surprise in her face. "If I get you into that bed, we won't leave this room for a week. Wedding or not."

Jilly shivered at the rough edge of need in his voice. When they sank down onto the couch, she made a sound of protest. "It's too small."

"I like it tight," he muttered. His hands opened, pulling her onto his lap. Their bodies moved, and her nightshirt rose higher as Walker coaxed her legs around his waist.

Desire pounded through her blood, sudden and sweet.

And yet, through the haze of her desire, Jilly fought against what he had said. It shouldn't *matter* like this. Caring so deeply frightened her.

She rested her forehead against his and sighed as he traced the curve of her breast. "Walker . . ."

"You have a problem with this? Because for me, there are no problems. Touching you like this is the best thing that's happened to me in a long time, Jilly."

What was she supposed to say to that? And how was she supposed to keep her thoughts clear and controlled when he touched her so carefully, so perfectly?

Jilly traced his jaw. "I'm not complaining about this. *This* is as perfect as I ever hoped to find. It's the rest of what you said, about mattering. I've never had anyone matter to me this way before. I don't want to screw that up, Walker. Even though there's next to no hope that we have a future." She sighed as his fingers traced the sensitive column of her spine and opened just below her breasts. Even then she fought to explain. "How can we? You live here. I live in Arizona and Oregon. There's my career, even though it doesn't hold much promise right now. There's also my health. I wish I could believe in happily-ever-after, Walker, but that's not my way."

Jilly felt him nod against her hair. "Yeah, that's all true. A whole lot of things should be keeping us apart. And yet here we are, with your legs wrapped around my waist and my hand buried in your hair. And I'm pretty damn sure it's the best thing either of us has ever felt. So we're going to forget about those questions, honey."

"How?" Jilly whispered, moving into his

touch, wishing there were no clothes separating them. "We can't exactly move your mountain to Oregon. And though I love Lost Creek, I couldn't see myself living here full-time. Plus, I'm not planning on a relationship. I'd be no good at it."

"Seems like we have a problem then."

But he didn't move. Neither did Jilly.

It felt too good to sit this way, safe in the curve of his arms and the heat of his body. It felt like a dream she'd glimpsed dimly but had never seen clearly. Now, with the full clarity of what she had found, and her joy in Walker's touch, it felt unspeakably cruel to have to give it up.

Temptation pounded through her. She could feel the strength of his body and the force of his need as the bond between them tightened, stronger than words.

He had seduced her from the first moment they met, captivating her with his calm strength and cool intelligence. And Winslow had claimed the last corners of her heart.

And right on the heels of that dizzying revelation came another. Jilly had never loved this way before. Her friends were her world, but that kind of love was calm and predictable, taking problems and laughter equally in stride.

This thing she had with Walker . . . would

never be calm or predictable. This was like a landslide after spring rains, toppling the cliffs above the cove. You could fling out your arms, but you couldn't hold your footing against it. It just forced you along in its path.

And for Jilly giving up control was the most frightening thing in life.

"Hey." Walker tilted up her face, staring into her eyes. She saw the heat and the racing desire, mirroring her own, but there was a trace of humor there as well. He almost seemed to be enjoying the situation in a dark way.

"You knew this would happen," Jilly said slowly.

"I hoped," he corrected.

"If you smile, or look smug, I'm going to punch you," she said thickly.

"I won't smile. Promise. But I may grin, just a little."

"This just doesn't — happen to me," she stammered. "Not like this, so I can't think of anything but touching you and being touched."

"I know just how you feel, honey."

"This messes *everything* up," Jilly said. "This feels important and I don't want important."

"Definitely feels that way." Walker kissed

the little hollow behind her ear and drew her body against him until there was no more space between them and her heart beat against his. He tugged off her shirt slowly and his hands opened on her breasts, rough calluses to soft, burning skin. "You're so beautiful."

She closed her eyes on a sigh as his hand slid up her leg and found her heat. He touched her with slow strokes until she gasped, pressing closer, driven by need.

"Stop arguing, Jilly. Let go."

And the plunge came in a heartbeat, thundering down, pulling Jilly in its swift, sudden violence right down toward the sea.

Control snapped. She gasped at the hot friction of his fingers against her sensitive skin, shuddering when she felt his finger slide inside her with perfect control. Pleasure slammed through her. Her back arched. Her hands dug into his hard shoulders. Dimly, dimly she heard him whisper her name, harsh with praise, while her body rose blindly against his.

Had a man with so much strength ever touched her so gently?

The answer hammered through her blood. Not like this. Never like this.

No other man ever would.

And then with a choked gasp Jilly stopped

fighting. She gave in to the pleasure and let her heart answer, raking his shoulders while desire broke in a storm, flinging her to shuddering oblivion.

Time trembled.

Jilly felt the minutes pass, marked in the pounding of her heart and the warmth of his breath against her face.

She didn't move. Couldn't move. Couldn't think straight, either. There was too much to understand and explore, but the effort was beyond her. She wanted to go on drifting like this, feeling his fingers in her hair and his strong body locked against hers.

How easy it would be to give up everything she was and start her life over from this second. And how dangerous.

Slowly she pulled free and studied him, seeing the calm pleasure in his eyes and the dark understanding of what had just happened between them.

"Walker." She took a short breath. "I — don't know what to say."

"I do," he said roughly. "Beautiful comes to mind first. Strong. Graceful. Incredibly stubborn," he added, smiling slightly.

"That's not what I meant."

"I figured that."

"I meant — what just happened. Like I said, that doesn't happen to me. Well, it has. Of course it has. But not like this, until my body simply melts and I can't think or stop wanting you to touch me again." Jilly caught a strangled breath. "Oh, hell."

Walker cut off her disjointed flow of words with a deep, searching kiss, his hands steady and anchoring. When they could finally breathe again, he released her. "There's no need to explain. I understand how fast a fire can start, and how fast it can race out of control," he added. "And that's about the nicest compliment you could pay me."

Jilly looked away, flushing. "But, Walker — you didn't —" Her face filled with fierce heat. "I mean, you haven't —"

He opened his hand and locked it over hers. "Not because I didn't think about it. Not because I don't want to. But right now things are too complicated between us. You put a lot of questions on the table, Jilly. Somehow we have to sort out the answers. We need to work this out as we go. Because it *matters*." His mouth feathered over hers and his tongue slid into a slow, heated entrance. Jilly felt her heart drop straight to her toes.

How did he do that so fast, so well? They weren't even in bed, for heaven's sake. They were sitting on the couch and Walker was still dressed. Even then he had her racing out of control, craving the blind heat of skin against skin.

Wanting whatever he would give her because she trusted him completely.

She closed her eyes, telling herself they would stop in a minute, and that the insanity wouldn't happen again. But not yet, not when touching him was so achingly new and her whole body sang with the joy of discovery.

She rested her palm on his chest, thrilled to feel the hammer of his heart. Leaning down, she kissed his shoulder, the base of his neck and an old silver scar below his collarbone. "Did it hurt when you were wounded?"

"It was a long time ago, honey."

Jilly traced another scar above his elbow and another near his wrist. Each one left her hollow inside. He had lived with danger and conquered it. Jilly wondered what the cost of that personal struggle had been. Could you ever leave those kinds of memories behind?

Her hand cupped his shoulder gently, where another scar gleamed in a jagged path. "Was Winslow there with you when it happened?"

"Always. He watched my back, and I watched his. He's the toughest marine I know," Walker said. There was no mockery or humor in his voice. Only deep emotion.

Jilly nodded. She understood the deep bond between man and dog now. She understood Winslow's unquestioning devotion and Walker's constant protectiveness. That kind of loyalty awed her.

Walker whispered her name and gathered her up against his chest, settling back on the couch until she lay stretched out against him. "We're not going to figure this out in an hour or a day, Jilly. Why don't we just enjoy what we have?"

"I think I just did enjoy myself," she murmured. She closed her eyes, listening to the rumble of his heart beneath her ear. She slid her leg between his, sighing when he ran his hand slowly down her spine and cupped her hip.

He was driving her wild with his control. She wanted to feel him, to touch all of him. "Why are you still dressed?" Jilly reached for the waistband of his jeans. "Take these off."

"Afraid I can't." Walker gave a rueful smile. "We don't have enough time."

Jilly frowned. "What do you mean?"

"Jonathan called while you were asleep.

We've got a wedding rehearsal dinner tonight, it appears. The ceremony is set. Tomorrow morning we get married in the chapel here at the resort. But Mamie kept everything small." His lips twitched. "She only invited two hundred and fifty of her closest friends and family. A whole lot of them will be at the rehearsal dinner tonight." He pulled her closer and kissed her hotly. His tongue slid over hers and he made a low groan of pleasure. "I'd rather be here, touching you, honey," he said hoarsely. "But we'd better get moving."

Jilly wasn't sure whether to laugh or cry.

But there was no going back now.

CHAPTER TWENTY-SIX

"You look tired." Jonathan paced the hall where the wedding rehearsal was being held. In the main room Mamie held court with a few of her closest friends — ninety-two at last count.

"I'm fine. Jilly and I are both fine. It's been a little stressful, that's all. And . . ." Walker reached a hand to his shoulder and frowned.

"What is it, Walker? Is your shoulder hurting again? Should I get the doctor?"

"No need. It's just this new medicine they're trying on me. It's pretty wicked on my system. But I'm good to go." Walker ran a hand through his hair and glanced out at the crowd assembled in the resort dining room. "Did Mamie really have to invite half of Lost Creek to this dinner?"

"This is nothing." Jonathan grinned. "Wait until you see the crowd tomorrow at the wedding."

"That's what I'm afraid of," Walker muttered.

From the first moment she stepped inside the dining room, Jilly was swept up in excited congratulations. The people here were amazing, she thought. They didn't judge or question. If they chose you for a friend, they simply welcomed you with open arms. You knew you could rely on them for anything.

At the front of the room Mamie watched every detail with quiet joy radiating from her frail face.

Jilly felt a hand touch her shoulder. She didn't have to turn her head to know it was Walker. The bond between them was humming, tighter than words. Once that knowledge would have frightened her, but now it didn't.

"You want to sit down?"

"No. I'm fine."

Walker studied the line of people who were still entering the dining room and shook his head. "Mamie sure knows how to throw a party."

"She certainly does. And I'm having a wonderful time. I think I should eat a little something though. I'm starting to feel light-headed."

"Are you feeling sick?" Instantly Walker's hand cupped her elbow, guiding her to a chair. "Sit down. I'll get a plate of food and a bottle of water for you."

"Walker, I'm fine. I just don't want to go too long without eating. I think that's been part of my problem. Or maybe I'm not so stressed so now I realize when I'm hungry."

"I'm going for food anyway. Don't move." Walker looked behind him and gave a low whistle. Winslow, busy entertaining half-a-dozen children with tricks, jumped up and bounded across the room. "Stay, Winslow."

Instantly the dog settled on the floor beside Jilly.

Walker said something low that she couldn't understand. The order made Winslow stretch out and rest his head against Jilly's feet.

No, she wouldn't be going anywhere. Winslow would see to that.

She looked down and ran a hand through the dog's fur. She didn't know how or when it had happened, but this whole town felt like home. Her real home was with her friends on Summer Island, in the small cobbled streets where she knew every corner and every house. But Jilly had discovered a new home.

And how in the world was she going to

leave this behind once their fake wedding
was over?

CHAPTER TWENTY-SEVEN

That night, while the rehearsal dinner was in full swing, Jilly and Walker slipped away. Jilly couldn't sleep, restless and lonely in her room. For the sake of appearances, Walker and Winslow were sleeping in another part of the resort.

She'd finally fallen asleep around 5:00 a.m., only to jump awake at the sound of loud knocking on her door. When she saw the clock, she gasped.

Ten o'clock? It *couldn't* be that late. Grabbing a robe, she walked to the door and peered out.

Mamie and Jonathan were waiting outside, looking anxious when Jilly answered their knock.

"Is everything okay? Your gown is done and the seamstress wants to do a last fitting. After that, Red will deliver food here to your room, so you don't have to leave. He's making a big ranch breakfast for you, Jilly."

Jilly put a hand on her stomach. She didn't really feel like spicy chili or *huevos rancheros,* not today. Why was she having bridal day jitters? This wasn't the real thing.

She forced a big smile for Mamie's sake. "It all sounds wonderful. Sorry that I overslept. I didn't sleep well last night."

Jonathan frowned. "That's odd. Walker said the same thing. He looked pale and stressed this morning."

"He didn't tell me anything," Mamie said sharply. "Is he okay, Jonathan?"

"I guess I woke him up too early. I went by around six."

"I should go see him," Jilly said quickly.

"No need. Besides, it's your wedding day. It's bad luck for the groom and the bride to see each other before the ceremony, remember?" Jonathan cast a telling glance at Mamie, making a little gesture behind her back as if to warn Jilly away from that plan.

"Oh. Right. Bad luck." Jilly wandered over to the couch. "Did he say what was wrong, Jonathan?"

"His shoulder, I think. He was rubbing it this morning. It gives him a lot of pain, and he won't agree to surgery. He said he knows too many people who have problems after shoulder surgery, so he's going to gut it out. Just like a marine." Jonathan said the words

341

with deep pride.

"I'm going to mention something to my specialist in Laramie. I think it would be a good idea for Walker to get another opinion," Mamie said quietly. "I'll set up a consultation as soon as the events here are over. But I feel terrible about this. If he's in pain, maybe we should delay the ceremony."

"No," Jonathan said quickly. "I'm sure Walker wouldn't want that. Besides, you're going into the hospital in a few days, Grandma. They won't want to get married while you're gone."

Mamie looked undecided. "I would hate to miss the ceremony. But I want to do the right thing. If Walker isn't feeling so good —"

"We'll send him off to rest for a while. No dancing on the tables tonight," Jilly said with a crooked smile.

"If you're sure. I am so looking forward to the ceremony. People are driving in from all over the west. I even located some of Walker's old marine platoon. One of them should be at the airport shortly. Several others are driving in from Arizona and California."

Jilly felt a stab of apprehension. This might not be a good thing to spring on Walker. She glanced at Jonathan, who had a similar expression of uneasiness. "Does Walker know?"

"I don't think he has seen his friends for months, not since he came to Lost Creek. I wanted to surprise him. If he doesn't like it, he can take it up with me."

There was no mistaking the determination in Mamie's voice. Since it was too late to change anything, there was no point in arguing.

Jilly turned around as she heard another knock at the front door.

"Room service. Eggs, bacon, two kinds of pastry and Lost Creek's best oatmeal." Red's voice drifted through the door. "Coffee, too."

Jilly would have killed for the coffee, but after cheating with that first cappuccino at Jonathan's coffee shop, she was determined to stay true to her promise. She would make do with tea.

"Jonathan, why don't you go check on Walker? I want to be sure he's okay."

"Will do." He gave a little two-finger wave and opened the door. Red was waiting next to a tall woman rolling a small suitcase behind her.

"Is this the bride's room?" she asked. "The seamstress is right behind me with the dress, and we need to get started. We only have two hours." The woman pulled her suitcase inside and studied Jilly thoughtfully. "I think you must be the bride." She opened a complicated makeup bag. With one expert movement she spread a dozen gleaming brushes on the kitchen counter. "Now then," she murmured. "Let's see what we have to work with."

CHAPTER TWENTY-EIGHT

It was a beautiful wedding.

The groom got sick.

The bride overslept. And the best man was a dog.

Mamie radiated joy in pearls and a dress of sky-blue silk. Jonathan hovered, looking anxious but surprisingly debonair in a formal black suit. His parents had come all the way from Aspen, and Jonathan was taking his duties as host seriously.

Jilly peeked out the door at the back of the chapel, watching more and more people cram the pews. Everything had happened so fast over the past week, and all she wanted was to have the ceremony over. She wasn't used to wearing makeup, and she never fiddled with her hair, but Mamie's friend had taken her job seriously. Jilly was stunned to see her image in the mirror, tall and serene, a vision of elegance in this exquisite gown with a wide satin sash. A single orchid gleamed in her upswept hair.

She didn't recognize herself. None of her friends would have known her.

The last stragglers were seated. Standing at the back of the chapel, Jonathan made a discreet gesture to Mamie, who smiled as Walker came to stand at the front of the chapel. Winslow was right beside the groom, elegant in a new red bandanna.

Everyone was here. Jilly took a deep breath as the organ music stopped. The achingly familiar strains of the *Wedding March* filled the chapel.

Her hands trembled. She stared down the long aisle and took a deep breath. Her mind told her this was just a performance, but her heart argued differently.

What if it had been a real ceremony?

What if she and Walker were promising to spend the rest of their lives together?

She closed her eyes. This was strictly an act, she reminded herself.

At the end of the aisle she saw Walker, tall and drop-dead gorgeous in a severe black suit that Jilly suspected was the creation of a very expensive Italian designer, well loved by Olivia. The suit made him look different — sophisticated in a way that he had not looked before.

"Are you ready?" Jonathan was at the

door, smiling. He looked pale, but determined to carry out his role. Red was going to walk her down the aisle.

"As ready as I'll ever be. Explain to me again why I agreed to this," she murmured.

Jonathan took her arm as row after row of delighted faces turned in their direction. "Take one look at Mamie's face. That's your answer. By the way, you look drop-dead gorgeous in that gown, Jilly. Seriously, I wouldn't have recognized you under all that makeup and puffy hair."

"Gee, thanks. *I think.*"

As they walked outside, Jilly focused to keep from falling in the strappy evening sandals the bridal expert had insisted she wear. Red waited at the last pew, a broad grin on his ruddy face. "Looking good, O'Hara," he murmured, sliding his arm under hers, as protective as any father.

And even more proud.

Every face turned.

Her tall groom, achingly handsome, smiled at her slowly from the altar.

Then the music swelled, and she walked out into the packed church.

The bride and groom offered their vows without a hitch.

No one stood up to protest the joining of

these two in holy matrimony. No one stood up to point an accusing finger and shout that this marriage was a hoax.

Jilly's nerves were a wreck.

There was a hint of humor in Walker's eyes as he slid a wedding ring onto Jilly's finger. "Almost done," he whispered. "You're so beautiful that I almost forgot my line. And it wasn't exactly a long one." His hand curved around hers and tightened. "I definitely do," he said.

Darkly handsome, tough and lean in that expensive suit, he looked like a character from a big-budget Hollywood action movie. He didn't look like the Walker she'd known, wearing scuffed boots, jeans and an old sweater. There was something different about this man. Jilly couldn't put her finger on it.

And then the beaming minister pronounced them man and wife. "You may kiss the bride," he added loudly.

Jilly's breath caught as Walker carefully lifted her gossamer veil of knitted lace. It was light as an angel's wing and just as beautiful. Walker seemed conscious of its delicacy, smoothing it back over her face and onto her shoulders with that careful touch that Jilly knew so well.

He stared down at her as if they were

absolutely alone and not standing in front of a church with more than two hundred people watching.

"You take my breath away," he murmured. And then he raised her face to his and kissed her, deeply and thoroughly, sliding his hands into hers. His finger traced her ring. When their lips met, Jilly almost forgot they weren't alone. She definitely forgot to breathe.

The thunder of the organ, booming through the chapel, brought her back down to reality.

"Ten more minutes," Walker said quietly, taking a breath and sliding his arm under hers. "Jonathan's got the car ready. We'll have some cake, offer some toasts. One dance, and then it will be done. You feel okay?"

Jilly nodded, hit by emotion.

Walker's hand opened under hers. "Good. Remember, you've made an old, frail woman very happy today. Now shall we go and meet most of the town of Lost Creek, Mrs. Hale?"

Chapter Twenty-Nine

Mrs. Hale.

For some strange reason Jilly kept remembering the final scene of the recent cinema version of *Pride and Prejudice.* It was the scene where Elizabeth Bennett told her new husband that he could only call her Mrs. Darcy when he was completely and incandescently happy.

Jilly wasn't much for movies, but that scene had knocked her socks off.

Now, looking up at Walker, she couldn't help herself from sliding a hand gently along his cheek. "Mrs. Hale," she murmured. "It has a nice ring."

She wondered what it would take to make Walker incandescently happy. She also wondered when it had become so important to do just that.

Unable to speak, she nodded at him, glad for the strength of his arm as unfamiliar emotions welled up. Around her she saw smiling faces. Mamie. Jonathan. Red and all the kitchen staff, along with at least twenty of the knitters from the retreat. Jilly thought maybe this was what family felt like, though she had no way to know. But maybe this unconditional support and acceptance was the very best part of being a family.

She glanced up at Walker, sensing something different about him. For a man who confessed that he didn't have a single suit in his cabin, he looked surprisingly comfortable in his beautifully tailored black jacket. When they passed one of the back pews, Jilly saw four very tall, very tanned men grinning at Walker. The closest man reached in his pocket, held up a satin garter and then tossed it to Walker, who smiled wryly as he caught it.

"Friends of yours?" Jilly murmured.

"Yeah, we spent some time together in the mud and dust over in Afghanistan. They're dumb as wood planks, but good men in a firefight. Mamie must have tracked them down. Hell, that woman can do anything."

Jilly's fingers moved along his. "It doesn't bother you, does it? Jonathan was afraid it might."

Walker seemed to consider his answer for a long time. "No. I thought it might. But today I'm in a surprisingly good mood." He looked down at Jilly. "Just fantasizing about a honeymoon, Mrs. Hale."

They kept walking through the crowded church, smiling and waving, nodding to all the people who seemed so proud to have their native hero married.

Suddenly Walker's eyes narrowed. Though no one else would have noticed, Jilly could read him now. She saw the tightening of his mouth, the stiffness that moved into his shoulders.

She glanced down the aisle and saw two children, three elderly men and four women. There was nothing to make him look upset.

"Walker, is something wrong?" she whispered.

A muscle worked at his jaw. Then he looked away, straight down the aisle to the back door of the church. "Everything's fine, honey. Let's go get some cake and make some toasts."

They were instantly besieged by people who offered good wishes and noisy congratulations. Jilly kept a watchful eye on Walker, remembering what Jonathan had said. He didn't seem to be in pain, but she noticed that he rubbed his shoulder once or twice. She watched to see if he glanced back at the row of people they had just passed, but he didn't.

Several of her friends from the knitting retreat closed in, admiring the intricately knitted veil. Jilly was caught up in their enthusiasm and descriptions of the interesting classes she had missed. How her friends would have gloated to learn that she actually regretted missing an afternoon of knitting.

When she turned around, Walker was gone. Probably he'd gone to talk to his marine friends, she thought. Then Mamie came to introduce the mayor of Lost Creek, along with the chief of police. There were toasts and congratulations and excited questions about the supposed honeymoon.

Jilly finally managed to escape. Where had Walker gone? She walked through the small meeting rooms, peeking into the offices that lined the chapel. Everyone seemed to be upstairs, where the wedding reception was in full swing. She could hear strains of a local band warming up, but down here everything seemed deserted.

Down the hall she saw a movement behind a partially opened door. Walking closer, Jilly heard the snap of muffled voices.

Angry voices.

One of those voices was definitely

Walker's. The other voice belonged to a woman who spoke fast and precisely with a definite New England accent.

Jilly stopped outside the door, wondering who the woman was and why they were arguing. She didn't want to eavesdrop, but if this affected Walker, she meant to stay close.

The woman paced angrily, and her voice drifted through the partially opened door. "Of course I saw the paperwork. It's my job to watch *anything* that affects the family. I couldn't believe you would actually consider getting married and not telling us. But you insist that this was all just an act." She laughed coldly. "Maybe for you it's an act, Walker, but no woman in her right mind would walk away from what you have to offer. Does she know that you're worth millions? Does she know about the estate in the Berkshires and the family homes in Provence? Does she know about the legacy that Grandfather left you? And the place in Bermuda?"

Jilly put her hand to her chest, struggling to understand what she had just heard. Millions? Homes scattered around the world? Who was this angry, impatient woman and what was she talking about?

Walker's answers were muffled.

354

The woman plunged right on, cutting him off. "You think she doesn't know? I'm always amazed at how naive men can be when it comes to a beautiful face and great legs. And she is stunning. I assume she has to be intelligent, too, if she managed to fool you. You're a superior catch for a regional chef whose restaurant and cooking career seem to be on the rocks. Yes, of course I checked her out. You thought I wouldn't?" She spat out questions like gunfire. "Did you do a background check on her? Did you get her to sign a prenuptial agreement? Because performance or not, your wedding was legally binding. I checked *that,* too. This O'Hara woman is entitled to half of *everything* you own now, Walker. But I'll be damned if a conniving little fortune hunter steals money out from under our noses. What were you *thinking?* Before you agreed to this ridiculous plan, why didn't you call me? I could have drafted language to protect our family," she said brusquely.

Jilly leaned against the wall, her heart pounding. Dimly she heard Walker cross the room.

His voice rose, colder than Jilly had ever heard it. "Damn it, Darrah, you've got this wrong. Jilly isn't after my money. She doesn't know or care."

355

"That's what they all say. Were you always this naive, Walker, or did it begin when you came back from Afghanistan?" The woman's heels clicked as she continued to pace angrily. "No, don't bother to answer that. You're intelligent enough when you choose to use your brain. So something else is going on here. Maybe this is your way of getting back at the rest of the family. Haven't you already done enough? After all, you've turned your back on all of us. Mother can barely stand to have anyone mention your name, and Father was crushed the day you left. He won't talk about it. But when you left, you broke his heart, too."

"It wasn't my choice," Walker said flatly. "He gave me no choice when I disagreed about my future. I won't go into politics, Darrah. I won't use what happened in Afghanistan to further a political career. Not mine or his. He couldn't accept that. So I left."

Father. Mother. This woman was Walker's sister, Jilly realized. A whole new world began to swim into view, along with a part of Walker that Jilly had never glimpsed. Blinking, she pressed one hand against the wall. She thought that she had known him, but the Walker she knew was as much an illusion as the ceremony that had just taken place.

Why hadn't he told her about himself? Why hadn't he given her any hint that his isolated life on the mountain was only part of who he was?

The woman tossed her expensive red handbag down on the table and crossed her arms. "There's one other thing you might as well know. Father is dying. He refused to have anyone contact you. He made us swear not to, but I was going to come and find you if you didn't answer my calls. Then I heard about this fiasco. You need to go home, Walker. He doesn't have much more time. The cancer is spreading, and the doctors think he may have less than a year." The woman's voice broke. Jilly saw Walker cross the room slowly and pull her against his chest when she began to cry.

"Darrah, I'm sorry. I didn't have a clue."

"Of course you didn't," the woman said in a broken, angry voice. "You didn't answer our emails. You wouldn't accept our calls with more than a few terse sentences. How in the hell were we supposed to let you know, by carrier pigeon?"

Father.

His father was dying. And in a sudden sweep of understanding, Jilly sank back

357

against the wall and closed her eyes.

His father was Frederick Harrison Hale, she realized suddenly. He was the scion of the Hale family, whose roots were as old as the country itself. Frederick Harrison Hale also happened to be the senior senator from New Hampshire. Jilly hadn't made the connection before because Walker seemed to have no link to that world of northeastern privilege and wealth.

How wrong she had been.

The knowledge left her shaken and empty, sick with a sense of betrayal. Jilly realized why he hadn't told her the truth. It was perfectly clear now. An insignificant nobody like her would *never* fit into a family like his.

The wedding was truly over, she thought blindly. She had done all she could for Mamie. They were supposed to leave on their fake honeymoon within the hour anyway.

No point in waiting to leave. Not after this.

She didn't want to see Walker trying to explain why he had kept all this from her.

None of that mattered now.

Jilly moved forward woodenly, leaving her bouquet on the chair outside the door. All she could see was the long shadowed corridor that led to the back of the resort. All she could think of was getting away before the tears began.

She should have known better. She had been colossally stupid, breaking her oldest rule not to trust a stranger, opening her heart when she should have been asking hard, pointed questions.

She clenched her hands, hating to see them shake. But she had her pride, and she clung to that pride now, moving down the deserted corridor like a sleepwalker caught in a horrible dream.

Walker was a millionaire several times over, the heir to one of America's largest fortunes. And Jilly, in all her stupidity, hadn't had a clue. What kind of life could two people so different have together? There would be no happily ever after here.

Jilly closed her eyes, rubbing away tears. She left the knitted veil carefully folded with a hasty note on the pastor's desk. She took her one small suitcase from her room and hailed a cab waiting at the front of the resort.

The driver studied her white gown in surprise. "You need a cab, ma'am?"

"I'm meeting somebody at the airport. They got in late," she lied. "I'm — in kind of a rush, too."

"There's no need for *you* to go. Give me

the name and I'll pick the person up. You don't want to leave your wedding."

"It's fine." Jilly's voice sounded low and hollow. "They'll wait for me. Besides . . . this shouldn't take long. Not long at all. In fact, I doubt that they'll even notice I'm gone."

"Hard not to notice that the bride's gone."

But he drove her anyway, though he did it with a questioning look. Jilly locked her hands on her lap, trying to be calm. As they wound down the mountain in the gathering dusk, the trees seemed to blur. Now the glistening snow on the high peaks only made her feel tiny and insignificant.

Suddenly she couldn't wait to get back to the Oregon coast.

To her small town and to her friends, the only place where she felt safe.

CHAPTER THIRTY

"You're completely wrong about this, Darrah. Jilly is no gold digger. I was going to tell her about all this. Then things just got out of hand. There was no time."

His sister, a powerful litigation attorney in Boston, rolled her eyes. "Give me a break, Walker. There's no innocence left in the world. You're a big boy. You should know that more than anyone. Everyone wants *something*." She stepped away, drying her tears with a carefully folded handkerchief taken from her pocket.

The linen was hand-embroidered with her initials, just like every piece of clothing in her wardrobe.

The Hales didn't do anything by half.

"But I'll clean up your mess anyway. I'll see that she's kept from doing any real harm, but I won't cut her off with nothing. After all, it looks like you two were very close. I suppose she's entitled to something after an affair like that."

"You still don't get it, do you?" Walker's voice was icy. He was glad that Jilly wasn't here to be assaulted by his sister's accusations. "You *won't* talk to her. You *won't* put out any fires. You'll do nothing, Darrah. I'll explain to her. And then I'll call our father." Not Dad. Nothing so informal. There was no love and precious little informality in the Hale household, Walker thought grimly. "You took the jet, I assume?"

"Of course. I'm not about to stand in line for security. Besides, I couldn't have gotten here in time without it." Darrah Hale smoothed her red suit and then picked up her small but exquisitely expensive leather portfolio, looking every inch the powerful lawyer that she was. "I'm going to the plane now. I'll expect to see you there in fifteen minutes."

"Don't wait for me. I've got to take care of this first." Walker turned abruptly, hearing a noise down the hall. Glancing outside, he saw something white on the little chair outside the door. Leaning down, he picked up a small circle of flowers.

It was Jilly's wedding bouquet. She had been carrying it the last time he saw her.

He stared down the shadowed hallway. She had stood right here. She had heard every angry word. How would these accusations feel to someone who was just starting to trust him?

"I'll talk to you later, Darrah. I've got to go."

"Walker, I mean it. I won't wait at the airport forever —"

Walker didn't look back. He broke into a trot, feeling an awful weight of guilt.

He was five minutes behind her every step of the way after that. He missed her at her room. He missed her at the taxi stand outside the main lodge.

And as he stood in the darkness at the airport, he watched the lights of the small commuter plane that had just taken off.

The attendant at the counter had remembered Jilly very well. She had been crying, though she'd tried to hide it. And the attendant was certain that the passenger had a bridal gown folded up inside a big paper bag. She definitely remembered *that* part. How many women carried an exquisite lace gown in a brown paper bag?

Walker looked down at his watch and cursed in impatience. The commuter flight was headed to Denver. He knew that from her gate information. He had tried to find out her next connection in Denver — he suspected either Scottsdale or somewhere in Oregon — but the gate attendant refused to tell him anything.

He wasn't going to let Jilly escape like this, in pain and hating him for the things that he had never mentioned. He had to find her and make it right somehow.

Out on the tarmac Walker saw the lights of a small plane, just as Darrah had described.

It just might work, he thought. But first he was going to have to break a promise made the day after he had come back from Afghanistan.

He would have to call his father and ask for a favor. He had sworn never to ask anything of the man who had wanted to profit by his son's military career and the brave marines who had fallen in that last firefight that had nearly killed Walker.

But there was no choice now. Walker had to find Jilly. And he was certain that his cold and devious father would make him pay dearly for his help.

CHAPTER THIRTY-ONE

"Senator Hale, please."

"Who may I say is calling?"

If he hadn't been so distracted by Jilly's flight, Walker would have smiled at the thought of his father's face when that particular message was delivered across his big mahogany desk.

Walker could almost picture the scene. The sun streaming through discreetly opened curtains made out of discreetly expensive silk that perfectly matched the discreetly expensive Persian rug.

He checked his watch in growing impatience. His father would probably keep him waiting, just to teach him a lesson. It was something that Senator Frederick Hale was very skilled at doing. Power and its uses meant everything to him.

Just as Walker expected, he was kept on hold for almost ten minutes.

There was no important business meeting. It was simply the senator's style.

"Lieutenant Hale?" The voice was deep and curt. There was no sign of the illness that his sister had described. Walker wondered if Darrah was capable of that kind of lie to bring the family back together.

He decided not. She had been too upset. As a litigator, she was a good performer, but tears were not in her usual repertoire.

"Well, Lieutenant Hale?" his father said curtly. No informality. No *son.* "To what do I owe the honor of this call? Your family hasn't heard a word from you in weeks. As I recall, the last time you and I spoke was over a year ago."

This was where the groveling began, Walker thought grimly. He would have to stow the anger. He had sworn never to ask anything of his father, but now he had no choice. His father could track down Jilly a lot faster than Walker could. "We parted on bad terms. I'm sorry about that. I'd like to talk about what happened. I'd like to make plans for the future, too."

A chair squeaked. "The future. Has Darrah spoken with you? Is she out there in Wyoming right now?" The old man's voice was hard with suspicion.

"Darrah? No, I haven't seen her. Is something wrong?" Walker played at ignorance.

His father would never welcome sympathy or commiseration.

"I see. And you're finally ready to talk to me? So fly back here this weekend. We can discuss your political future and the future of this family. You won't have a penny from me while you continue in this pigheaded manner, turning your back on everything that eight generations of Hales have lived and died for."

"I don't want your money," Walker said coldly. His grandfather had left him more than he needed. They both knew that. "I won't be going into politics, either." His father knew how to dig the knife in deep. Doing what was best for the family *always* meant what Frederick Hale thought was best. No one else's opinions ever mattered to the senior senator from New Hampshire.

"In that case, we have nothing to discuss."

"No. We have to talk. I'll listen to what you have planned. But first . . ." Walker cleared his throat. "I have a favor to ask."

The chair squeaked again. Walker's father barked out a laugh. "A favor? You're asking this of the man that you called a cold-blooded political scavenger, the man who you said was a disgrace to the Hale name? Why in the hell should I do anything for you?"

"Because I'm asking you to." Walker opened and closed his hands, trying to rein in his temper. It was never easy around his father. "And because I know you'll ask a favor of me in return. And I'm prepared to accept your terms."

Silence. The chair squeaked a third time. "Anything I ask? Anytime I ask, the conditions to be determined when I ask you? Are you really prepared to do that?"

Oh, yes, Frederick Hale drove a damnable bargain. He would delight in holding this promise over Walker. It would be an excellent means of manipulation.

And then Walker thought of Jilly, standing alone at the airline counter with an exquisite lace dress shoved inside a brown paper bag. Crying, but trying to hide it. "I agree. One favor, whenever you ask."

The senator chuckled, but the sound was cold and flat. As his laugh trailed off, he gave a dry, hacking cough.

This was something new, Walker realized. For the first time his father sounded like a sick man.

"Very well. Now what is this information you find so crucial? Are you asking about the upcoming military appropriations bill? I know every detail, of course. I suppose you're trying to help someone in your old command. Why exactly is it that you have more loyalty to the men you served with than to the family who raised you?"

"It's not about appropriations. I need information on connecting flights that will be made for a passenger when she lands in Denver."

"*Cherchez la femme.* So this is about a woman. Am I permitted to know what your relationship is?"

"I'll explain when I'm in New Hampshire. Right now I don't have time. So . . . will you help me or not?"

"Very well. A favor from me now in exchange for a favor to be granted by you at any time, the terms of my choosing. Agreed?"

"Agreed." Walker said the words stiffly. His shoulder was hurting again, but it was nothing against the pain of losing Jilly.

"Very well. What is this woman's name?"

"Jilly O'Hara. Her flight left Lost Creek, Wyoming fifteen minutes ago. She had a connection in Denver." Walker rattled off the commuter flight number. "I need to know where she is headed after Denver, and her addresses in Oregon and Arizona, as well as the addresses of her friends in case I need them. Home phone numbers, too."

"That's all?" Frederick Hale gave another

dry laugh. "Give me their names and ten minutes. Let's see how much juice the old man still has."

The senator called back six minutes later.

Walker was pacing anxiously at the gate where Jilly had left. He pulled out his phone, relieved to see the New Hampshire area code. "Yes?"

"I have the residence in Scottsdale. Also one in a town called Summer Island in coastal Oregon. Your Jilly O'Hara's flight from Denver routed through Portland. If you hurry, you might even catch her. I'll keep tabs on the airplane for you. I will send you those addresses next."

Walker felt a surge of relief. One thing he couldn't deny, his father had a network that extended everywhere in the world. "I appreciate it."

"Oh, don't thank me yet. Not until I ask my favor. Then we'll see how thankful you are, Lieutenant Hale. You're not walking away from this family."

Walker grimaced. He glanced at his watch, making his plans. The sound of his father's little laugh stopped him.

"One thing you might want to know. Your mysterious lady friend was carrying a wedding gown in a brown paper bag. She was

370

also crying. What the hell is going on, Walker? Is she pregnant? Did you leave her at the altar?"

Walker's hands closed to fists. He fought a wave of self-loathing at the thought of Jilly crying. "No, she's not pregnant. And I didn't leave her at the altar. I did something much worse. I broke her heart. But I'm going to fix it, no matter what it takes."

Walker ran down the hall, glancing at his watch.

It was going to be damnably tight. With his sister ready to raise a fuss when she found out what he had planned, things were going to get sticky.

But Walker knew who to call when things got sticky: four tough marines who'd fought in Afghanistan. They would be wondering where he had gone after the wedding. And he knew they were always up for a good adventure.

He frowned, realizing he didn't have their current cell phone numbers. He hadn't spoken to any of them since he'd left the hospital. But Red would track them down.

He dialed quickly on his cell phone.

"Walker, is that you? Jeez, what happened to Jilly? Where the heck *are* you?"

"It's a long story, Red. And I don't figure

371

in it too well. I have to make things right, and I have to do it fast. I need a favor."

"You name it, I'm all over it."

Walker had to smile at that, remembering his father's cold, grudging help. Could two men ever be more different?

"Those four hard cases at the wedding ceremony, my marine buddies from Afghanistan, are they still there?"

"Oh, yeah. Draining the bar dry and eating their way through the buffet. You need me to get them?"

"I'd appreciate it. Before they're too drunk to walk without falling," Walker said dryly.

"Anything else I can do?"

"Keep an eye on Mamie. Tell her that . . . something came up. Jilly and I had to leave early."

"You got it. There's nothing wrong, is there? Someone said they saw Jilly waiting for a cab, but I told them it had to be somebody else. She just went back to her room to change, right?"

Walker rubbed his neck. "It's complicated, Red. I'll explain when I can. Meanwhile, can you find my friends? I need to get moving."

"They're right here. Hold on."

Walker heard static as the phone was

passed over.

"Lieutenant? We thought you were off on your honeymoon. Something wrong?"

"I need your help, Cudahy. Call it a little diversionary action. Are any of you sober enough to drive right now?"

"You bet, Lieutenant. What's our rendezvous point?"

Once a marine, always a marine, Walker thought with quiet pride. You didn't forget ties and a brotherhood like those forged under fire.

He stared out at the little jet on the tarmac. Darrah hadn't arrived yet, thankfully. If his friends moved fast, they could carry off this crazy plan.

"Ask Red for a car. Pick up Winslow, okay? Then get yourself over here to the airport double time. Park the car and call me. I'll tell you what to do next."

"Roger that, Lieutenant. We're boots to the ground. You need firepower?"

Walker shook his head at the man's enthusiasm. "No firepower necessary. We're using brains today, Cudahy. I know it may be a novel experience for you four, but it's a good time to start."

"Ah, jeez, Lieutenant. We can be smart when we want to be. We just don't want to be. It's more fun charging around and letting people think we're idiots." At the sharp laughter that boomed across the phone, Walker knew that the other three men had heard the comment.

Some of his uneasiness lifted. These men were tough and smart. They would divert his sister and give him time for what he planned to do next.

Because there was no way in hell that Jilly was going to get away from him. Not if he had to track her all the way to Tibet.

"Okay, move out. Call me when you're in the car with Winslow. And leave any weapons at the resort. You're going to be entering the airport, and I don't want any security problems." Walker smiled coldly. "Only the problems that I make myself, that is."

Then he headed for the stairway that led out to the Hale family's private jet.

CHAPTER THIRTY-TWO

Time seemed to shift and jerk, moving in a blur.

Jilly sat stiffly in the cramped seat of the commuter plane with the brown paper bag on her lap. So far she had managed to keep from crying. She was pleased about that.

All her thoughts were focused on getting home to Summer Island, to the friends who would offer support, with no explanation needed. The events of the day had been too much to take in. Her mind simply shut down.

But like a hangnail that you couldn't ignore, whenever Jilly closed her eyes she thought of Walker, tall and devastatingly handsome in his dark suit. She thought of the look in his eyes when the minister had pronounced them man and wife.

And then she thought of the slow intimate kiss that had followed.

Her hands trembled. She locked them

hard on the arms of her seat.

"Is everything okay, ma'am?" A concerned flight attendant leaned down, frowning at Jilly. "Can I get you an air sickness bag?"

Jilly shook her head. Throwing up wasn't going to make her feel better. She was pretty sure she would get over this betrayal, but Walker would be with her forever, haunting her with what happiness might have been hers.

She shook her head. "No, I'm fine. Just tired. Suddenly I'm very, very tired."

Walker had to admit, his men were still razor-sharp. They'd been working hard to adjust to civilian life, just the way he had, but some moves you never forgot.

"Do you have that straight, Cudahy? She'll be the one in the red suit. Pretend that you're the police or something. Do whatever it takes. Just keep her away from that jet. Don't hurt her. Just detain her until we've taken off. You got that?"

"Jeez, Lieutenant. That's your sister? You didn't tell me she was such a babe."

A babe? Walker had never thought of Darrah in those terms. He was pretty sure that she would cringe at the description, too.

"She's one of the best litigation attorneys in the country, Cudahy. Don't mess with her. She'll rip you four to shreds before you realize she's there."

Walker heard the sounds of laughter. "Hell, we won't hurt her, Lieutenant." Cudahy chuckled. "Finesse. Charm. This is going to be fun."

Walker shook his head, wishing he could be around to see what Darrah did when she realized the jet was gone. But he didn't have any more time. Jilly's plane was landing in Denver in less than twenty minutes.

And he was going to be right behind her.

Darrah Hale frowned at the tall man in a camo jacket who was blocking her way. He flashed some kind of a badge and held out a cell phone.

"Miss Hale? I'm Riley. Military police. We've got a problem with your brother."

Darrah frowned. "My brother? What's wrong?"

"He's on the phone. He wants to talk with you. And I think you'll want to have this conversation someplace private."

What in heaven's name had Walker done now? He had screwed up his life enough. Since he had come back from Afghanistan, Walker had wanted nothing to do with any of them.

And now this thoughtless marriage with

377

no protection for his assets. What was it about men and a pretty face? There were gold diggers on every corner. Couldn't men see that?

She had been surprised to see how tired he looked and how much weight he had lost since she'd seen him last. If she hadn't been so irritated, she would have worried about how he was going to recover, both in mind and in body.

But Walker had always been strong. He had never welcomed her worry. And he had turned his back on the family without ever once calling for help or news.

So she wouldn't waste time worrying about him. Her brother would not expect or welcome that kind of concern. In her family, weakness was ruthlessly rooted out. It began young, as soon as you were old enough to understand the difference between yes and no.

Between having and not having.

Darrah gave her head a little shake, forcing her thoughts back to the present. "Where *is* Walker? What's happened? Has he been arrested?" Instantly, all her instincts for litigation flared to life. "What's he being charged with?"

The man's eyes narrowed. "He has not been arrested, ma'am. I'm afraid it's worse than that." He gestured down the hall to a quiet alcove. "You can talk to him in there. He said you would want to keep this quiet."

Oh, there was no mistake about that. The last thing Darrah wanted was to see her brother's problems blazing on the pages of a national tabloid.

And yet . . .

Something didn't seem quite right here. It wasn't like Walker to ask for help. And if he was in trouble, why hadn't he called her himself?

She stopped short, reaching for her cell phone. She didn't know anything about this man. And her family had always been a target for kidnappers.

She turned around. "I forgot something in the car. I'll be right back." She picked up her pace, her eyes on the big double doors at the end of the hall.

"I'm afraid I can't let you do that, ma'am." His strong hand gripped her arm. "So we're going to go over here in the corner, nice and quiet. You're not going to make a fuss, either. Because if I have to, I have restraints. Duct tape makes a fine gag."

Darrah stared at him in disbelief. What was Walker involved in now? Frankly, she was getting sick and tired of his problems. If he chose to stay here in this backwater town like a hermit, that was his problem. But her skills of persuasion were legendary.

She didn't expect to be here long at all.

She smiled at the man in the camo jacket. "I'm certain we can work out this misunderstanding. You do know who our father is, don't you? Senator Hale?"

Usually mentioning the name was enough. Her father's reputation could unlock all kinds of doors.

But this man had no reaction. "I know who he is. A downright bastard, from all I hear. Now if you'll just step this way, ma'am."

"But — you *can't*. I have a plane to catch. I'm in the middle of a complicated litigation —"

"Not now you aren't."

Suddenly Darrah Hale was surrounded by four tall, unsmiling men. One look at their faces told her all the arguments in the world would not help her. But . . . oddly, they looked familiar now. She realized that they had been at her brother's wedding earlier that day. What was going on here?

She glanced outside to the tarmac, hearing the drone of motors. A small, private jet was turning to taxi out to the runway.

Darrah cursed. That was her family's jet. And it was going to leave *without* her.

The hand tightened on her arm.

"That's my plane! He's taking off without me."

"Sure does look that way, doesn't it?" The man in the camo smiled slowly. "Must be somebody very important on that plane."

And that was when Darrah Hale realized how thoroughly she had been outflanked by her brother.

CHAPTER THIRTY-THREE

Oregon

Jilly made it through the Denver airport by sheer grit. She had no energy and no appetite. When her legs felt jittery she stopped for a yogurt and a granola bar before boarding her flight to Portland.

Some small part of her brain kept making her turn around, checking to see if Walker had followed her.

But the rest of her brain warned that he wouldn't come after her. He wouldn't care. It had all been a performance anyway. She would never fit in with a rich, successful family like his. Running away as she had would give him the perfect excuse to bring their performance to an end.

Once, walking past a crowded gate, Jilly almost thought she heard him call out her name. But she kept right on moving. The time for happy ever after was over. She was back to *her* world now, and in her world heroes were an extinct species.

Besides, Jilly told herself that she didn't want Walker to come after her. A clean, fresh break was best. She kept telling herself that over and over again.

It didn't stop the pain or the crushing sadness.

The sky was gray, spitting with rain when she landed in Portland.

Jilly arranged for a rental car and then broke her caffeine promise, loading up with a large cup of coffee. Without it she had no hope of driving all the way to Summer Island.

Right now all she could think of was being home, caught in the warm circle of her friends. When her big Samoyed puppy barked, licking her face, maybe she would start to feel normal again.

Olivia pulled back the dusty curtain at the window, her hand on her hip. "Caro, did you notice that car? It's been parked there for a while, but the driver hasn't gotten out."

"What car?" Caro wore long rubber cleaning gloves up to her elbows and her hair was caught up beneath a hand-knitted hat. They had been hard at work all afternoon, cleaning and renovating the front room of the old Harbor House. "If it's one of the teenagers from town hoping to graffiti our back wall, I'm going after them with a bucket of cleaning solution. I've washed off that wall twice this month."

"I don't think it's a teenager." Olivia put down her dust cloth, frowning. "I'm going to check it out."

"You're *not* going out there alone. It could be a thief. Or a stalker."

Olivia laughed dryly. "Who would have any interest in robbing us? There's nothing of value to steal. I doubt we're attractive targets, either. Seriously, have you seen my bank account lately? Every penny is going into renovating this dilapidated old place. Stalking me would be pointless."

"A stalker isn't exactly sane," Caro said uneasily. "I'm going with you." She picked up her big broom. "Let's go."

They used the back door and circled around so they could approach the car from the rear. There was indeed someone sitting motionless in the driver's seat.

And Olivia was the first to realize who it was. She ran forward, smiling. "Jilly, when did you get back? Why didn't you call us?"

She flung open the driver's-side door, and her breath caught when she saw Jilly's face, pale and slick with tears. "Oh, Jilly, what's wrong? Is it your heart again? I'm going to call 911. We can have an ambulance here fast. Better still, move over. I'll drive you straight to the hospital. Does it hurt much?"

Jilly gave a sad laugh, her hands gripping the steering wheel. "Oh, it hurts. It hurts more than anything I've ever felt," she whispered hoarsely. "But it's not my heart. At least, it's nothing a cardiologist can cure."

"What do you mean?" Olivia sank down beside her. "What's happened?"

Jilly wiped shaky fingers across her face. "It finally happened, the thing you three kept telling me would happen. I met him. He's the man I wanted to spend the rest of my life with. He's the man I wanted to marry. I even thought about having children with him, though I'd be the worst mother in the world. But — it was all a lie. I never knew him at all. And now . . . I just want to crawl into a hole and die."

They didn't waste time with questions or arguing. Caro and Olivia simply caught her arms, pulled her from the car and guided her inside. Within seconds she was curled up in the Harbor House's only comfortable wing chair with a blanket across her lap and hot herbal tea steaming on the table beside her.

Now the questions could begin.

"Who is he? If he hurt you, I'll kill him. I'll stick knitting needles in his throat. I'll rip out his fingernails," Olivia said fiercely.

"Ditto that for me," Caro cut in. "Did he work in the resort? A chef maybe?"

"No, he lives in Lost Creek. His name is Walker. He's an ex-marine."

"Oh, right. You mentioned him when you called." Caro glanced at Olivia, who was heating soup on the stove. "How did you meet him? I doubt he was there for the knitting."

"No, he's a local celebrity. A true hero." Jilly's voice broke. She looked down and grabbed a tissue, blowing her nose loudly. "Everything happened so fast. But he was perfect. And he has the most amazing dog named Winslow." Jilly gave a little smile. "I'm going to miss Winslow. In fact, I miss him already." She rubbed her eyes. "Is it possible to fall in love with a dog?"

"What have you eaten today?" Olivia said worriedly.

"Some yogurt and half a granola bar in Denver. Not much else."

Her two friends shared more anxious glances. "And you're definitely not feeling any heart symptoms? No chest pain? No nausea?"

Jilly shook her head. "It's not like that. This is worse than high blood pressure or sudden dizziness. And why aren't you two laughing? We always used to argue about falling in love. I swore it would never happen to me. I was completely smug, no romance for Jilly O'Hara," she whispered. "Then I met Walker. Now here I am. A wreck."

"We'd never laugh at you, Jilly." Caro handed Jilly another tissue, frowning as Jilly tore the wet paper into small pieces and stacked them in a little pile.

"You know what the strangest thing is? When we were together . . . I actually felt like I belonged somewhere." She took a drink of her tea and squared her shoulders. "But it was a lie. I thought he was a regular person, but he's not. He never got around to telling me that his father is Senator Hale from New Hampshire, the most powerful man in the Senate. His family probably owns most of the northeastern United States. Talk about bad choices. A man from that kind of family — and me. How could *that* ever work out?"

"You're a celebrity, too," Olivia said loyally. "Your Jilly's Naturals line is sold everywhere. You may not be rich yet, but you're going to be."

"Olivia's right. He'd be lucky to have you," Caro said firmly. "But I don't like this part about lying. He didn't tell you anything about his family?"

Jilly shook her head tiredly. "He hinted at some tension there. He told me they weren't close, but no details. Nothing about *which* Hale family he belonged to. Everything happened very fast, and we weren't exactly concerned about our distant relatives or life stories. For the first time in my life I stopped asking questions. I decided to trust him. Stupid me."

"Oh, honey." Olivia rubbed Jilly's shoulder. "Maybe — well, maybe there's more to it. Have you talked to him?"

"No point. I heard enough to know everything I need to know. His sister told him that I'm a gold digger. That I only married him for his money and his assets."

Olivia nearly fell off her chair. "Wait, you two are *married?*"

Jilly smiled crookedly. "Oh, yeah, I forgot to mention that. It was a favor we did for a friend at the resort. Something to cheer her up before she goes into the hospital. It wasn't meant to be permanent, but yes, it was legal and binding. A crazy idea." Jilly rubbed her eyes. "I knew if I got back to Summer Island I'd be safe. Now I just want to sleep. But first, where is Duffy?"

"He's with Dr. Peter over at the animal shelter. We can take you to see him on the way to my house," Olivia said. "I'll make you something to eat and then you can sleep as long as you want."

Jilly nodded, too exhausted to argue about anything. "I miss Duffy. Can we go now?"

"Right away," Caro said. "Why don't you and Olivia drive back to her house? I'll go and get Duffy myself." Caro shot another worried glance at Olivia. "You two go ahead. I'll be right behind you."

Jilly yawned again, looking pale and vulnerable.

The rest of their questions would have to wait.

CHAPTER THIRTY-FOUR

"What are we going to do about her?"

Olivia paced the immaculate kitchen of the old renovated farmhouse she had bought two years before. She stopped to straighten a set of teacups and smooth the fresh roses in a crystal vase. "She has to sleep, Caro. Then she needs to eat. Most of all . . . we have to drive that pain out of her eyes. This man — she called him Walker Hale? — has hurt her very badly."

"I want to strangle him for that. But you know, our Jilly isn't always an easy person to deal with. As angry as I am right now, I can see there could be more to this."

"The questions will have to wait." Olivia watched Jilly's big white Samoyed wolf down his food. "She's already asleep. I'll take Duffy up after he's eaten and gone for a run on the beach. He'll love that." She straightened a dishcloth hanging from the door of her sleek stainless-steel refrigerator.

"I still can't believe they got married. I was hoping she'd relax up in the mountains, but this is a new Jilly. I've never seen her this open or vulnerable."

"We'll find out all the details tomorrow, after she's rested." Caro frowned at the brown paper bag that Olivia had brought in from Jilly's rental car. "There's something white in there." Caro opened the top of the bag and caught a sharp breath. "Olivia, you need to see this."

Her friend pushed in beside her and gave a low whistle. "That's one gorgeous wedding dress. So they really *did* get married in Wyoming. I'm going to kill her for not telling us." Olivia looked at Caro, her eyes filled with worry. "How did this man get through Jilly's defenses so fast? That's what I want to know. Jilly doesn't open up to anyone. It's taken us *years*."

"Tell me about it." Caro's lips set in a flat, angry line. "Can I use your computer?"

"Sure. Why?"

"I'm going on a hunting expedition. I'm going to find out everything there is to know about Walker Hale and his illustrious, driven, filthy rich family." Her eyes narrowed. "Gage always tells me you have to know your enemy better than your friends. I figure we should start right now."

■ ■ ■ ■

When Caro wandered out of the living room
half an hour later, she looked more confused
than ever. She accepted a cup of tea from
Olivia and sank into the beautiful chintz
chair near the window. "Jilly's sleeping. She
seems more relaxed now. Duffy's curled up
on the bed next to her, snoring in dog
fashion."

"So why the big frown?"

Caro stabbed a hand through her hair.
"Because there's next to nothing on the
internet about this Walker Hale. Oh, I found
a boatload of press releases and interviews
with his famous father. It looks as if the
whole family is in politics or law. His sister
handles litigation for a big Boston law firm,
but Walker has stayed out of the limelight.
He was in the marines serving in Afghanistan. He did two tours of duty there. Then
he was hurt and he came home. That's all
there is. Something doesn't add up here,
Olivia."

"So we'll dig deeper. Since he was in the
marines, maybe you can email Gage for
more details."

"I sent him an email ten minutes ago. But
if he's out in the field, I may not have an

answer soon." Caro's eyes darkened.

Olivia reached over to grip her hand. "Don't worry about him. He's a smart man and a good soldier, too. He's going to make it through this and come home safe and sound. I'm going to be dancing on the tables when it happens."

Caro summoned a smile. "I'm holding you to that. I can't wait to see the elegant, always impeccably behaved Olivia Sullivan dancing half-drunk on a table."

"Who said anything about *half*-drunk?" Olivia muttered.

And then the two women froze. Duffy rocketed down the stairs, barking loudly as a black SUV pulled into the driveway. The car had rental plates and the logo of a national chain. A man in jeans and a black sweater got out and stretched slowly, then rubbed his neck, studying the house.

He was a tall man, lean and unsmiling. There was an intensity about him that Olivia could feel even at a distance. "Well, well. What have we here?"

Caro crossed her arms tensely. "I'd say that's Mr. Bigshot Hale himself. About time he showed up. Let's go ask him some hard questions."

CHAPTER THIRTY-FIVE

Caro grabbed a big porch broom, and Olivia armed herself with a spackling gun.

They burst onto the porch together, looking tough and very angry. For long moments they studied the lone man leaning against the SUV in the gathering darkness.

"What do you want?" Olivia demanded roughly.

The man didn't seem surprised by her question. He just looked tired, Olivia thought. Tired and also very worried.

"My name is Walker Hale. I'm here to see Jilly O'Hara."

"She's not here."

The man frowned. "She isn't? But her flight landed in Portland. I assumed that she came back here. She told me how much she loves Summer Island."

Olivia shook her head. "She drove back to Scottsdale. She left an hour ago."

"I wanted to speak with her. No, I *need* to

speak with her." He frowned at the dark sweep of the ocean. "She's not answering her cell phone. I tried calling her all the way from Wyoming."

Olivia slid her spackle gun from one hip to the other. "What do you want to talk to her about?"

He rubbed his right shoulder. "I hurt her. There were things that I should have told her."

Caro angled her broom against the side of the porch and crossed her arms. "What kind of things?"

"Who I am. Who my family is. But more than that, I should have talked about our future. Because I want a future with Jilly. I want her in my life. We haven't come close to working out the details, but I'm not going to let her walk away and pretend that nothing happened between us. She'll try to do that. She's strong enough and stubborn enough to succeed for a while, but it will cost her. And then she'll end up settling for less than she could have. Because no man will love her as much as I do," he said roughly. "I think she's had to settle enough in her life."

As Caro studied him, she felt her heart soften. "What makes you think she wouldn't be *settling* with you, Walker Hale?"

"Only one thing, ma'am. But it's important." He took a deep breath. "I love her. I think I loved her the first second I saw her overturn her suitcase and spill two dozen Tastykakes all over the airport floor back in Lost Creek. I knew I loved her when she took time out to befriend my dog. She's smart and stubborn and generous and often impossible." He stabbed a hand through his hair. "And there's no one I'd rather spend the rest of my life with."

Olivia blew out a breath and set her spackling gun down on the big porch glider. "Well." She shot a look at Caro and then shrugged. "That's quite an explanation, Mr. Hale."

"Call me Walker, please. You must be Olivia. You're the architect. Jilly described you. And I think you must be Caro." Walker nodded slowly. "Your husband is in Afghanistan. Jilly told me about you, too. She was very proud to have such tight friends to support her."

"One thing I don't understand. How did you know my address?" Olivia asked.

Walker gave a tight smile. "I called in some favors. Sorry to turn up on your doorstep like this." He reached through the window as something moved inside the car.

"What are you doing?" Olivia asked sharply.

"Just giving Winslow some water. He's tired from all the traveling." The man tapped lightly on the sill of the open window. "Sit up and say hi to Jilly's friends, buddy."

The brown dog rose on the seat. There was a red bandanna tied around his neck, and his eyes were alert.

Olivia felt another cold wedge of anger begin to melt. "Nice dog. You shouldn't keep him cooped up in there. The ocean's just down the hill. Take him for a walk while my friend and I go inside. We need to talk."

"I'll do that." Walker frowned. "But if Jilly's on her way to Arizona, I can't stay long. I'm going after her."

Olivia studied him in silence. "Why should we help you? Explain that to me again."

Even in the gathering shadows of night it was impossible to mistake the way his eyes darkened. "Because I love her, damn it. And I'm getting tired of explaining that to everyone I meet. We may be oil and water. We'll probably fight once a week and disagree on everything. I don't want anyone else but Jilly — and I'm going to make her happy, whether she wants me to or not," he said grimly. "*That's* why you should help me."

Caro glanced at Olivia and then put her hands on her hips. "Don't go anywhere just yet. Take your dog down to the beach and then we'll talk."

"He's serious. Did you see his eyes when he talked about having Jilly in his life?"

"I saw." Olivia attacked her counter ruthlessly with a sponge. Then she refilled the teapot and added more Earl Grey tea. "It could be an act. After all, Jilly said he broke her heart and lied to her. Maybe we should just send him away. We could send him on a wild-goose chase to Arizona."

Caro sipped her tea thoughtfully. "That's what I meant to do. That's what part of me still wants to do. But what if we're wrong? What if he *is* the one for her? What if we screw that up?"

Olivia rolled her shoulders. "Don't look at me. You're the queen of the relationship department. I'm a failure, remember?"

"One or two misfires don't make you a failure. And we're going to work on that relationship stuff," Caro said firmly. "Just as soon as we get Jilly sorted out." She glanced through the big picture window that faced the beach.

He was still down there.

He had run his dog up and down half-a-dozen times. Now he was on the ground, flat on his back, wrestling with the big brown dog.

Caro sighed. "I don't care. I like him. I'm probably biased. He's a former marine, after all. But he's serious about Jilly, and that's what counts. It may hurt her to see him again so soon, but being alive means being hurt. I vote that we let him in."

Olivia gave the counter another vicious cleaning. "Remember what she said? His family is about as powerful as they get. You know how sensitive Jilly is about being an orphan and a foster child. What would that be like for her? How will she ever fit in?"

"We can't keep her here forever, wrapped up and protected. We may want to, but we can't." Caro pointed to the beach. "Take a good look down there. That quiet man may be her very best chance at happiness. That's the problem with trying to do the right thing. There's a chance you can make things worse." Caro sighed. "I wish Grace were here. She would know what to do."

"Well, she's *not*. So it's up to us." Olivia tossed her sponge into the spotless sink and crossed her arms. "So does he go or does he stay?"

■ ■ ■ ■

Jilly tossed restlessly, caught in dreams of big brown dogs and tall, quiet men.

There was no particular order to the dreams. There were no faces or names or voices. Everything felt blurred as she walked through a quiet mountain twilight, feeling lost, wanting things that she had never put a name to before. She had learned how to want and hope and wish while she was in Wyoming.

After a long time she heard a low voice call her name. She spun around, but there was only darkness. There was no one waiting for her, no one to share her hurts and hopes with.

With a low sound of loss, she let the images go and sank back into sleep.

CHAPTER THIRTY-SIX

"I've made up my mind." Caro stared up toward the bedroom where Jilly was sleeping. "Let's go."

"Go where?" Olivia frowned at her friend. "*What* did you decide?"

"You'll see." Caro gestured for Olivia to follow her out to the front porch. She moved quickly now, a woman with a purpose.

"I don't understand. Did you hear something from Gage? Did he send an email about this man, Walker?"

"No, I haven't heard anything yet, but it doesn't matter."

"We need to discuss this." Olivia shook her head. "There are still questions. I don't want Jilly to be hurt any more."

Caro didn't answer, pushing open the front door. They were greeted with a gust of clean sea wind and the muffled sound of barking from the beach.

"He's the one." Caro took a deep breath. "That's all I know. I don't know how I know it, so don't ask me to explain, but every cell in my body is warning me not to let him leave. So I won't. It may not work out. They may both be hurt, but that's the cost of being alive. Jilly has to accept that. So do you, Olivia. Life isn't neat and tidy. It isn't a dirty counter that you can scrub clean twice a day. So just get over it." Caro stalked down the path toward the beach and smiled when the big dog ran toward her, barking and circling her in excitement. "My, you are one beautiful dog."

Walker Hale jogged up behind Winslow. "He needed that run on the beach. I guess we both did. Thanks for the suggestion." He was watching the women, waiting for a sign of what would happen next.

"You hurt Jilly," Caro said flatly. "What are you going to do to make that right?"

Walker met her gaze directly. "I'll start by telling her the truth. Everything that happens after that will be her decision as much as mine."

Caro considered this and then nodded. She ignored Olivia, who was digging her elbow into Caro's side. "Jilly didn't go to Arizona. She's asleep upstairs. She was exhausted when she got back and very upset. So a word of warning for you, Mr. Hale. Treat her right. If you hurt her again, we'll be coming after you with paring knives and knitting needles. And that's not something you want."

Walker didn't smile. He didn't act as if it was an empty threat, either. "I understand. And I'm not going to hurt her. We're going to work this out somehow. The only thing is . . ." His voice trailed away.

"Don't tell us that you're an ax murder," Olivia said coldly. "Or you already have two wives. Let's hear everything right now, before you go upstairs to see Jilly."

"It's my family. We pretty much put the *D* in *dysfunctional*. I'll do all I can to buffer Jilly from that, but there are going to be moments when she wishes that she'd never met me."

"Do your best. That's all Jilly would want from you. And be ready to tell them to back off."

Walker's lips curved slightly. "I'll remember that." He looked down as Winslow whined, glancing at the front door.

"She's upstairs. Olivia and I were just leaving. We'll take Jilly's dog, Duffy, with us. If he sees a stranger and another dog here, it would be World War III. Give us five minutes to clear out. Then you can go in."

Caro's eyes narrowed. "And remember what I told you."

Olivia started to protest, but Caro grabbed her arm and tugged her back into the house, closing the door firmly behind them.

The women were gone in under five minutes. In the sudden silence, Walker stood uncertainly, hands in his pockets, wondering if he was making the right choice. Could he be sure that Jilly wouldn't get hurt?

If their involvement became known, Jilly would be hounded by reporters, biographers and political hacks looking to make capital off his father's career. How was he going to protect her from that?

He gripped the porch rail, frowning. Maybe he should leave now. Maybe it would be best for Jilly to get over him and move on with her life. His driven, complicated family thrived on secrets and power plays. Jilly would hate to have any part of that.

Undecided, Walker turned, watching the moon rise over the restless cove. Winslow bumped against his leg, whining softly, alert as ever to Walker's moods and emotions.

"What do you say, buddy? Do we go or do we stay? My heart is telling me not to leave. But my mind, the mind that knows exactly what my family is capable of, is shouting for me to go before Jilly finds out what life with the dysfunctional Hales is like."

Wind blew up from the harbor, whistling over the quiet porch. Every gust seemed to carry whispered words of sadness and warning. Walker heard his own dreams carried in that low whisper. He felt the pain of dark memories of war and too much death. But since meeting Jilly he had learned to turn his eyes from the past and look at the road ahead.

Winslow whined. When Walker didn't move, the big dog rubbed against his leg, staring restlessly at the house in longing to go inside.

Walker blew out a breath. "I know how you feel, buddy. I'm right there with you. So — it's boots to the ground. Let's go inside and see what it takes to make this right."

Walker climbed the stairs slowly.

He had picked and measured his words all the way from Lost Creek. From the moment he'd found Jilly's bouquet, forgotten on the chair outside the room where his sister had cornered him, he had tried to imagine all the ways to soothe her.

He still didn't know where to start.

The truth would always work best, he thought wryly.

Pushing open the door at the top of the stairs, Walker saw a shadowed room. A pink blanket and pink walls. And then he saw Jilly.

He would have laughed if he hadn't been so worried. She slept with the same driven energy that she did everything else. The blankets were tangled across her feet. A pillow was jammed under her shoulder. One arm stretched out as if she was flipping omelettes in a busy kitchen.

She didn't change.

Walker didn't *want* her to change.

She looked exhausted, so deep in sleep that she hadn't felt his presence, and he couldn't bring himself to wake her. So he sank down onto a frilly chair of bright pink chintz and studied the room, taking in Jilly's single suitcase and the brown paper bag in the corner near the bed.

The wedding dress she had worn in Lost Creek hung neatly behind the door, wrapped in plastic, ready to send back to Mamie.

Hell.

Quietly he nudged off his boots and motioned for Winslow to sit beside him. From the chair he had a sweeping view of

406

the Summer Island cove and the scattered fishing boats at sea. But he saw none of it.

All he saw was Jilly. She had touched him that way from the first moment they had met. His shoulder had ached and he had been exhausted from a difficult training mission, and yet her energy had touched his life, changing him forever.

When she was in a room he saw nothing else. When her laugh drifted through the air, it dug straight into his chest, playing havoc with his pulse and sanity.

And when they had touched, with her legs wrapped around him and her mouth soft against his lips . . .

Nothing else in his world had ever come close. She stirred his blood with only a smile.

And where did that leave them? This was about more than sex, even though he could already tell that the sex would be off the chart.

Walker closed his eyes. No, it was about far more than sex. And she wouldn't open up easily to the future he had planned. She would never welcome interference, so he had to move very slowly. Nothing too obvious.

To a point.

If she endangered her health, he would be

all over it. And it wouldn't be a smooth trip. They had a lot to learn. So much to experience.

But he wouldn't have it any other way.

This was about trust, about being partners as well as lovers. He wanted to build a future that would inspire them and provide safe haven as long as they lived. Walker wouldn't accept anything less than forever with Jilly.

On the bed she stirred, whispering words he couldn't understand, drifting up from sleep like a tired swimmer surfacing from deep water. The pillow slid out from under her head.

She sat up sharply and blinked.

Her eyes widened when she saw him. Shock. Joy. Relief.

And then complete and total *fury.*

Her pillow came shooting straight toward him.

"Get *out!*"

CHAPTER THIRTY-SEVEN

Jilly tossed the blankets back and stood up, her long legs flashing. She grabbed the quilt and tossed it in Walker's face. "Go away!"

"Jilly, we have to talk."

She didn't listen. Wildly, she grabbed whatever was close. A book flew at his head. Olivia's new Italian leather sandals hurtled toward his chest. "Leave!"

"I will. But first —"

Muttering, Jilly grabbed his boots, shoved open the window and tossed them over the edge. His sweater went next.

She couldn't bear to see the shadowed figure in Olivia's favorite armchair. She didn't give him time to explain — or herself time to change her mind. "You have nothing to say to me."

"I can understand your anger, Jilly. I'm sorry you had to learn about me the way you did, through the angry words of an angry woman."

"I'm not going to listen to this. It's *over.*"
She stood behind him, her shoulder to his back, shoving him to the door.

And then she slammed the door behind him.

Walker had expected angry.

He hadn't expected *insane.* Then he remembered Jilly's mocking self-description. She had called herself a screamer. Not far off the mark, he thought ruefully.

"She's mad at us, Winslow. I should have guessed. Fortunately I came prepared." Walker reached into the duffel he had stowed at the top of the stairs. Once the fuming and pacing stopped inside, he tapped lightly on the door.

"Go away."

"Fine. But I have something for you. I'll leave it here, just outside the door. Come on, Winslow." Walker made loud noises as he walked down the stairs. But he stopped near the bottom, motionless and silent.

The doorknob turned. A hand appeared. Jilly peered out, saw no one on the stairs, and then leaned down to grab the small box tied with a red ribbon. "It won't work anyway," she called out. "I don't trust liars."

She closed the door. Paper rustled. Walker

heard her small sigh.

"No. That's . . . not fair."

"Chiltepins. Nearly the hottest wild peppers known," Walker said, climbing the stairs. "Extremely rare. Now preserved in the mountains of the Coronado National Forest in southern Arizona."

"I *know* what they are," Jilly called back. "And it doesn't change a thing."

The box rustled again. He heard her mutter. "That's *really* not fair."

"Single origin. Fair trade. Organic coffee that's low in caffeine and acidity. I had some help tracking it down. My father pulled some strings." Walker grimaced at the memory of that particular conversation. But whatever it cost him would be worth it. "I know how you love your coffee, so I figured you might give it a try."

"Oh, that's *so* dirty." The door opened slowly. Jilly stared at him, pale and tired and vulnerable. "Fine. You can come in. You can talk. But you only have two minutes." Her mouth set in a determined line. "Then you have to go."

"Fair enough. But not until I've said the things I came here to say."

At his side Winslow whined. He strained toward Jilly.

She flushed and then walked back inside,

411

sitting stiffly on the edge of the bed. "Go on. Talk. Just make it fast."

"Winslow wants to come, too. He's been restless the whole trip."

Jilly looked guilty. "Of course he can come in." She leaned down when Winslow trotted toward her, excitedly bumping her leg. Jilly kissed his head. "Hi, there, honey. Come and sit here beside me. Just for a minute." But when she looked at Walker, her eyes were cold. "Don't drag this out. There's no point, Walker. The performance is over. You don't fit in my life, and I sure as hell won't ever fit in yours."

"Most people would agree with you," he said quietly. "They look at us and see a wealthy, powerful man with prospects and connections. Then they look at you and see a struggling chef, racing to follow her dreams. Some people would even whisper that I was slumming," he said harshly.

"They'd be right," Jilly said.

"No, they'd be as wrong as people could be." Walker studied her face in the shadows. "Because you're the wealthy one. You have great friends. You have a job you love. You have a passion you won't compromise. You've had some bumps on the road, but you're handling it. In fact, you've got your whole life in front of you, with no manipulative family. No ghosts you can't bury," he said quietly.

"So what does that make you? A poor little rich boy?"

"Just a loner who's looking for something he never knew he'd missed. Just a man who found himself struck by a force of nature. Because one night a woman with wild dark hair and a big bag of Tastykakes blew into his life. She knocked him down hard and taught him about laughter. About food and friends and real courage. Winslow fell in love with her first." Walker cleared his throat. "But I wasn't far behind."

Winslow raised his head, looking between the two intently.

Jilly raised a hand to her chest. "Don't, Walker. No more. We both know this will never work. You're from the big, illustrious Hales of New Hampshire. I haven't a clue who my parents are and never will. Why don't you go on back to Lost Creek and get on with your life? I'll stay here and do the same. Maybe we can exchange cards at Christmas," she said coldly.

"So you plan to plow right on, pretending we never met, forgetting what we had."

"What exactly did we have? An evening of laughter. A few minutes of lust. We certainly didn't have any trust. If we had, you

413

would've told me about yourself and your family a whole lot sooner. Instead I had to hear about it from your sister's angry accusations."

"I can't take it back. I wish I could. All I can say is that things happened too fast, Jilly."

She stood up suddenly, her hands gripping the pillow. "Sorry, not interested." Her eyes were dark and unreadable. "And your time's up." She pointed to the door.

Between them Winslow stood stiffly. He didn't move, looking confused.

"You'd better take him," Jilly said hoarsely. "Don't make it harder."

"I plan to make it a lot harder," Walker said. "I love you, Jilly. You can tell me you don't care, but it would be a lie. And you make a very bad liar. When you touch me, your hands tremble. Your skin glows with heat. You want exactly what I want."

"Stop," she whispered.

"And no man will ever touch you the way I do. No man will want you like this. It won't be smooth or easy, but it will be the most amazing adventure you'll ever hope to know. I can give you all that."

She closed her eyes. One hand slid to the bed.

Walker saw her head slide forward as she

dug her fingers into Winslow's fur. "How can it ever work out? We're from two different planets. I'm afraid . . ."

"We'll make it work. We'll talk it out and get the details right. And then we'll sink into a big, soft bed and make love until we can't walk or even breathe." Walker leaned down and took her hand. "I want you in my life, Jilly. I want forever. No conditions or compromises."

She looked up.

Her cheeks were slick with tears. But her smile began and slowly grew until it filled her eyes and maybe her whole body. "You're sure?"

"I never had a single doubt."

"But I'm — just a cook."

"You're the woman I love," Walker said fiercely.

She whispered his name and slid her arms around his shoulders. "Kiss me, Walker. Take me to bed and let me feel your body. Don't let me get away this time."

"Count on it, honey. This one's forever."

His mouth met hers, hungry and searching. His hands slid around her waist.

Jilly sighed while her clothes slowly fell onto the floor.

An hour later Olivia and Caro returned.

The black SUV was still outside. The lights in the house were all off.

"No broken windows," Caro said. "No door broken in. Always a good sign." She slid one arm around Olivia and smiled. "Let's go over to my grandmother's house and have chili. Something tells me those two are going to be in there for a *very* long time."

EPILOGUE

It was nearly dawn.

Walker had been gone for almost three weeks. Jilly knew his time away had been difficult, including a trip to visit his family in New Hampshire and a thorough medical consultation in Washington. After a trying week, he had flown to Virginia for training work with Winslow.

When car lights turned up the drive near midnight, her white Samoyed had raced outside to greet the tired travelers. Walker's truck was streaked with dust, and Winslow had bounded out to greet Duffy and then Jilly with enthusiastic canine kisses. Then Winslow and Duffy had raced off for an excited romp on the beach.

The kiss she and Walker had shared left her brain reeling. Even now with a single touch he sent her straight into hormone overdrive. By the time they had rounded up the dogs and unloaded Walker's bags, Jilly's head had cleared enough for her to see that he was exhausted.

So she had sent him straight to bed. No arguing allowed.

And he had rested for all of four hours.

When he awoke, he had dragged her down onto his chest without a word. With calloused hands he settled her against his hard body. Slowly he kissed every inch of her aroused skin, and Jilly had sighed in pleasure.

She held nothing back while need beat a reckless rhythm between them. When Walker turned, pinning her beneath him, Jilly sighed his name. Their joining was hot and fierce. He had brought her to a mindless release and then they had collapsed together, fingers entwined, in the darkness.

Now Jilly stood in her silent kitchen, listening to the waves whisper out in the cove. There was no light yet, but in an hour the sea would be burnished silver, aglow with pink.

This was her favorite time of day, full of possibilities and endless beauty. The world seemed fresh and unspoiled in these moments before dawn, when pink slowly burned away to gold and a new day began.

Today Walker would be here to see it with her.

She had already sent off two long emails that had been weighing on her. In the end she had decided to sell the restaurant in Arizona to her two closest friends from cooking school. They would work out details for the sale in the next few weeks, but meanwhile the business had responsible people who could take charge and make decisions. Jilly had felt a weight removed as soon as she had pressed the send key.

Quietly she moved through the darkness and stood in the doorway while her eyes adjusted to the shadows in her room. Walker was asleep on her bed, the pillow beside him on the floor. Her blue knitted blanket was draped across his chest. One hand was stretched out, as if searching for Jilly's heat.

Time seemed to stop, and Jilly felt her heart overflow with welcome and joy. This *mattered,* just as Walker had said it would. He mattered. She accepted that now.

There would be no going back.

Jilly smiled down at the tweed sweater folded in her hands. It had taken her several weeks, but she had managed to sneak his grandfather's old sweater out of his bag. With the help of Grace and Caro she had mended the snags and carefully reknit the holes at the neck and elbow. It didn't look new. Nothing could restore the stitches to the way they had looked decades before. But now the mended spots added a sense of age and texture that enhanced the sweater's beauty. As the tweed brushed her fingers, Jilly realized what she had not seen before, though it had been in front of her all along.

She had mended the old stitches, following their twists and flow, in the process creating a newer, stronger set of attachments. And that was exactly what Walker had done to her. She would never be brand-new, never pristine and unaffected by the challenges of life. Her youth had left her with wounds that would never heal.

But Walker had mended those holes and smoothed the gaps. With his love and his calm strength he had made Jilly whole again. He had taught her how to trust completely for the first time in her life.

Duffy was asleep in his bed in the living room, but she heard the scrape of a metal bowl in the kitchen. Smiling, she peeked around the door and saw Winslow bump his dog dish, their agreed sign that he wanted a run on the beach. Jilly ran her hand along his neck, rubbing the sensitive spot behind his ear, and was rewarded by a little growl of pleasure. Winslow was more active and less stiff now. He could almost keep up with Duffy. Jilly liked to think she had helped make that happen.

Without warning hard hands circled her waist. Warm thighs anchored her hips and she felt Walker's chest against her back. "Hey. Come back to bed."

Jilly smiled. "For a recluse, you turned out to be a very sociable guy."

"So people keep telling me. I owe it all to you." His hand moved, tracing the curve of her breast. "The moment I saw you raining Tastykakes in the airport, I was lost."

"Now I understand. You want me for my Tastykakes, is that it?"

"Pretty much. Although there are a few other . . . attractions." He leaned down and kissed the rise of her nipple. "As you may have noticed."

Jilly sighed with pleasure, sliding her hands into his hair. "I've missed you so much, Walker."

He straightened slowly. His eyes gleamed with desire. "So have I, honey. Let's go back to bed. We have some unfinished business."

"If we have any *more* business, I may have to sleep for a week."

Walker bit the lobe of her ear gently. "That could be arranged."

"Promises, promises." Jilly traced his jaw. "How do you turn me inside out like this? When you're gone for a day, it feels like a lifetime."

"Only nineteen days." He rested his chin on her head and slid his arms around her back. "Seven hours and forty minutes," he muttered. "Not that I was counting or anything."

He looked down, feeling the tweed sweater crushed between them. "What's this?"

"Your sweater. The one your grandfather gave you. I — I mended it."

Walker's hands moved over the sweater. "You didn't have to do that."

"I know. I wanted it to be a surprise."

"I don't know what to say." Walker's voice tightened. "I loved the old codger. He was the only one in my family who understood me. And that sweater is the only thing I have of his. Thank you, Jilly." He brushed a strand of hair from her cheek. "And there's something else." He studied their laced fingers. "I love you. I intend to tell you that quite a lot in the future." His voice turned husky. "I intend to show you, too."

Jilly closed her eyes as he pulled her closer. "I certainly hope so." She slanted a slow kiss over his chest. "Have you heard from Mamie? Jonathan said she had a new specialist."

"It looks like they have an arterial stent lined up. They think it will give her considerable relief. He asked me about that therapy thing you do on my shoulder, too. He wants to learn it. It seems that he caught Mamie cleaning windows again, and it took Red and two more staff to make her stop."

Jilly shook her head. "That is one strong woman."

"Yeah. Just like another woman I know," Walker murmured. "So what did your specialist in Portland have to say after your last visit?"

"It's . . . good." Jilly took a slow breath. "There are more tests to be done, but he thinks that medicine and lifestyle changes will be enough. For now," she added quietly.

"Now is where it all starts." Walker's hands tightened. "That's the best gift I could have." His lips curved. "I hope you won't have to give up your exercise program?" His thighs moved between hers.

"Exercise is important. Medically and psychologically." Jilly lifted one leg, letting their bodies move in slow seduction. She sighed as need flared.

"Good. Because I had something in mind." Without a word Walker lifted Jilly and carried her back to bed. Still surrounded by his arms, Jilly sank against his aroused body. Their legs tangled.

She watched dawn paint the hard lines of

his face as he studied her in silence. Then he brought their bodies together in a slow, powerful thrust. Jilly's breath caught.

She realized that Winslow had trotted off to the kitchen. "How did he know that we — well, this? Did you give him some kind of sign?"

Walker kissed the tip of her breast, his hands circling her waist. "Didn't have to. That dog is smart enough to recognize a field action when he sees one," Walker said hoarsely.

And then he moved beneath her, filling her perfectly until the air seemed to hum around them, gold and pink and alive as it had never been before.

Jilly brought his hand up, opening it over her heart.

Over the heart that Walker had made whole again.

She whispered his name as she watched the promise of a new day — and a brand-new life — shine from his eyes while they tumbled over the edge of passion together.

AUTHOR'S NOTE

Thank you for joining Jilly and Walker on their journey. Strong and stubborn, these two have surprised me at every turn. Somewhere along the path of writing, they claimed a spot among my very favorite characters. (Even though they made me tear at my hair!)

And Winslow . . .

No words needed there.

He carries his own kind of magic and courage.

I hope that Summer Island continues to touch you as it has touched me, beginning with my story in *The Knitting Diaries* and again in *A Home by the Sea.* In those fog-swept coves and quiet streets friendship runs deep.

For readers in search of a detailed look at the inspiration for Jilly's amazing desserts, try *Bittersweet,* by Alice Medrich (New York: Artisan, 2003). Decadent and delightful, the book is rich with baking secrets and chocolate lore. For a second helping of dessert, enjoy Sherry Yard's *The Secrets of Baking* (New York: Houghton Mifflin, 2003), a master course for all adventurous cooks.

And if you want up-to-date recipes right from Jilly's kitchen, visit my website. I'll be offering new recipes regularly.

To learn more about service dogs in action, track down *US Army Field Manual 3-19.17 Military Working Dogs* (2005), a basic resource about training, protection and utilization in combat.

If you are intrigued by the gentle movements that Jilly used on Walker, I highly recommend the tissue techniques developed by Tom Bowen. Or email me at my website (www.christinaskye.com) for more information. The Bowen system has a truly impressive record of success. While you're at my website, have a look around. And drop by frequently for new book updates, free knitting patterns and contest news.

Meanwhile, a new Summer Island book is already heading your way. As summer sunlight fades into winter storms, Olivia will find her world shattered by lies. And when she least expects a gift, she will stumble into a man who holds the healing touch of love.

For her nothing will ever be the same.
I'll be watching for you down at the cove.

With warmest wishes,
Christina

SKYE

Skye, Christina.
The accidental bride
Park Place ADU CIRC
01/13